"I assume you've got information for me on Dana Turner."

"Yeah, Jace, there's plenty on the woman. Her legal name is Dana Howard Turner. Female Caucasian, twenty-seven, last known residence Fielding Women's Prison, San Bernardino, California, on a murder conviction. After she'd served seven months, the case was reopened and the judge vacated his verdict. She went free at the end of April."

Jace had to pull over to the side of the road.

"Jace? Did you get all that?"

"I did," he murmured, still trying to assimilate the fact that she'd spent seven months behind bars. The time frame made it impossible for her to have had any contact with the killers during their crime spree.

What about before and after, Riley? Questions bombarded him from all directions. Were the killers originally from California? Was one of them in love with Dana? Had they visited her at the prison?

Jace's chest tightened. Either Dana was guilty as sin and had been released on a technicality, or she was a total innocent, sent to prison by mistake.

Until he knew the truth, he wouldn't breathe freely.

And if it's the wrong truth, Riley?

He refused to think ab

Dear Reader,

I've heard people say, "There aren't any mountains in Texas!" Well...I'm here to tell you that statement couldn't be further from the truth. The Rocky Mountains definitely run through the western part of Texas. In fact, the Davis Mountains of the Lone Star State have been nicknamed "The Texas Alps."

On top of Mt. Locke at 6800 feet where the air is dry and clear sits the McDonald Observatory owned by the University of Texas at Austin. This area is renowned for having one of the darkest skies in North America and is therefore perfect for viewing the heavens. I've modeled my own fictitious setting after this one.

My hero, Captain Jace Riley of the Texas Rangers, is truly a hero. Rangers have a heritage that can be traced to the earliest days of Anglo settlement in Texas. They've often been compared to four other world-famous law-enforcement agencies: the FBI, Scotland Yard, Interpol and the Royal Canadian Mounted Police.

Prior to the Civil War, there was a real Texas Ranger with the first name Jace and another whose last name was Riley. I liked both names so much, I put them together to create my hero. Former Captain Bob Crowder has described the Rangers this way: "A Ranger is an officer who is able to handle any given situation without definite instructions from his commanding officer or higher authority. This ability must be proven before a man becomes a Ranger." I think you'll agree that Jace Riley is a perfect example of that.

I hope you'll enjoy Jace's story—and his romance with Dana Turner, first introduced in *My Private Detective*.

Rebecca Winters

P.S. If you have access to the Internet, please check out my Web site at http://www.rebeccawinters-author.com

Beneath a Texas Sky
Rebecca Winters

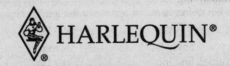

HARLEQUIN®

TORONTO • NEW YORK • LONDON
AMSTERDAM • PARIS • SYDNEY • HAMBURG
STOCKHOLM • ATHENS • TOKYO • MILAN • MADRID
PRAGUE • WARSAW • BUDAPEST • AUCKLAND

ISBN 0-373-71034-8

BENEATH A TEXAS SKY

Visit us at www.eHarlequin.com

Printed in U.S.A.

To Ann, an invaluable resource and a great friend.
I couldn't have done it without you!

CHAPTER ONE

As CAPTAIN JACE RILEY of the Texas Rangers loaded up his van, sweating under a hot July sun, he heard someone call to him.

"Hey—you there!"

Jace turned around in time to see a man, about thirty years old, come out of the service station in Fort Davis.

The brown-haired stranger rushed toward Jace's brown, heavy-duty van. Jace didn't think the man had a weapon in the overnight bag he carried, but you never knew for sure.

"I overheard you tell the mechanic you were on your way to Cloud Rim," the stranger said.

"It's my last stop."

It had been six months since two men had robbed an armored car in Austin of a million dollars before gunning down three people. One of their victims was Jace's longtime friend and mentor, retired Ranger Gibb Barton. Jace was desperate to track the killers down. But so far none of his travels in the mountains of West Texas had turned up evidence of the two killers or their stolen plane. The body of the original pilot had been dumped over the Davis Mountains and the killers had vanished.

In the days after Barton's death the whole department mourned him, but it was Jace who'd felt the loss on a personal as well as professional level. His efforts to track the killers while doing his regular work had been exhausting.

Frustrated and disappointed, he'd become so miserable even his colleagues had begun to avoid him. After several months of this, his superior called him in to the Austin office for a chat.

"You know something, Riley?" Tom Haster eyed him shrewdly. "You're one of the best, but you've worn yourself too thin. It's everyone's considered opinion those murderers made it to Mexico."

"My instincts tell me something different," Jace replied.

"We're all aware of that." Tom leaned back in his swivel chair. "So what do you want?"

Jace had understood the question. If he didn't get his act together, his job was on the line.

"The time to go after them."

"I was afraid you were going to say that." They'd stared at each other for a full minute. "All right— I'm going to grant your wish. You're not the only one who cared about Gibb."

Thank God. "Is that effective immediately?"

"Yes. I'll put you officially in charge of this case for two months. If you haven't turned up anything by then, I want you to let it go and come back to us. I assume you've already worked out a plan?"

Jace nodded. "If you could make arrangements with Instant Parcel Service, I could work as a summer relief driver and search the Davis Mountains for evidence. The job with IPS would be a good cover and give me the chance to explore the area. And I could hook up with Pat Hardy. He was a good friend of Gibb's, and now that he's retired from the Rangers, he's the sheriff in Alpine. He could be my backup man. With your permission I'd like to handpick some officers and P.I.'s funded by our department here to work behind the scenes with me and Pat.

"He'll have his own staff of officers, of course, but we're going to need a lot more help than that when I've picked up their trail."

"You've got anything you want."

"You're a good man, Tom."

"Bring the bastards in and I'll agree with you."

That conversation had taken place over six weeks ago. As Jace finished loading the van, he realized he had less than two weeks on the case before he had to go back to his normal duties. Eleven days to solve what his colleagues had been saying was an insoluble case.

His tension rising, he shut the van doors.

"Hey, I guess you didn't hear me. I need a ride."

Jace had barely noticed the clean-cut stranger in the button-down shirt who'd followed him to the driver's side of the van.

"I'm on my way up to Cloud Rim to see a woman. You know how it is." He flashed Jace an ingratiating smile, but Jace didn't buy it. In fact he couldn't relate to the man's problem. Jace had buried his wife seven years ago.

Cassie had been the sunshine in his life. When

he'd had a bad day, her quiet loving helped chase the demons away.

After her death from ovarian cancer, there didn't seem to be much point in going home anymore. Work and more work filled the hours and pretty soon it became his whole life.

"The clutch on my car wore out." The guy pointed to a silver Volkswagen Jetta parked at the service entrance. "The mechanic won't be able to replace it until tomorrow. I have to get up there today. What's it worth to you?"

There was always a chance that giving this stranger a lift to a small town where a stranger couldn't help but be noticed might lead to information on the killers. If so, it was worth more than money could buy.

Jace was open to anything that could shed light on the case, even this arrogant preppy type who appeared to have the hots for some woman. He reminded Jace of guys who never outgrew their college fraternity. People like him irritated the hell out of Jace. If it was a con, it was a good one.

The department didn't have a description of the killers. The driver of the armored car, who'd been badly wounded, said the men had been wearing ski masks and the older of the two gave all the orders. He thought they could be anywhere from twenty to forty years old. That was all he could manage to tell the paramedics before he died.

"You can ride with me. Hop in."

He unlocked the van and climbed behind the wheel where he released the master lock so the stranger could get in the other side, and then they were off.

Jace found himself hoping that this guy was one of the killers. Jace wanted evidence so badly, he'd gotten to a place where he fantasized about their capture with every male stranger he met.

Anxious to find out more about the guy, Jace decided to concentrate on his passenger and take him to Cloud Rim first, then finish his deliveries.

"What's your name?"

"Tony Roberts."

Which might or might not be his real name. Jace could check the guy's car registration later to find out the truth.

"What's yours?"

"Jace."

At the intersection he turned onto Highway 118. They passed a sign that read Exit to Cloud Rim in 10 Miles.

"Short for—"

"Just Jace."

It had been the first name of one of his great-great-grandfathers who'd been a Ranger before the Civil War. The family theorized its origin might be a distortion of the initials J.C.

"Must have been a rough childhood."

The guy's condescension was getting old fast. "Who's the woman you have to see in Cloud Rim? Maybe I've heard of her." In a town with a population of less than eight hundred, it was possible.

Since Monday Jace had taken over as the relief driver of the route while IPS's regular driver went on vacation. Today was Thursday. In that short amount of time, he'd not only made a ton of deliveries, he'd amassed an amazing amount of information about the area. But until Tony had asked for a ride, he hadn't stumbled across anything or one who made him suspicious.

"Dana Turner."

Jace nodded. "She lives in a trailer on the Mason property."

The guy's head whipped around. "You've met her?"

Why did Jace get the impression his passenger didn't like the idea?

"No, but I've left several packages for her at the ranch house. In fact, I have another delivery for her on the truck."

"I thought this was my unlucky day. Looks like I was wrong. Meeting up with you has solved the big problem of tracking her down."

It didn't sound as though the woman was expecting him. If she was the guy's wife, ex-wife or girlfriend, maybe she didn't want to be found. Maybe she was married to someone else. Maybe she was on the run. By now Jace's curiosity was fully aroused.

"Your first visit to Texas?"

"Why do you ask?" the other man asked aggressively.

So…press the right buttons and the guy had a short fuse. Paranoia dogged most angry people with something to hide. "Just making conversation."

Jace upped the volume for KALP, locally known

as the Voice of No Choice, broadcast out of Alpine where he rented a furnished apartment.

His passenger shifted in the seat. "Is that all you can get out of that thing around here?"

"Afraid so."

The other guy grunted. "This is one godforsaken place."

Jace figured he'd seen the last of his passenger's fatuous smile. So far the jerk hadn't said thanks or offered money for gas. Jace hadn't liked the guy right off. The reasons kept accumulating.

The Davis Mountains were green and rugged. Every time Jace drove up and down over the passes of his route, he marveled at the scenic views. One of his favorite spots was the breathtaking vista at the crest of the summit just before the drop into Fort Davis.

His passenger had to be totally eaten up with whatever was driving him not to be impressed with such magnificent scenery.

They passed the occasional suburban and SUV as the van continued to climb to the six-thousand-six-hundred-foot level. At this altitude, scattered clumps of ponderosa and piñon pine, mixed with oak and juniper trees dotting the rugged terrain, stood out in dark relief against the leaf-green grass.

Around one of the many curves of the blacktop two-lane highway he spied some vultures circling a jackrabbit that lay dead at the side of the road. He figured they were the same pair that took advantage of the roadkill yesterday.

All of creation had a purpose. That was what Jace

had been taught from childhood. But life had dealt him enough blows; he didn't know what he believed anymore. The only thing that felt good was the thought of catching up with Gibb Barton's killers.

If his passenger turned out to have anything to do with the case, he was going to pay…

"DANA? It's Glen Mason. I've been waiting for you to come home. Open up. I've got something you need."

"Just a minute!"

Dana Turner had heard the knock on the trailer door, but didn't answer at first. Since a month ago when she'd started renting from his grandfather, Ralph Mason, Glen had been making a nuisance of himself. The pathetic twenty-three-year-old had developed a crush on her.

Clutching her cell phone tighter, she said, "Dad? Someone's at the door. I have to go, but I'll call you back."

"Let me know when you get those pictures I sent you."

"I'm dying to see them. Don't worry, I'll phone you the minute they come. I love you, Dad."

"Me too, honey. Talk to you later."

Clicking off, she walked to the front of the trailer from the tiny kitchen where she'd been fixing lunch. When she unlocked the door, she noticed Glen was all spruced up in a western shirt and cowboy boots. His cologne was too much.

His blond hair was parted in the center and fell to his shoulders. She assumed he wore the small goatee to offset his baby face in an effort to appear older. He had a thin body that was only an inch taller than her five-foot-eight frame.

All in all she found him completely repulsive. To make things worse, his hazel eyes always looked at her with an expectant expression. No matter how many hints she'd thrown to make him stay away, he kept coming over on one pretext or another. This time he held a brown sack in his hand.

"What is it, Glen?"

"Grandad said you called about that special light that went out over the sink. As soon as I heard, I drove the pickup into town and got a replacement. If you want, I'll put it in now."

"That won't be necessary. I can do it myself." She took the sack from him. "I'll pay for the part when I mail him my next month's rent."

There was no way she was going to drop the check off and risk running into Glen. Renting the trailer had seemed such a perfect solution in the beginning. How was she to know it came with a price? Glen was four years younger than she was. He reminded her of a lonely, needy little kid, yet he was grown up enough to be loathsome.

"Fine." He rocked back on his heels. "Is there anything else I can do for you?"

"Not a thing."

His hands went to the pockets of his jeans. "Grandad told me to take good care of you."

"That's very kind of him, but I'm not anyone's concern." She started to shut the door.

"He told me to ask you over for dinner tonight. If you're not busy, that is," he added.

Dana was convinced Glen had made that up. "I'm afraid I am. Goodbye," she said pointedly.

Two ruddy patches broke out on his cheeks before he wheeled away.

She closed and locked the door.

Dana liked his kind eighty-eight-year-old grandfather. He had macular degeneration of the eyes and could barely get around the front room of his house with his walker.

If Glen wasn't living with him, she'd drop over once in a while to see how he was doing. But his grandson's obsession prevented her from doing anything he could misconstrue as interest on her part.

After putting the sack down on the kitchen counter, she poured herself a glass of milk from the fridge, then grabbed her tuna fish sandwich and sat at the table to eat.

The living room of the trailer wasn't much bigger than her prison cell had been, but since she'd been acquitted and freed, she felt as if she'd entered paradise.

Before her incarceration, she'd always pictured the Bible's version of that resting place beyond mortality.

After the judge ordered the handcuffs removed and told her she was a free woman, she realized paradise could be anywhere on earth, even inside this tiny space she called home. As long as she was free to be alone, free to breathe pure mountain air that didn't smell of disinfectant or urine, free to listen to the crickets instead of the clank of prison doors closing or other women being sick in the night it was paradise to her.

Free to fix herself something to eat any time she wanted, free to lie on soft sheets, free to sleep in or stay up late. Free to make a phone call in the middle of the night, free to lock her own door against the outside world, free to come and go at will, free to choose how to fill each minute, free to make her own associations.

The list was endless. Since gaining her freedom just months ago, she counted her blessings on an hourly basis like a litany, wondering if the day would ever dawn when she'd stop thinking about the horror of the past.

Thank God for work. During those precious hours when she was immersed in it, she forgot everything else. It was her salvation.

Reaching for the latest *Royal Astrophysics Journal,* she turned to her article about the discovery of a brown dwarf. She had submitted it before her imprisonment. With the advent of sophisticated light sensors and adaptive optics at Mt. Palomar, where her father worked as one of the head astronomers, she'd had access to the powerful tools needed to resolve smaller, dimmer objects near stars.

Pleased to see her words in print at last, she settled down to read the piece while she peeled an orange for dessert.

Fresh fruit. Something rare in prison. She couldn't get enough of it or fresh, crisp lettuce, which she'd piled inside her sandwich and devoured like a rabbit.

But her enjoyment of the juicy fruit was short. She couldn't help but picture Consuela Juarez, the woman in the next cell, lying on her bunk right now while she sobbed for her daughter, Rosita.

The poor thing cried for her child every day after lunch. Thinking about it tore Dana's heart out. Even the distance stretching between California and Texas didn't ease the pain.

Dana stopped reading, unable to concentrate.

Since her release, she'd been to Anaheim, California, a dozen times to spend the day with the five-year-old who was being raised by her aunt Paquita. The impoverished woman had more children than she could handle.

Dana always slipped her money to take care of Rosita's needs, but there were some problems money couldn't solve. It wouldn't be long before an overwhelmed Paquita placed Rosita in foster care.

Yet every time Dana visited Consuela at Fielding Women's Prison outside San Bernadino, she chose to tell her only the good things about her adorable daughter.

Consuela was a twenty-two-year-old mother in for fifteen years on a manslaughter charge. Dana was convinced the woman had killed her drug-riddled, abusive, maniac ex-husband in self-defense. But she'd had no high-priced lawyer to defend her.

By the time Consuela lived out her prison sentence, her daughter would likely be a troubled young woman. By then it would be too late to help her. Dana knew Consuela would give up on life long before then.

Dana could relate to that state of mind better than anyone else. She'd talked to her best friend Heidi Poletti about Consuela. Heidi in turn had talked to her husband, Gideon, the San Diego homicide detective who'd been responsible for getting Dana freed from prison. It was Heidi who asked her husband to look into Consuela's case and see what he could do.

So far there'd been no word; however, Dana knew Gideon was working on it. These things took time.

Time was all you had in prison. Time to grieve endlessly for her beloved sister, whose undetected brain tumor had caused such tragedy. Time to think about killing yourself to end the agony. Like Dana, Consuela lived with the additional burden of believing it was a sin to commit suicide. Which meant there was no alternative but to tough it out until you'd done your time.

No one knew what that was like unless they'd been locked up. At the thought, Dana broke out in a cold sweat and felt sick in the pit of her stomach.

She started reading the article again, then heard another knock on the door. It had to be Glen with some other trumped-up excuse to see her. He could stand there till doomsday. She continued to sit there and read.

This time there was a distinct rap on the door. "Ms. Turner?" a deep, unfamiliar male voice called out. "Delivery!"

She shut the journal and hurried over to the door. When she unlocked it, the first thing she saw was a tall, black-haired, rock-solid man in a khaki-brown uniform. He filled her vision.

For a moment she thought he was one of those legendary Texas Rangers. Was that a subpoena in his hand? Had he tricked her into answering the door?

She thought she would be sick in front of him. Too late she read the inscription on his badge and realized he was a driver for IPS, not a police officer!

JACE COULDN'T IMAGINE what he'd done to cause the willowy brunette to react like that. The blood had all but drained from her lovely face. Right off, the woman's vulnerability disarmed him.

"Are you all right?"

"Yes, of course. I just wasn't expecting anyone."

He felt a stab of guilt. Tony stood near the other end of the trailer listening, hoping to discover if the woman who answered the door was the one he'd come to see.

"I noticed the Toyota next to your trailer. It's the first time I've seen a car parked here all week, so I assumed you were inside."

"I came home for lunch today. N-normally I stay at work," she stammered. "You have a package for me?"

He nodded. "If you'll sign here." Jace handed her the clipboard. As she put her signature on the line, her fingers trembled. He wondered what caused her fright.

Though he tried not to be obvious, he couldn't help but gaze at her classic features. If she ever smiled, she'd be a raving beauty.

⸻ssed in a pale pink blouse and jeans that she
⸻ly, she had a femininity that appealed

strongly to the male in him. He took in her long legs—the kind he admired on a woman.

When she gave the clipboard back to him, he found himself so distracted by her flowery scent he almost forgot to put the package in her hands.

Clutching it against her chest like a shield, she said, "I'm glad you found me at home. From now on, would you please leave any deliveries for me outside my door, even if I'm not here? No one's going to steal them, and I don't want Mr. Mason over at the ranch house disturbed because of me."

He looked into her translucent gray eyes fringed by dark lashes and realized he was staring.

"I'll be happy to do that."

"Thank you."

As she started to shut the door on him, a voice called out, *"Hello, Dana."*

Jace had all but forgotten about his passenger. He couldn't remember the last time he'd lost his focus simply by looking at a woman. It shouldn't have happened.

"What are you doing here, Tony?"

She sounded…outraged, yet she'd spoken in a controlled voice. Jace watched her eyes darken as the other man approached from the side of the trailer where the van was parked.

"What do you think?" He flashed her his vacuous smile.

She didn't show fear, but judging from her wintry reception, the guy was persona non grata. That came as no surprise to Jace. What *did* surprise him was to hear her invite Tony inside the trailer.

Having no excuse to linger, Jace disappeared around the front end of the trailer, then stood close by, hoping to hear more conversation. But if they were talking, he couldn't hear them.

He let another minute pass before he climbed in the van and did some paperwork while he listened through the open window. There was no sound coming from the interior of the trailer. That bothered him a lot. Anything could be going on in there.

It might not have to do with the case he was working on, but he sensed trouble. After hanging around as long as he dared, Jace started the engine and headed back toward town.

He didn't like Tony Roberts. Worse, he couldn't abide the thought of the two of them together, shut away in such an isolated spot.

The street ended just beyond the Mason house. There weren't any other neighbors, just dense clusters of junipers and pines.

Jace had about an hour's worth of deliveries to make in Cloud Rim. When he'd finished the last of them, he'd drive back to the trailer. He could always use the pretext that he needed her to fill out a form allowing their company to leave packages without getting a signature. That way he could check things out.

DANA PUT the overnight package from her father on the table. She was still trying to recover from the shock of thinking the IPS driver was a police officer. She wondered how long it would take her to control her fear every time someone in law enforcement crossed her path.

The only reason Dana had let Tony inside the trailer was to avoid a confrontation with him in front of the stranger. Now that she'd heard the van drive away, she could concentrate on getting rid of her unwanted visitor as fast as possible.

He'd set his bag on the floor and was looking around as if he intended to stay for a while.

To think there'd ever been a time when she'd dated him, let alone kissed him. It had been a short, stormy month that had ended when she discovered he'd only been using her to get in good with her dad. Looking at him now, he was as pitiful as Glen, only for different reasons.

"Months ago my father informed me you were told to get your Ph.D. somewhere other than Cal-Tech. You have your gall showing your face here," she said coldly.

"I came to patch things up between us. It was all a misunderstanding."

"You committed a crime!" Her anger rose quickly.

"I know that's what your father believes," he said in exasperation. "But he would never listen to my side of it."

"You didn't have a side, Tony. While I was in prison, Dad figured out what you'd been up to. It was your insatiable ambition that did you in—using the material off my disks to pass off as your own work. How sad. You were a graduate student with a lot of promise."

"I know that's what it looked like, but I was only trying to advance your theories while you couldn't work on them yourself. Don't you see? I put my name on a few projects you'd shared with me because *you* couldn't."

Dana moved closer. "You should have visited me at least one time if you expected me to fall for that fairy tale now."

"How could I do that? After the fight we had before you were arrested, I was afraid you'd refuse to see me."

She shook her head. "That bald-faced lie isn't even worthy of you. I can see it in your eyes. Despite my innocence, you still haven't made up your mind if I murdered my sister or not. What's worse, you don't give a damn, because all you've ever cared about is *you*."

"That's not true. If I felt guilty, do you think I would have come to this backwater in the hope of becoming your assistant? I thought we could start over again. We made a great team."

"You're delusional. You'd do anything to get back in my father's good graces. You'd be the last person I would ever hire for any reason. Please leave. The door's right behind you."

He flashed her the phony smile that had gotten her into trouble the first time. "I can't go anywhere. My car's broken down in Fort Davis. I got a ride with the IPS driver, and now he's gone."

It was just like Tony to use someone else rather than pay for a rental car. He was insufferable.

"That's tough. I guess you're going to have to

hoof it back to town and take your chances that the motel isn't full.''

"Come on, Dana,'' he pleaded. "I was hoping to sleep on your couch tonight. For old times' sake.'' He closed the distance and pulled her into his arms before kissing her.

Revolted, she pushed him away. "'For old times' sake' implies there were some good ones.''

With that comment, the mask fell away, revealing the depths of his anger. It must have been humiliating to have been given the boot by her famous father.

"You've changed.''

"Betrayal does that to a person.''

"You're as hard as your old man.''

Tony was nothing more than a spoiled brat who'd never learned the meaning of the word *no*. Clearly, he thought this was some kind of game he could win.

"He could have brought you up on criminal charges. Be thankful you got off lightly. Now get out!''

A strange glitter entered his eyes. "Not yet.''

What happened next came as a total surprise. One second she was standing there. In the next, he'd grasped her shoulders and pinned her down on the couch. His hands were everywhere.

Realizing he was out of control, she summoned enough strength to fling her body lengthwise on the couch. She grabbed beneath the cushion at the far end and whipped out her father's handgun.

At the sight of the weapon pointed at him, he pulled back far enough for her to get to her feet.

She pushed the hair out of her face. "Maybe now you'll change your mind about leaving."

Her dad had insisted she keep his Glock nine millimeter in the trailer in case there was an intruder. Until she'd spent time in prison, she hadn't understood the need for a woman to protect herself.

The bloodcurdling stories she'd heard from her fellow inmates had taught her lessons she wouldn't have learned elsewhere. She paid attention to her father when he taught her how to shoot.

For the first time since she'd known Tony, Dana saw astonishment on his face. He got up slowly from the couch.

"It's against the law for an ex-felon to be in possession of a firearm."

"I was pardoned."

He darted her a wild-eyed expression. "You even know how to use that thing?"

She stood her ground. "Shall we find out?"

After a moment he must have realized this wasn't an argument he was likely to win. He picked up his overnight bag. "I'm going."

"Good. Don't ever come near me or my father again."

His menacing expression was a revelation. "The judge made a mistake when he let you out."

"Tell that to God. Goodbye, Tony."

CHAPTER TWO

AFTER THE TRAILER DOOR closed behind him, Dana's legs almost gave way. She put the weapon on the coffee table, then ran over to lock up after him.

Had she really pulled a gun on Tony?

When her strength returned, she ran back to the table for her cell phone. She needed to talk to Heidi. The distance between Texas and California didn't seem as great when she could call her closest friend at virtually any time.

Once she'd punched in the digits, she paced the small space waiting for her to pick up.

"Hello?"

"Heidi?" she cried.

"Dana—what's wrong?"

"You'll never believe what I just did." Her voice shook. "*I* don't believe it." In a torrent of words, she told her friend everything.

"I bet Tony's never been so terrified in his life," Heidi blurted. "I would have loved to see that! He's probably halfway to Fort Davis already. Wait till I tell Gideon."

"No—don't!"

"Why not? After what Tony tried to do, you

would have had every right to shoot him in self-defense.''

"That argument didn't work for Consuela."

After a slight hesitation, "Point taken," Heidi said in a subdued tone. "Let's just be thankful Tony felt threatened enough to leave."

"Believe me, I am. Who would have guessed at all that anger?"

"According to Gideon, the guys who walk around with wide smiles and phony handshakes are like ticking bombs on the inside, ready to go off. Something bad must have happened to Tony in his childhood, but he's no longer your problem. I'm so thankful your dad insisted you keep that gun."

"Me too." No telling how far Tony would have gone in his rage if she'd had no protection.

"Is that strange kid next door still pestering you? You know who I mean. The one who looks like General George Custer without the hat."

Heidi had met Glen when she'd helped Dana move in to the trailer. The description was so perfect, it made Dana laugh at a time when she didn't think laughing was possible. "Yes. Glen was here earlier trying to get me to eat dinner with him and his grandfather tonight. He refuses to go away."

"Then I'm doubly glad you've got that gun."

"Heidi!"

"Let's face it, Dana. You've had your share of lowlifes with Glen and Tony. Where are all those tall, tough, tempting Texan males I've always heard about?"

Dana's gaze darted to the overnight package. She

knew of one fitting that description who drove an IPS van. No doubt his wife was waiting for him to get home from work.

How would it be to welcome *him* into your arms every night? Heidi would never stop teasing her if Dana told her the IPS man looked like a god.

"Dana? Are you still there?"

"Yes."

"Are you holding out on me?"

Heat crept into her face. "No. Of course not."

"Yes you are. You always say of course not when you're telling a blatant lie."

"I have no interest in men anymore, Heidi."

"That's because you're afraid. But the right man will help you get over that. You'll see."

"I have to get going now. Thanks for listening to me."

"I'll call you later tonight to make sure you're all right. Maybe by then you'll be willing to tell me about this blue-eyed wonder."

"They're dark brown," Dana said before she realized her mistake.

"Mmm, nice. Blond hair or black?"

"I don't remember."

"Liar, but I love you anyway."

Tears filled Dana's eyes. "I love you too. I owe you and Gideon my life."

"Aren't we past that yet?"

"No—I still can't believe I'm free." She took a deep breath. "Has Gideon said anything about Consuela?"

"Not yet. I swear I'll phone you the minute I hear

anything. Don't forget we're driving out to see you next week. We'll probably arrive in Cloud Rim next Thursday around noon, but I'll keep you posted.''

''Can't wait till you get here.''

''Me too. Talk to you tonight.''

Once they'd said goodbye, Dana put the gun back where she'd hidden it. After grabbing the overnight package, she left for work, anxious to see what her father had sent her.

So far her new Toyota performed without flaw. She drove a half mile toward town, then turned left on the dirt road. If you weren't a local, you'd never guess the divider road between two small ranches eventually wound its way to the top of Mount Luna. Its summit was two hundred feet higher than the town of Cloud Rim.

High up at six thousand eight hundred feet lay her family's private property with its white observatory. She paused a moment before going in. Here the world lay at her feet in every direction. Such magnificent vistas were a constant wonder to her. She could breathe in all the pure, dry mountain air she wanted. And for someone who'd suffered from claustrophobia since childhood, the open expanse came as pure relief every time she got out of the car.

Dana first discovered her phobia for enclosed places during a submarine ride at Disneyland. Later she shied away from entering any haunted houses at Halloween.

Some things she could tolerate fine, like an elevator or her trailer. What she couldn't abide were places like tunnels, where she couldn't see daylight.

On her trip around the world with Heidi several years before, she hadn't been able to go inside the pyramids in Egypt or see the catacombs of Rome. When they were in Austria viewing the salt mines, Heidi had been forced to take the underground train ride alone.

But prison was the place Dana had suffered the most. Every time she heard the gates lock after the inmates had been allowed in the yard for a minimum of time, she felt entombed.

If it hadn't been for the medication the judge had ordered the prison doctor to give her, Dana was positive she would have died in that hellhole. When she thought of Consuela still locked up in one of those airless cages away from her daughter, she could hardly breathe. The only thing that helped was knowing Gideon was working on her case.

Without wasting any more time dwelling on her friend's pain, Dana unlocked the entrance to the observatory with its thirty-foot dome and went inside. It had been built last year to her father's exacting specifications with the newest state-of-the-art equipment. All expenses for its construction had been privately funded by various companies with interests in future findings.

Dana thrilled to the custom-made forty-inch reflector telescope; its mirror represented the latest in astronomical technology.

Housed with special observational computers that would enhance the imaging, the place was a joy to operate while she worked on her Ph.D. in astrogeology. Now that the computers had been hooked up to Cal-Tech's at Mount Palomar, she had constant access to their data, and vice versa.

Two offices, a rest room, mini kitchen and store-room had been built.

This place was home to her, not the trailer. She'd bought a futon and bedding, which she kept in her office. Many nights she slept here after finishing her observations.

The night sky over the Davis Mountains was one of the darkest on the North American continent. It brought the heavens so close, there were times she felt she could reach up with her hands and pull down a cluster of stars.

Her father always chuckled when he told people the story of her first look through the telescope when she was five. Apparently she'd begged to touch the rings of Saturn.

"I'd like to touch them too, honey. But they're too far away."

"But I want to see them up close."

"You can."

"How?"

"By looking at some new pictures we've just re-ceived from a camera on board the *Voyager I* space-craft."

"Can I see them now? Please?"

"All right. Come on. I'll take you to my office and show you."

According to her father, her interest in the planets had been insatiable. That night marked the beginning of her great love affair with the heavens.

She sat down at her desk in the swivel chair. As

she opened the package her father had sent her, an image of the man who'd brought it to her door came back to her in full force.

Since he was an IPS driver, they'd probably see each other again sometime. Though she'd already decided he belonged to a wife or girlfriend, it seemed her heart hadn't gotten the message yet.

Frustrated because her mind kept dwelling on their encounter, she gave an impatient tug at the package. Out came three large photographs of Jupiter's moon, Europa. Each one showed an icy surface riddled with fissures and cracks.

After studying them for a few minutes, she got so excited she had to call her father on her cell phone. He would see her caller ID. She hoped he wasn't too busy to answer.

To her delight he picked up on the third ring. "Dana, honey? Are you all right?"

That was his stock question whenever he heard her voice these days. Prison had affected their family's life in untold ways. However, one positive manifestation was the stronger outpouring of love between her and her parents. There was more talking, more sharing.

"I just opened your package. *Daddy!*" she shouted with excitement.

He laughed. "Those pictures are tantalizing, aren't they? Although some impact craters are visible, I'd say their general absence indicates a youthful surface."

"I agree. When you look at the youngest ridges, like those features crossing the center of the pictures, you can see aligned knobs and central fractures along with those dark irregular patches. In my opinion they could indicate cryovolcanism. More than ever I believe there's been volcanic activity on Europa in the past.''

"I think you're right, honey. I'm just as convinced a liquid ocean lies beneath the crust.''

"If both are present, then—''

"Then we've got a moon with an environment for the existence of li—'' Her father stopped midsentence. "Uh-oh. Dr. Harbin just came running in to my office with one of those problems that needs solving right away.''

"We'll talk later. Thanks for the pictures, Dad.''

"You bet, honey.''

After they said goodbye, she pinned the photos to the corkboard wall where they would be on constant display. Inspired by what she could see, Dana opened up the computer file on the Europa project and began entering her observations.

She'd told Glen she had other plans for the evening, so she would stay here and work straight through until dark.

At some point tonight, Heidi would be calling. Her friend would be relentless with her questions about the IPS man. Until then, Dana would try to put him out of her mind, but deep inside she knew it was impossible.

JACE HAD JUST CLIMBED in the van when Art Watkins, owner and pharmacist of Watkins's Drug, came hurrying out the back entrance of the building with a box in his hands.

What now? Jace checked his watch before rolling down the window. It was after three. Though he'd hurried to get everything done so he could check up on Dana Turner, he was already running late.

"Could you do me a favor, Jace?"

"If I can. What is it?"

"While you're out there doing your deliveries tomorrow, would you mind leaving a few of these flyers at the different stops on your route?

"My wife and I found out we're losing our renter this weekend. We don't like the apartment to be vacant and we're using every means we know to spread the word.

"It's a real cozy half-basement unit with a new kitchen and full windows in the living-room portion. There's a private entrance and garage around the back of the house."

"It sounds nice. I'll be glad to help you out." He reached for the ream-size box and put it on the passenger seat.

Jace would have agreed to the request anyway, but Art had just provided him with a legitimate excuse to get in some new places and ask questions even if he didn't have a pickup or delivery to make.

In all these weeks, he hadn't spotted any plane wreckage. For that matter, he hadn't heard of anyone who'd inherited a fortune recently or was spending one. No businesspeople were talking about a show of big bills being flashed around.

Maybe Jace's instincts were shot and the killers *had* gone to Mexico.

"I can't thank you enough." Art pulled a couple of twenties out of his wallet.

Jace shook his head. "I appreciate the gesture, but keep your money. See you tomorrow." Flashing him a grin, he closed the window before the older man could drop the bills inside the door.

As he started the engine and drove down the alley, he glanced in the van's side-view mirror and could see Art waving to him. He waved back.

To some degree Art reminded Jace of his own father. A good, kind, hardworking family man. Honest to a fault. Always pleasant to be around. The contrast in nature between the two older men and someone surly, like Jace's passenger of a few hours ago, was amazing, to say the least.

That situation had been preying on his mind. Anxious to find out if Dana Turner was all right, he headed for the Mason property. As soon as the trailer came into view he noticed that her white Toyota was missing. It could mean several things, but there was no point in speculating.

He pulled off the road as he'd done before, and reached for the form he would ask her to sign. Fastening it to a clipboard, he got out of the van and walked up to her door.

"Ms. Turner?" He knocked several times and waited. When there was no answer, he rapped on the door harder and called out to her again. Still no response.

Jace walked around the trailer. The curtains were

drawn at all the windows, so he couldn't see inside. Suddenly worried, he went back to the van for a certain set of tools. With no one to witness his actions, he could slip inside her place for a quick look and be out again in seconds.

If for some reason she and Tony were in there and hadn't felt like answering the door, he would have to show his credentials and explain there was a manhunt on for the killers. He hoped it wouldn't come to that, since he'd be blowing his carefully created cover if it did. There was too much at stake to risk it prematurely.

He grimaced when he realized the lock was too damn easy to release. Anyone could break in here while she was sleeping. She'd never know what hit her.

There were times when the law allowed an officer to enter a private residence without a search warrant if an emergency arose. In his judgment, this was one of those times. He realized he was relying on instinct more than on evidence, but his gut feelings had rarely steered him wrong.

He drew his weapon and opened the door, entering in a crouch position. To his relief, the place was empty. He moved silently through the interior, past the empty bathroom to the bedroom.

Except for an empty glass and plate on the table, she kept a spotless place. Had she fed her uninvited guest before they left? He saw no evidence of a struggle, but that didn't necessarily mean there hadn't been one. The package he'd delivered earlier was nowhere in sight.

He peered through the curtains of both side windows to be sure the way was clear before letting himself out. When he'd secured the lock, he headed back to the van.

It would help if he knew where she worked. Ralph Mason would have that information. Jace pulled into the man's driveway and hurried to the front door. After ringing the bell several times, it was clear the old man wasn't going to answer. He'd probably fallen asleep.

Ralph had a grandson who was living with him, but Jace hadn't met him and it didn't look as if he was around now. The blue Chevy three-quarter-ton pickup he'd seen parked next to the house on several occasions was missing.

There was no more time to waste. Jace got back in the van. After ten minutes of driving around town looking for her car, he called Pat, his backup man, who'd been only too willing to help Jace with this case.

The sheriff had brought in extra help for Alpine's regular department business so he could concentrate on Gibb's case and be available to Jace on a twenty-four-hour basis.

"Pat, in case there's been foul play, I want any officers working within a hundred-and-fifty-mile radius of Cloud Rim to watch for a new white four-door Toyota."

He gave Pat descriptions of Dana and Tony, plus the license number that had been taped to the rear window. She didn't have Texas plates on her car yet and could have purchased it under the name Howard or Turner.

If anyone spotted the vehicle, they were to follow it and get the information back to Jace.

With a feeling of foreboding, he left Cloud Rim and started down the mountain, watching for any white car that came into sight, parked or moving.

He was looking so hard he almost missed Tony Roberts, who stood at the side of the road halfway to Fort Davis with his overnight bag in hand, thumbing for a ride.

When he saw Jace's van, he waved him down. Jace didn't know whether to be relieved or not. He wouldn't rest easy until he knew Ms. Turner's whereabouts and had been assured she was all right.

Some criminal types got a high remaining visible. Jace wouldn't let up on Tony Roberts until he had proof he was wrong about him.

After slowing to a stop, he put his head out the window. "Come on. I'll give you a lift." While Tony went around the van, Jace put the box of flyers on the floor behind the other seat.

His passenger climbed inside and shut the door, placing his bag across his legs. He turned to Jace. "I figured I might catch you on the way back."

Jace started up the van again. "You didn't stay very long."

"Nope."

If Jace wanted to get any information out of this guy, he needed to play whatever hand he was dealt. Unfortunately, Tony remained silent for the next five miles.

By the time they'd crested the summit to drop down into Fort Davis, Jace had seen one white car go by, but it wasn't a Toyota.

Tony finally turned to him. "Where exactly is Indian Lodge?"

"About three miles south of here."

"Hell."

"What's wrong?"

"It's the only place I could get a room for tonight while my car's being fixed."

"Then I'll keep going and drop you off there."

After another couple of miles Jace turned onto a road leading to the pueblo-style lodge.

"As you can see by the number of cars parked, you've come at the height of the tourist season."

"You think I don't know that? When I started out, I assumed I wouldn't be needing a room."

This was the opening Jace had been waiting for, but they'd arrived at the front entrance to the lobby. "Your girlfriend's a beautiful woman. It's too bad you couldn't have won her around. Maybe next time."

"There won't be a next time," Tony muttered.

"Why not?"

"For the last six months she's been hanging out with trash, but I never thought I'd see the day she'd pull a gun on me. That's the biggest turnoff I can imagine. Thanks for the ride," he said before getting out of the van and walking off.

What in the hell— Jace reeled.

Tony had been planning to stay with Dana Turner, but had ended up walking back to Fort Davis.

Maybe Tony, for all his strange behavior, had been telling the truth. So what did that say about Dana—whoever she was?

What kind of woman stayed alone in the mountains away from people? Why did she have a gun? Who were the criminals Tony had referred to? Where were they? Jace had seen no evidence of anyone else living with her in the trailer.

Were the seven months Tony had mentioned pure coincidence?

Or had there been a third party connected to the armed robbery that had taken place six months ago? Had Dana been one of the killer's girlfriends, or an accessory?

Perhaps she'd sheltered the killers for a time and knew where they were. It might explain why she didn't want Tony around and had gotten rid of him in a way guaranteed not to bring him back.

And maybe you're so desperate to catch Gibb's killers, you're grasping at anything and have lost your mind.

Before Jace could be sure of anything, he needed a lot more information about both Tony and Dana.

On a fresh burst of adrenaline, he drove out to the highway and turned back toward Fort Davis. Ten minutes later he pulled into the service station where he'd picked up his passenger earlier in the day.

After leaving some of Art's flyers with the attendant, he got a look at the silver Jetta's California license plate. When he climbed in the van, he phoned in the information to Pat.

"I'll run a background check on Roberts as soon

as we hang up, Jace. As for an update, no officers have called in about the Toyota yet, but they're staying on it. We've learned one thing—the woman in question listed herself as Dana Turner on her new license. And before that, she held a California license plate also under the name of Turner.''

Jace gripped the phone tighter. ''Run a California statewide check on her and see what comes up. Motor vehicles. Vital records. Anything you can find.''

''Will do.''

Jace checked in at the IPS office in Alpine, but his mood was so black he headed for his apartment without saying a word to any of the other drivers.

Once he'd let himself inside, he flung off his shirt and reached for a cold can of beer from the fridge. He blamed his frustration level on the fact that, despite his suspicions, despite his instinctive fears, nothing that happened today seemed to have anything to do with the killers.

But it wasn't until he stood under the spray of the shower that the real source of his frustration hit him like a ten-ton truck.

He'd felt an instant attraction to the woman who'd opened her trailer door to him earlier in the day. It had gone deep, awakening something inside him he thought had died with his wife.

A groan escaped his throat. Why did the line between innocence and guilt have to be blurred where Dana was concerned?

As he stepped out of the shower, he heard his cell phone ringing. He grabbed a towel and dashed into the bedroom, checking the caller ID before he answered.

"What have you got, Pat?"

"Hey, Jace, your guy came up pretty clean. His name is Anthony Roberts, twenty-nine, Caucasian male resident from Irvine, California. He's received three speeding tickets in five years. No outstanding warrants for his arrest."

Jace sucked in his breath. "What about the woman?"

"Nothing on her yet. The guys are still combing the area for her Toyota. I'll get back to you the minute I hear anything."

"Thanks, Pat."

"Sure thing."

No sooner had he hung up than the phone rang again. It was Buck, his younger brother. They'd always been close, but since Jace had taken a leave of absence, they'd only touched base once.

"Buck? How're you doing?"

"Everything's fine at home. What about you?"

"Not one piece of hard evidence has turned up yet."

"That's tough, Jace. I figured you'd phone if there'd been any good news. I know how much Gibb meant to you."

Jace's jaw hardened. "Only eleven days to find the killers before I have to report back to Austin."

"That means you'll miss the family reunion again this year."

"When is it?"

"Next weekend."

"I forgot."

"At least this time you have a legitimate excuse to stay away."

"What do you mean?"

"This is Buck, remember? I know how painful it is for you to be at big family gatherings without Cassie. Maybe by this time next year you'll have met someone."

"I already have," he muttered before he could catch himself.

The silence on the other end was tangible. Finally, "Are you saying what I think you're saying?"

"Don't get too excited, Buck. This is a woman who might be involved in Gibb's murder. I'm waiting to hear what the background check turns up on her."

"How in the heck could yo—"

"It wasn't a conscious act on my part," Jace broke in. "She just...happened to me."

Buck whistled. "I can't believe what I'm hearing. You honestly think she's mixed up in the case in some way?"

"The only thing I know is that I don't *want* to believe it."

"I won't say a word to anyone," his brother assured him.

"I can always depend on you. Tell the folks I'll call them soon."

"I will. Be careful, Jace."

A vision of Dana Turner flashed before his eyes. "You're probably too late, but it's the thought that counts. Thanks for phoning, Buck."

GLEN MASON DROVE the pickup to the rear of the ranch house and let himself in the back door. He'd almost made it to his bedroom on tiptoe when his grandfather called out.

"That you, Glen?"

"Yeah, Grandad. Go back to sleep."

"That's the second time this week you've come in at three o'clock in the morning. Aren't those pretty late hours you're keeping with Dana Turner?"

"I told you. She has to work late. We don't even leave for Alpine until nine. What do you expect?"

"Don't talk to me that way, Glen."

"Sorry."

"Mr. Jorgenson phoned tonight."

"Yeah?"

"According to him, you've been coming into work late and taking longer lunch breaks than you should. Now I can see why. If you're staying up half the night courting, there's no way you can be at the grocery store by eight in the morning to stock shelves."

"I get the work done."

"That's not the point. Since you came to live with me, you've lost one job after another. Mr. Jorgenson took you on as a personal favor to me. I promised him you wouldn't let him down. You know how hard it is to find a job in Cloud Rim. You're lucky to have this one."

"I know."

"No you don't, but that's your daddy's fault for abandoning you. Listen, Glen—if you want to go on living with me and have the use of my truck, you're going to have to do everything you can to show Mr.

Jorgenson you're not a sluggard. In order to make certain you get your sleep, I'm putting you on a midnight curfew.''

"Midnight—"

"If I don't hear any more complaints from Mr. Jorgenson after a month has passed, I'll change it to one o'clock. Do we have a deal?''

"I'm almost twenty-four, Grandad.''

"That may be, but you can't take care of yourself yet, let alone anyone else. Before I die, I want to see you hold down a steady job and become responsible.''

Tears stung Glen's eyes. "You sound like Mom before she took with one of her boyfriends. She said I'd never amount to anything—that I'd end up a drifter just like Dad.''

"Don't talk that way, Glen. You had a hard life, but I believe in you even if she didn't. Otherwise I wouldn't keep trying to help you. But you've got to do your part to be successful.''

"Don't worry. I'm going to be successful. A lot sooner than you think,'' he muttered under his breath.

CHAPTER THREE

UNANSWERED QUESTIONS about Dana Turner kept Jace tossing and turning throughout the night. If he slept, he didn't know when it happened.

At six he was up and out of the apartment. After grabbing breakfast at a drive-thru, he arrived at the small IPS branch office to start loading his van before the other staff reported in.

He didn't want to see his co-workers or the other driver who covered the town of Alpine. No doubt they'd ask him what he was doing for the weekend and invite him to join them. They were nice guys, but he had other plans no one could know about.

After making deliveries at several ranches outside Alpine, he drove to the Chihuahuan Desert Research Institute and Visitor's Center. Along with the usual deliveries, he left some of Art's flyers. From there he stopped at every facility he hadn't been in before in order to leave IPS company brochures and the flyers.

Each time he talked to someone, he asked questions about new people in the area, new businesses springing up. To his chagrin, he never got the answer he wanted.

So far he still hadn't heard from Pat about the

background check on Dana. By the time he'd reached
Fort Davis, he was tied up in knots. After he'd finished his business there, he drove by the service station, unable to resist.

The silver Jetta had made it to the top of the lift.
No telling where Tony was while he waited to get
out of here.

Halfway to Cloud Rim, Jace's cell phone rang. His
gaze swerved to the caller ID. When he saw it was
Pat, his heart slammed into his ribs as he realized
this was the moment of truth.

Now that it had come, he dreaded hearing the
words if they weren't the right ones. Yesterday Dana
Turner had done something to him, something he
couldn't explain. If Pat had bad news, it was going
to take a long time before the name Dana no longer
meant anything to him.

He pressed the talk button. "Pat? I assume you've
got information for me."

"Nothing on the Toyota yet, but there's plenty on
the woman. Her legal name is Dana Turner, female
Caucasian, twenty-seven, last known residence Fielding Women's Prison, San Bernadino, California, on
a murder conviction.

"After serving seven months of a thirty-years-to-
life sentence, the case was reopened and the judge
vacated his verdict. She went free at the end of April
of this year. Before her arrest, her last known address
was Pasadena, California."

At this point Jace had to pull to the side of the
road. Listening to Pat was like flying over the ocean
in a jetliner that suddenly went into a twenty-

thousand-foot crash dive, then by some miracle righted itself enough at the last second to prevent utter annihilation.

"Jace? Did you get all that?"

"I did," he murmured, still trying to assimilate the fact that she'd spent seven months behind bars. The time frame made it impossible for her to have had any contact with the killers during their crime spree.

What about before and after, Riley?

Questions bombarded him from all directions like matter being sucked into a black hole.

Were the killers originally from California? Was one of them in love with Dana? Had she committed other crimes with them? Had they visited her at the prison and made arrangements for her to come to Cloud Rim when they heard she was free? Had she threatened Tony so he'd stay away?

Jace's chest tightened.

Either Dana was as guilty as sin but had been released on a technicality that came to light only after her incarceration…

Or, she was a total innocent—one of the unfortunates of this world sent to prison by mistake while the real culprit ran around committing more crimes.

Until he knew the truth, he wouldn't breathe freely.

And if it's the wrong truth, Riley?

He refused to think about that just yet.

"You're awfully quiet."

Jace had been too stunned by the unexpected news to make conversation. "You had to do a lot of digging to come up with that much information." Pat was thorough and meticulous about police work. It's what had made him such a great Ranger in his day. "I owe you."

"Forget it. We'll keep looking for that Toyota."

"Thanks."

At two-thirty Jace drove into Cloud Rim. Dana said she didn't usually eat lunch at the trailer. He decided he'd buy a hamburger at the local café, then get all his deliveries and pickups done first. Around five, when most people got off work, he'd drive out to see her.

"Hi, Millie," he said as he sat down at the counter. The café was named after the middle-aged widow who knew a lot of the people in town. So far she'd been his greatest source of information.

She smiled before pouring him a cup of coffee. "Hamburgers get boring, Jace. For once, why don't you live dangerously and order my egg salad sandwich with a bowl of chowder on the side."

"Why not. It sounds like a nice change."

"Coming right up."

There were only a few people at the booths and no one else at the counter. It appeared the lunch crowd had already passed through.

When an old sixties song played from the jukebox, Jace glanced in its direction. A strange-looking guy with long blond hair was feeding coins into the slot. Wearing well-worn cowboy boots, jeans and a cowhide vest with no shirt, he reminded Jace of someone out of an old western film.

"Here you go. Hope you like it."

Jace smiled. "I wouldn't come here every day if

I didn't approve of the food *and* the service." He bit into his sandwich and proceeded to devour it.

"Since I run the only café in town, you don't have much of a choice."

"Sure I do," he said. "I could pack a lunch. But then I start thinking about your caramel pecan pie."

"I'll see if I have one left."

"Before you check, do you happen to know that blond guy over by the jukebox? He looks like Jimmy Stowe, one of my younger brother's friends who used to live in Alpine. But the last time I saw him, he'd joined the army and wore his hair in a buzz."

She shook her head. "That's Glen Mason, Ralph Mason's grandson."

"You're sure?"

"Positive. He's been here since Christmas. I understand he's had a terrible family life. Ralph's felt so bad about his own son abandoning Glen, he's been trying hard to play father and straighten him out."

Jace stopped chewing.

Christmas?

"I'm glad I asked you first, Millie. The resemblance is uncanny."

"They say everyone has a look-alike somewhere."

"I've heard that too. Not to change the subject, but your chowder's superb."

She eyed him shrewdly. "I can take a hint. I'll go look for that pie."

Jace could see the Mason boy through the mirror behind the counter. He had to be in his early twenties. The way he leaned against the jukebox was a study in loneliness. The awful kind that spelled bad parenting, isolation, neglect. The type of abuse that turned fragile children into gang members, drug addicts and worse.

Millie brought him his dessert, which he finished off in no time. He put three five-dollar bills on the counter.

"That's one too many." She tried to hand it back, but he moved away.

"This is my favorite stop of the day. Don't ruin it for me. See you on Monday."

He would have liked to leave her a much bigger tip for the unexpected information. Since Jace had been driving this route, Glen Mason was the first male he'd heard of who'd come to this vicinity in roughly the same time period that the killers had disappeared over the mountains.

The news by itself didn't necessarily mean anything, but the fact that Dana Turner lived on the Mason property presented some new possibilities Jace needed to check out. No matter how remote, if he could establish a connection between Dana and Glen, he might be on to something.

As Gibb had once told Jace, "Working a tough case is like trying to get a ring off your finger that's too tight. You wiggle it this way, you wiggle it that. You apply leverage. When nothing works, you get out the soap. Use different brands. If none of them do the trick, you pour on a little olive oil and nudge away.

"Once you've tried everything and it's still stuck,

you get real inventive and take pills to lose water. As a last effort you fast for twenty-four hours. Never cut it off unless it's down to the bone and killing the circulation.''

After six weeks in West Texas without a glimmer of a clue, Jace decided he was at the inventive stage.

Both Dana and Glen were new to the area. Both had troubled pasts. If there was a link between them…

Too bad Dana had asked him not to leave any more of her packages at the ranch house. Was that because Glen didn't want strangers like Jace coming to the house, chatting with his grandfather, who had no idea what was really going on? Maybe Glen had warned her to keep a low profile around Ralph so he wouldn't be suspicious of their prior association.

Without a legitimate reason to ring Ralph Mason's doorbell, Jace would have to drum up a viable excuse to talk to the older man when Glen wasn't around.

Jace could drive to the ranch house right now. However, Glen might decide to pull in right behind him in the blue Chevy truck. Jace could see it parked outside the grocery store across the street from the café. When he made a delivery at the bank next door, he'd jot down the license-plate number for future reference.

After five o'clock today, Jace would be free for the weekend. During his search for the missing plane, he'd keep an eye on Glen's comings and goings. At the opportune moment, he'd approach the man's grandfather.

If Ralph could tell him anything about Glen's

whereabouts before he showed up in Cloud Rim, it would cut down on the time it took to provide him a lead, assuming there was one.

That was the rub.

Time was one commodity Jace was running out of fast. For now, he'd ask Pat to run a statewide background check on Glen and see what came up.

Three hours later, he'd finished his shift with a big delivery for Art Watkins. The druggist handed him a six pack of Coke on his way out. It was his way of saying thanks for distributing the flyers.

Relieved to be back at work on the case, Jace headed for the Mason property, hoping to catch sight of the Toyota.

No such luck.

He made a big turn at the end of the road and passed the ranch house where the blue pickup stood in the driveway. The *wrong* person was home.

The IPS van would attract attention if Jace stayed put for very long. He drove back toward town, planning out the rest of the evening in his mind.

It seemed the only way to get to the highest point in the area was to take the lonely dirt road coming up on his left. He could follow it now and take a good look around, then drive back to Alpine for his own car. When he returned to Cloud Rim to make camp, he'd call on Dana first, if she was at her trailer. So far, the police hadn't spotted her car yet.

SINCE HER RELEASE from prison, Dana had embraced her freedom to the exclusion of almost all other considerations. But after her conversation with Heidi last night, she realized that even working in this glorious setting still couldn't fill every human need.

For the first time since she'd come to Cloud Rim, she was aware that it was a Friday night, and she was alone. She could blame her restlessness on the IPS driver. Her reaction to him proved how vulnerable she was to an attractive male.

Dana had no idea if he was married, separated, divorced or living with someone. It didn't seem to matter. Too many times today, she'd found herself thinking about him.

He probably wasn't as wonderful as her imagination had made him out to be. In the past, Dana had dated her share of mediocre men. No one truly memorable. Of course there'd been a couple of losers sprinkled in. Tony was a case in point.

Though she didn't believe he'd show up again, she decided it might be a good idea to take Heidi's advice and get away for the weekend. She could drive to Fort Davis and stay at the Pride Ranch for the night. That way she'd be certain to avoid Glen as well. The next time he came by, she would warn him off in no uncertain terms.

According to Millie, the Pride Ranch served a terrific buffet that included prime rib, barbecued ribs and the most mouthwatering strawberry pies you ever tasted. That sounded good to Dana who was tired of her own cooking.

As for tomorrow, she could swim and go horseback riding. Meet some fun people. She'd heard about the Pride's summer-camp program for young astronomers. This would be a good chance to check it out.

Depending on a variety of factors, she might allow small groups to visit the observatory for a look through the telescope. There was no greater thrill for a youngster.

With her mind made up, she turned off machines and lights, locked up, then walked out to her car. It was only six o'clock. She had time to throw a few things in her overnight bag and reach her destination well before dark.

She put the car in first gear and let gravity do the rest. Around and down the summit she went, passing the sign that said, "Private property—No trespassing beyond this point." By fall the area would be fenced and a gate installed like most of the private property in the area, but everything took time.

Coming around the bend of a curve Dana was surprised and delighted to see an IPS van coming toward her on the narrow road. Her heart did a little dance to think it might be the same driver.

As she drew closer, she realized it *was* the same man from yesterday. As their vehicles came alongside each other, they both slowed to a stop. Filled with nervous excitement, her hand trembled as she pushed the button to lower the window.

"Hello again."

His window was already down. She moaned inwardly. Those dark brown velvet eyes were as gorgeous as the rest of him. She hadn't exaggerated one detail about him to Heidi.

"Good evening," he responded pleasantly. "Are

you just coming home from work?'' As he asked the question, he reached a tanned arm of solid sinew out the window to adjust the van's side-view mirror. She noticed his left hand was ringless.

"Yes, I'm all through for the day, but I'm surprised to see you here. I'd have thought you'd be done with your deliveries by now." She was talking too fast. "Do you have a package for me?"

His black eyebrows formed the hint of a frown. "No. If there'd been a delivery for you, I would have left it by your trailer door."

So he *hadn't* been looking for her. She'd just assumed it because he was driving on this particular road.

Why did I stop? Now he thinks I'm flirting with him. Other women probably do it all the time. Damn.

She started up the engine. "Well, have a good evening."

"Wait," he called to her. "I think I'm lost. I had one last delivery for a Shelby Norris. Someone in town thought he lived out this way. Does that name ring a bell?"

"Afraid not. But I only moved here a month ago. If you go to the café the owner, Millie Johnston, might be able to help you. She's lived here most of her life and is acquainted with everyone. Good luck."

JACE SAT THERE in stunned surprise as she put her car in gear and pulled away.

He'd made up a lie about looking for Shelby Norris. There was no such person, but he'd needed an excuse to be out on the road so Dana wouldn't think he was looking for her. Now she was gone.

He'd seen guilt do crazy things to people. Dana Turner acted guilty as hell over something. Otherwise she wouldn't have taken off like a frightened doe caught in the headlights.

What kind of work did she do way up here, far removed from civilization?

Much as Jace wanted to go after her, he decided it would be better to leave it alone for now. By the time he could turn the van around and try to catch up with her, she'd be long gone.

Letting out a sound of exasperation, he phoned Pat and told him to call off the search for the Toyota. It had been found.

She'd been found.

Jace had hoped that on a second meeting the appealing traits he'd gradually endowed her with throughout the night would have lost their allure.

What a joke that was. If just looking at her again could make him feel this way...

He reached for one of the cans of pop that Art had given him. After quenching his thirst he drove on, determined to find out where this road led and why she'd been on it.

The van wound slowly up to the peak. At one point he passed a No Trespassing sign. Disregarding it, he kept on going.

"Good grief," he muttered when the observatory popped into view. The white-domed structure stood out in stark relief against a landscape of clustered trees that resembled giant green polka dots.

The building stood perched above rugged vistas that fell away in every direction. The magnificent sight took his breath.

Turning off the engine, he got out of the van and walked all around. The area looked deserted. He saw no sign of human life. Nothing moved.

What did Dana Turner have to do with this place?

As his keen eyes swept the landscape, he didn't detect anything that would suggest pieces of plane wreckage. When the killers' charter disappeared, police helicopters had spent days flying over miles of mountainous terrain. They'd come up with nothing.

The Mexican authorities had been cooperating with the Rangers. To date, no evidence had turned up to prove the plane had made it across the border.

More than ever, Jace had the gut feeling it hadn't crashed at all. One of those killers had been a pilot. He'd found a place to land it and hide it. That meant he'd been familiar with the terrain ahead of time and knew exactly what he was doing once they'd reached the mountains.

Jace's gaze darted back to the observatory. He saw the remains of building materials and tire tracks, indicating recent construction, yet the structure appeared abandoned. Walking over to the door, he tried the handle but it was locked up tight.

Dana Turner obviously had access to the building. Did she work for the construction company that built it? For two men hiding out in these mountains, this would make a perfect rendezvous spot, especially if they were using her for their eyes and ears.

After a few more minutes of pointless speculation,

Jace got in the van and started back to town. When he reached the turnoff, he decided to drive by Dana's trailer.

If she was there, he'd invite her to have dinner with him at the café. That way he could get to know her better while he asked Millie for directions to the Norris place in front of her.

It was vital he allay any fears Dana might have about his being on the road to Mount Luna at the same time she passed him. The last thing Jace wanted was for her to be suspicious of an IPS driver while he was supposed to be on the job.

He'd told himself she probably wouldn't be home, yet his disappointment was greater than it should have been when he drove down the street and discovered her car wasn't parked next to the trailer.

Since he wanted her to know he'd come by, he pulled to a stop across the road. Once he'd found an IPS release form for her to sign, he got out of the van.

"Well, well, well. What have we here?" he muttered when he saw Glen Mason letting himself out of her trailer. The man had discarded the vest in favor of a western shirt.

As the two made eye contact, Jace said, "Hi, you're the guy I saw at the café earlier today."

For someone who'd been caught by surprise, Jace had to give the guy credit for keeping his cool. Except for the ruddy spots that broke out on his cheeks, he behaved as if he had every right to come and go from her trailer.

"Yup. I live next door. Dana rents this trailer from my grandad, but I do the upkeep."

"I've met your grandfather. He's quite the gentleman."

"If you've got something for her, I'll make sure she gets it," he said without acknowledging Jace's remark.

"There's no package. I'm leaving her some information." He stepped around Glen to press the sticky end of the IPS form to her door.

"Aren't you working kind of late?" Glen had put his hands in the back pockets of his jeans while he rocked on the heels of his cowboy boots.

His attitude recalled Jace's childhood. There was always some troublemaker out on the playground. Dana Turner's guard dog might not be a heavyweight, but he was definitely protecting what he considered his.

"Afraid so. Maybe you can help me. I have a package for a Shelby Norris. After an hour of driving around trying to find him without success, I thought I'd pay a call on your grandfather. Maybe he'll recognize the name."

Glen shook his head. "There's no need. I've lived here on and off all my life. That name don't mean nothing to me."

"No matter. Before I leave town, maybe you could help me out with something else."

"What's that?"

"Since you and your grandfather are on such friendly terms with Ms. Turner, I wondered if you knew if she's living with a guy or seeing one on a regular basis.''

Glen kicked his toe against the dirt. ''I don't figure that's any of your damn business.''

''Hey,'' Jace smiled. ''I'm just trying to find out if I've got serious competition. She's a good-looking woman. The best I've seen on my route so far.''

His hazel eyes narrowed. ''You're not the regular driver, so I guess you don't know.''

Ralph's grandson didn't miss much. ''Know what?''

''About Dana and me.''

''You two have something going?'' Jace couldn't imagine it under any circumstances.

''Yup.''

''Then what about that other guy yesterday who came to spend the night with her?''

He watched Glen's Adam's apple bob several times. Jace's question had thrown him, just as he'd hoped it would.

''What other guy are you talking about?'' he challenged. The ruddy patches had more color now.

''The one who hitched a ride with me from Fort Davis yesterday because his car broke down. Sorry to have to be the one to tell you, dude. Forget I said anything.''

Jace started across the street. By the time he'd climbed inside the van, Glen had caught up to him.

''Who's the guy? What's his name?'' he demanded through the open window.

''I don't know. You'll have to ask her those questions.''

"How old was he?"

"Thirtyish."

"Did he have dark brown hair?"

Jace nodded.

"Was he about six feet?"

"Yes."

Glen's face screwed up before he wheeled away. By the time Jace had made a U-turn to head back to town, the Mason kid whizzed past him in the blue pickup.

Though Jace had been describing Tony Roberts, Glen had been describing another guy, and his jealous reaction proved beyond doubt he and Dana weren't an item and never had been.

Maybe there was no link between Dana and Glen. But Glen might have seen one of the killers hanging around her. The description fit the general statistics given by the armored-car driver before he died.

At this point Jace couldn't help but wonder if Dana knew her landlord's grandson was letting himself in her trailer with his own key when she wasn't there. No matter what excuse he might come up with if asked, it was called trespassing.

He watched for Dana's white car on his way out of town. She didn't seem to be anywhere around. The same could be said for Glen. Twenty minutes later, as the sun dipped below the horizon, Jace rounded a curve on the mountain road and saw the blue pickup in the far distance. They'd both passed Fort Davis, so he imagined Glen was headed for Alpine.

Deciding to cover all his bases, he phoned Pat, who was having dinner with his family.

"Sorry to bother you at home."

"Hey, you know better than to apologize. I'm sorry I don't have anything on Glen Mason yet."

"I wasn't expecting results that fast. Will you put one of your men on his tail? I'm about three miles out of Fort Davis. He's driving his grandfather's sky-blue '92 Chevy pickup and will be coming into Alpine before long at a pretty fast clip.

"Tell him not to give Glen a ticket. I'd like to know where he goes, who he sees, without him having any idea he's being followed." He gave Pat the license number.

"I'll get on it right now."

"Thanks. I'm headed for IPS to leave the van and get my car. Then I'll drive to my apartment for dinner and a change of clothes before I head back to Cloud Rim.

"I'm spending this weekend in the mountains to see if that plane's been hidden inside someone's barn."

"I'm with you on that, Jace. If there'd been wreckage, the guys would have sighted it at the very beginning. Good luck."

"With so little time left, I'm going to need it. I'll be back in Alpine Sunday night."

"The second there's any news, I'll phone you."

"Can't ask for more than that."

After they said goodbye, Jace pressed on the accelerator. If he hurried, he might find Dana home and could have a little chat with her tonight before he starting scouting around.

As much as he told himself that making contact

with her was all in the line of duty, he knew it was far from the truth.

He'd been with a few women since Cassie, but they'd only helped him pass the time. Any real feelings had died when his wife took her last breath.

But if that was the case, then what magic did Dana Turner possess to resurrect his deepest needs and desires after all this time? For all he knew, she was up to her luminous gray eyes in the kind of trouble he didn't even want to think about.

CHAPTER FOUR

SATURDAY EVENING a sunburned Dana drove into Cloud Rim and headed straight for the observatory. It wasn't until she'd wound to the top of Mount Luna that she realized she was avoiding the trailer because she didn't want to have to deal with Glen Mason.

The overnighter in Fort Davis would have been wonderful if she'd been able to share it with a man. She'd found out fast that despite the many friendly tourists who included her in the ranch's activities, she felt dissatisfied, lonely even. Again she questioned if her restlessness wasn't the fault of the IPS man whose image continued to haunt her.

In any event, when her car came to a stop at the observatory, she was glad to be back where she could concentrate on work.

There'd been one pleasing outcome as a result of her mini trip. After talking to the enthusiastic leaders of the young-astronomers camp, arrangements had been made for the kids to be driven up on Tuesday night for a view of the heavens. She decided to plan a star party, with something to satisfy every child.

Excited by the prospect, she climbed out of the car. However, she'd forgotten how sore she was from spending too much time in the saddle. As she hobbled toward the door, a car came around the curve.

Relieved it wasn't the blue pickup, she waited to see if the visitor was someone she knew from town, or simply a lost tourist who was looking for a place to turn around.

A man got out of the car. A tall man with curly black hair and the kind of hard-muscled physique a woman didn't forget. Though he wore a knit shirt and jeans instead of a khaki uniform, she'd know him anywhere. With the late sun gilding his rugged features, Dana could hardly breathe.

"Good evening, Ms. Turner."

"Good evening. I'm afraid you have me at a disadvantage."

He moved toward her, his brown eyes intent on her face. "Yesterday you drove off too fast for me to introduce myself. My name's Jace Riley."

Jace. It was an unusual name. She liked it.

"How do you do."

Her hand disappeared in the strong warmth of his before he released it.

"I'd just filled my car at the corner gas station when I saw you turn on this road. So I came back up. I hope you don't mind."

Dana steeled herself not to jump to any conclusions. She could tell he wanted something from her. She just didn't know what.

"Is there a particular reason you needed to talk to me?"

"Probably the oldest one known to man." His eyes were smiling.

Heat swept through her body.

"How would you like to have dinner with me at the café?"

She blinked. "You mean now?"

"Yes."

His invitation thrilled her, but being arrested and imprisoned had made her cautious. She didn't trust that his interest in her was the result of chemistry alone. That mistake had already been made with Tony.

Though she might ache for a meaningful relationship with a man, her prison experience made her different from other women. She had a history that could weed out even the most ardent suitor. Even someone who seemed as together and confident as Jace Riley.

"That sounds very nice, but I've already eaten and I have work to do tonight."

She felt his gaze wander over her features. "Is that your polite way of telling me you're committed to someone else?"

"Look, Mr. Riley—"

"The name is Jace."

"All right then, Jace—my work is wait—"

"Before you tell me to mind my own business," he broke in on her, "I should let you know I've been by your place several times hoping to find you home. When I drove over there after work yesterday, I found Glen Mason on your doorstep. He intimated you were his girlfriend."

"That's absurd!" she blurted. "He's my landlord's wayward grandson who's been making a nuisance of himself ever since I moved in to the trailer.''

Jace nodded. ''I thought it had to be wishful thinking on his part, but I took Tony Roberts a little more seriously when he told me *he* was your boyfriend. That is, until I was driving back to Alpine and saw him thumbing for a ride. For a man full of plans to be with his woman, he didn't stay in Cloud Rim very long.''

Her face went hot. ''I was never his woman. We dated briefly last year, then I broke it off. If Tony had been alone when he came to see me, he would never have made it inside my trailer.''

''In other words, you were trying to spare *me*.'' Jace's subtle teasing made her smile.

Dana wouldn't have put it past Tony to have told Jace about the gun. If that were true, then Jace didn't scare off easily. The first time she saw him, she had the feeling he was a man who could handle anything. That impression was growing stronger.

''What do you have to work on tonight?''

Jace had asked the question while she'd been mentally comparing the two men. Of course there was no comparison. Hopefully, Tony had gotten the point and had gone away for good.

''Tony didn't tell you?''

Her question seemed to surprise him. ''He was intent on finding you, period. If he could have done it without me, I have no doubts he would have preferred it that way.''

''He should have rented a car!''

''Then I might not have met you,'' came the quiet

response. Their eyes met. "Mind if I come in with you for a while, or do you work better alone?"

No and yes in that order. "If you'd really like to."

"I thought I'd made it clear I wanted to get better acquainted with you."

She'd noticed a gold band on his right hand. "Are you divorced, Jace?"

"No. My wife died of cancer seven years ago."

"I'm so sorry." She averted her eyes. "Do you have children?"

"No."

That one word conveyed a wealth of emotion. It spoke of living and loving. Of shattered dreams... Dana could relate.

She unlocked the observatory door. "Welcome to my world."

Jace's eyes widened in surprise when she turned on the lights.

He'd been concentrating so hard on the case, trying so desperately to get a handle on it from any conceivable angle, he'd assumed the observatory was a newly erected shell, still empty on the inside.

Good Lord. If this was her world, then that meant sh—

"If you'd like to go into my office there on the right side of the telescope, I'll bring you something to eat from the kitchen."

Staggered by the realization he'd been this far off base where she was concerned, he entered her office in a daze.

Dozens of fascinating photographs of the planets covered the walls. There were all kinds of computers, machines, printers and screens. The place was an astronomer's paradise.

On her desk she'd propped small framed photos. He saw one of Dana with a man and woman he suspected must be her parents, though they were blonde.

There was another photograph of a very attractive-looking couple. The man appeared to be about Jace's age. The woman looking up into his eyes had the most amazing red hair.

There were other photos. One of a cute little Hispanic girl around four or five. Another of a teenage boy with a dog. The last showed a blond teenage girl. Were they her siblings?

"Here you go." She set a package of nacho chips and a bottle of Orange Crush on her desk. "I hope you don't mind canned jalapeño bean dip. This is about the extent of my offerings until I go grocery shopping on Monday." She popped open the lid and placed the can next to the chips.

"Please, have a seat. I'll get another chair out of my dad's office."

She was off and running before he could stop her.

"You're not going to eat with me?" he asked when she reappeared with a swivel chair exactly like hers and sat down.

"Not right now. I stayed at the Pride Ranch last night. This afternoon, just before I left, I had dinner at their buffet. I'm so full I couldn't eat or drink anything."

He'd wondered where she'd gone. Feeling happier and happier with every answer, Jace ate a few chips with dip. "So that's where you got your sunburn."

"Yes. I laid out by the pool too long. Then I rode horses for the rest of the day. Now I'm miserable."

He drained half the bottle of pop before he asked, "Were you on a date with someone?" He *had* to ask her.

She eyed him frankly. "No. I decided to take a little break. But my reason for going was to visit the camp." She told him about her plan for the young astronomers.

"When did *you* become an astronomer?" Everything about her charmed and fascinated him. Jace couldn't hear enough.

She tapped a finger against the group photo. "My dad's one of the head astronomers at Mount Palomar near San Diego, California. He got me interested when I was just a little girl."

Jace shook his head in wonderment. "Isn't that part of Cal-Tech?"

"Yes. I moved to Pasadena so I could get my master's there."

"In what, specifically?"

"Astrogeology."

At some point in her studies, she'd gone to prison. It made no sense.

"Did Cal-Tech build this observatory?"

"No. This property belonged to my mother's family since way back. She was originally from Texas."

The pieces were falling into place faster than he could fit them.

"They were ranchers who owned a lot of land near Big Bend, then sold it off in parcels. My grandparents held on to this piece on Mount Luna, then willed it to Mom.

"She gave Dad the land for a wedding present. It's probably the best place in the western hemisphere to study the stars.

"Recently he built this observatory with private funds. It's linked to Palomar. In a few years he and Mom will both retire and build a house here. Until then, I'm running the place while I work on my Ph.D. in astrogeology."

"Why the change?"

"Because I've always had a fascination with volcanoes as well as stars. This way I can have my cake and eat it too." When she smiled at him this time, it reached dark places inside him that hadn't felt the sunshine in years.

"What project are you working on right now?"

"When I started graduate school, I began studying one of Jupiter's moons called Europa. You can see the pictures on the corkboard. Those large blowups were in the package you brought to my trailer. Dad sent them."

"I take it there's something special about it."

She nodded. "Very."

"Tell me."

"I don't want to bore you."

"That wouldn't be possible."

"Did you ever take astronomy in college?"

"No."

"That's why you can say what you did with such certainty."

He chuckled. "All I'm asking for is a layperson's explanation."

"You really want to know?"

His expression sobered. "I wouldn't have asked otherwise."

"Well, astronomers are no different than the fictional characters on *Star Trek* who search for life on other planets. There is evidence that the possibility of life could exist on Europa."

"What sort?"

"I'm not talking about aliens," she teased.

"I didn't think you were."

"Okay. To make energy, which is essential to life, you need fuel and something with which to burn it. Earth has a supply of oxidants which are energy sources. As it turns out, data from the spectrometer reveals the presence of sulfur on Europa, a known oxidant on Earth.

"The reddish-brown area on the surface you can see in those pictures suggests that another oxidant, sulfuric acid, might coexist with the sulfur. What I'm attempting to do now is prove that the acid is coming from Europa's hot interior beneath its icy crust.

"I believe the material is either being ejected by sulfuric acid geysers, or else it's being funneled through cracks in the ice to the surface."

"In other words, volcanoes."

"Yes. There's one theory that the volcanoes on Io, Jupiter's fiery moon, have been ejecting sulfur atoms into the magnetic environment around Jupiter that eventually whirled toward Europa."

"But you don't think so."

"No. So far my data suggests that sodium and magnesium sulfates have worked their way from underground oceans. When they reach the surface, they are altered by an intense radiation field. The pictures Dad sent me, which were taken by one of the probes, support my theory.

"Since I came to Mount Luna, I've been monitoring volcanic activity on Europa twenty-four hours a day and recording my observations. That's about it."

"I'm sure that's only the tip of the proverbial iceberg."

She smiled. "It's the only part that's interesting. The rest is physics. What about you, Jace? I've been doing all the talking. Tell me about your life."

I've already told you some of it, Dana Turner. But there's a lot I can't reveal. Not yet.

"I tell you what. I know you came up here to work. If you're not busy tomorrow evening, how about having dinner with me at the café, and we'll take up where we left off."

She sat back in the chair. He flinched when she crossed those gorgeous long legs of hers. Being with her had made all his senses come alive.

"I'd like that very much, but there's something you should know about me first. After you hear what I have to say, you may not want to see me again, and that will be all right with me."

At her unexpected remark, his heart skidded sideways.

She reached for the picture of the blond teenage girl. "This is my younger sister, Amy, my only sibling. Last year she took a lethal overdose of drugs, lit her bedroom on fire and died. She made it look as if I had murdered her.

"The prosecuting attorney convinced the jury I was guilty, so I was given a thirty years-to-life sentence and locked up in Fielding Women's Prison outside San Bernadino."

After putting that picture down, she showed him the couple photo. "If it hadn't been for my best friend, Heidi, and her husband, Gideon, a homicide detective in San Diego, I would still be in prison.

"They found new evidence to get my case reopened. The judge ruled my sister's death a suicide. I was acquitted and set free at the end of April.

"Before I did anything else, I went through some intensive counseling. Among other things, it taught me that even though I knew I was innocent of any wrongdoing, there'd always be people who would believe I was guilty, or at least entertain doubts about me.

"However, I've learned the hard way that my past will always cling to me. The truth is, I've spent seven months in prison. It's a fact of life, and it has changed mine forever."

Jace heard her take a steadying breath, evidence of what it had cost to be so brave. Her honesty spoke straight to his soul.

"Rather than say anything now, why don't you think about what I've just told you, Jace. Tomorrow evening I'll go to the café at six. If you're there, fine. If you're not, I'll understand."

He didn't need time. But a woman who'd been wrongfully imprisoned *did*.

Dana fit the typical profile of an innocent weighted with the fear that people would always see her as a felon. Jace would give her the space she needed for her sake, not his. Little did she know her unsolicited confession had filled him with joy.

"Six it is."

Tonight he would fill in the dark hours hiking around. While people were asleep, he could look around the more isolated ranch areas without being spotted. During the day, he'd sleep. It was a plan that would keep him from jumping out of his skin until he could be with her again.

By tacit agreement they walked to the door of the observatory. When she opened it, he saw the soft breeze tousle her shining dark hair around her shoulders. With classic features set in the smooth oval of her face, she was a truly beautiful woman. He rebelled at the thought of having to leave her for any reason.

"How soon are you going back to your trailer tonight?"

Her eyes met his. "I'm not. The project I'm working on requires me to stay at the telescope. I'll go home in the morning."

Perfect. He'd noticed the observatory came with a state-of-the-art electronic locking device. He was satisfied she had more than adequate protection against predators like Glen.

"Good night, Dana. After I make camp and stretch

out in my sleeping bag, I'll look up at the heavens and think of you.''

"You're going to camp tonight?" she cried.

"That's right. When I've been penned up in the van all week, there's nothing I love more than to get out in nature.''

"Where?"

"I don't have a set destination. I like to explore. When I see the right spot, I'll know it.''

"I guess I don't need to tell a grown man like you to be careful, but my mom warned me there are black bears and mountain lions roaming these mountains. They stay in the caves.''

He grinned. "Don't I know it! If I don't show up at six tomorrow night, you can send out a search party.''

"That's not funny, Jace!"

What he'd said had upset her. *Good.*

He walked to his car with the sure knowledge that she cared. In his gut he had the feeling she cared as much as he did.

"Thanks for the snacks and the drink," he called to her from the open window.

"You're welcome," she answered.

As he started the engine and headed around the downward curve, he glanced in the rearview mirror. She was still watching him.

How long had it been since he'd wanted a woman to watch him, to worry about him....

The feeling was indescribable.

By the time he'd reached the crossroads in Cloud Rim, it was dark out. Another hour and he'd follow the fire road highlighted on his forest service map. It would take him to the southeastern portion of the area for a search. In the meantime he'd check things out at the Mason property and see what was going on.

When Pat had phoned him earlier in the day with his latest report, Glen appeared to be clean of any warrants for his arrest as far as the state of Texas was concerned.

An officer had tailed him to a bar in Alpine. He drank beer and played pool with some local guys before getting in his truck and heading back to Cloud Rim at eleven-thirty.

Thinking back to his conversation with Glen, Jace recalled his jealous reaction to the mention of another man in Dana's life. Jace had been talking about Tony Roberts—but who had Glen been thinking of? None of those local guys fit the description.

It looked as if nothing was going on, but Jace and Pat thought differently.

With time to spare, Jace parked his car in front of the café, then walked along the side of the road until the trailer came into view. The first thing he noticed was the IPS tag missing from her front door.

Since Dana hadn't stopped there on her way home from Fort Davis, only one other person could have removed it. Glen would probably use it as an excuse to come over and see her when she was home.

He flicked his gaze to the ranch house. The pickup wasn't there. Now might be a good time to pay a visit on Ralph. But no sooner had Jace made up his mind to walk over there than he heard the sound of an engine coming down the road.

Thankful for the darkness, he moved behind the trailer and waited to see who it was.

Jace didn't have to wonder very long. Glen turned into Dana's driveway and pulled the truck alongside the trailer as if he lived there. Within seconds he'd let himself inside her place.

A light went on. Jace guessed it lit the corridor between the kitchen and bedroom. He tiptoed around the other side.

Glen was doing something in the bathroom. Whatever he was up to, it didn't take long before he turned off the light and locked the trailer. Until he'd gone back to the ranch house for the night, Jace didn't move from his vigil behind the trailer.

When all was quiet, he walked back to town and drove his car as close as he dared to the edge of the Mason property. His tools and flashlight were in the trunk. He got out what he needed, then crept over to the trailer.

This was another one of those times the situation called for an immediate search. Once he had the door open, he rushed to the bathroom.

Glen had come in here for a reason. There was nothing on the walls or ceiling but the smoke alarm. Jace turned on the flashlight so he could see to remove the cover.

His fingers found a minicamera with a pinhole lens and a ten-hour tape. Where did Glen get the kind of money it took to buy a device like this? *Bastard!*

In a rage, Jace grabbed it at the edges and pulled

it out, wrapped it in tissue and put it in his pocket. He probably wouldn't be able to get any good prints off it, but the hard evidence was stacking up big time against Ralph's grandson.

After Jace put the cover back on the smoke alarm, he moved to the bedroom to see if she was being filmed in there too. But a thorough search didn't reveal anything else. He walked through the entire trailer checking for listening devices. When he was satisfied there was nothing more, he locked up and took off.

Dana had been renting for a month. Who knew how long that vile little vermin had been watching her. Jace broke out in a cold sweat, as if his own body had been violated.

He wouldn't tell her what Glen had done, but Jace would fix it so Glen never got his jollies at her expense again.

Picking up his cell phone, he called Pat and told him what he'd uncovered.

"It's time to call in the P.I.'s to set up a twenty-four surveillance on Glen Mason. I want to know every move he makes, every person he talks to. Pictures. The works!

"He's at the ranch house right now. I presume he'll be there until tomorrow morning. By first light I want those guys ready to follow him to work, wherever he goes. After he's left the house, I'll have a chat with his grandfather.

"Hopefully, Ralph will be able to tell me something that will help us trace Glen's movements before he came to Texas."

Pat heaved a sigh. "You can bet that if he's into breaking and entering to do garbage like that, he has a record a mile long."

"It's only the tip of the iceberg," Jace muttered emotionally. He still hadn't recovered from his find. Maybe he never would.

"At this point it doesn't matter whether he has anything to do with Gibb's case or not. I'm going to make sure Glen gets put away for what he's been doing to Dana. When I think—"

"Don't go there, Jace," Pat broke in. "I know how hard this has hit you, but I think you're on to something big with Glen. He's got the profile of a bona fide criminal."

"I know. He's a pathological liar, which makes him particularly dangerous."

"And shrewd," Pat added. "I've been asking myself how come he's been able to stay out of trouble since he came to Texas."

"That's easy. He knows he's a wanted man. He's trying to be extra quiet about whatever it is he's doing."

"Exactly. It's the only reason a twenty-three-year-old hellion would turn up at his grandpa's after years of no contact, offering to take care of an eighty-eight year-old man."

Jace's hand tightened on the cell phone. "Forced to keep a low profile, he gets his kicks from spying on his neighbor and harassing the hell out of her!"

"It's all part of a pattern, Jace. A little more patience and who knows where this could lead."

"If it were anyone but Dana..."

"You want to get this off your chest now?"

That was all the encouragement he needed to confide his feelings. Pretty soon Pat knew everything.

"Tell you what. When I contact the P.I.'s, I'll warn them that if it looks like Dana could be in danger from Glen, they're to call me so my officers can intervene in time. We'll keep her safe."

"Thanks, Pat."

IT WAS CLOSE to 10:00 a.m. when Dana let herself in the trailer. Normally she'd be exhausted after staying up all night. But Jace's presence in her life had knocked everything off kilter. She felt wired.

The fear that he wouldn't be at the café made her too restless to concentrate. If he didn't show up, it would be a disaster for her emotional life, even though they'd only known each other a few days.

She wanted too much. She wanted it too soon.

One moment she wished he'd never come into her life. The next, she didn't know how she could wait to see him.

It was absurd, ludicrous how much she cared. But Jace Riley wasn't like any man she'd ever met.

The plain truth of the matter was, she'd taken one look at him and had fallen for him.

If it was a biological drive for a woman to seek a certain type of man in order to perpetuate the species it had kicked in the moment she'd laid eyes on Jace.

"Dana?"

That was Glen knocking at her door. She whirled around, furious that she couldn't come home from work and have five minutes' peace before he was chasing after her.

It was time for a little talk.

She marched through the tiny living room to the door and unlocked it. "Hello, Glen." That awful cologne he wore filled the room.

"Hi. I've been waiting for you. Where have you been all weekend?"

That's absolutely none of your business.

"I brought you this." He handed her an IPS tag. "The driver left it for you."

How odd. Jace hadn't said anything to her about it.

She'd had it with Glen!

"As long as you're here, I'd like to talk to you. Come in for a minute."

"Sure thing." He stepped inside and sat down in the upholstered chair with his hands clasped between his knees.

Dana remained standing. "When I signed the lease with your grandfather, he told me that if I had a problem I could call and you'd fix it."

"Yup. That's the arrangement."

"So far there haven't been any problems, Glen, and yet you've probably been over here at least once every other day since I moved in."

His head reared back. He had to smooth the long blond strands out of his eyes to see her. "Well, yeah, I'm just being friendly. There's no harm in that, is there?"

"Do you find me coming over to your grandfather's house every day wanting to see you?"

"No."

"What does that tell you?"

He shrugged.

"Just so we understand each other, you're never to come over here again, not under any circumstances. If I need a plumber, I'll hire one. If a light burns out, I'll take care of it.

"So far I haven't informed your grandfather of what you've been doing. But if you knock on my door one more time, I'll have you charged with harassment. You'll not only have to explain to him, you'll be in big trouble with the law. I hope I've made myself clear."

"Yes, ma'am." He sat there sullen faced. "Just tell me one thing. How long have you been seeing Lewis?"

She frowned. "Who's Lewis?"

"Come on," he muttered angrily. "I found out he was here. He rode up from Fort Davis on Thursday with the guy in the delivery van."

"How do you know about that?" He'd confused Tony with someone else, but that didn't matter as much as the fact that Glen Mason had stepped way beyond the bounds.

"I caught the delivery guy hanging around here waiting for you yesterday. He wanted to know if you and Lewis had been sleeping together."

That was an outright lie.

Completely appalled by this little creep, she said, "Get out of my trailer. As long as I pay rent, this is my private property. Remember what I told you.

Don't show your face at my door again or you'll regret it.''

"I'm going."

She waited until he'd stepped clear of the trailer before she shut the door and locked it. Just knowing she had the gun gave her a certain measure of calm. If he ever came near her again, she'd call the police.

Being around him made her feel dirty. She hurried into the shower and washed her hair. After blow-drying it, she fixed herself an early lunch, then climbed into bed with her cell phone to call home.

Dana knew her parents had felt an instant attraction for each other when they'd first met. She needed to talk to her mother about it. Deep down she was craving reassurance that Jace was one of those rare people who would accept the judge's decision as the truth.

It would take an awful lot of faith. Probably too much.

CHAPTER FIVE

"GRANDAD? My chores are done. I'm leaving now."

"Where are you going?" The old man glanced up from his recliner, positioned in front of the television.

"Dana and I are taking a Sunday drive down to Alpine. We'll get a burger and be back by dark."

"Why don't you bring her over here after? I like talking to her."

"That all depends if she's got work to do."

"You mind your manners with her, Glen."

"I will, sir."

"She's a real lady like your grandma was."

"That's what you keep saying."

"Because it's true. She's refined, educated. You don't come across a woman like Dana Turner every day. You get my meaning?"

"Sure I do, Grandad. You want me to pick you up some of that pipe tobacco while I'm in Alpine?"

"I'd like that. Thank you, Glen."

"Sure. See ya later, Grandad."

"Drive carefully, now."

An hour later he pulled into the parking area of the Gray Oak Bar in Alpine. Live country-and-western singing on Sundays brought in a capacity crowd.

There was no sign of Lewis's Harley, but that didn't mean he wasn't inside drinking.

Impatiently looking for parking, Glen was about ready to ram some dude's Porsche out of the way when a couple of guys in shirts and ties left the bar. He wheeled into their spot and jumped out of the truck.

Once inside the place, his eyes had to adjust to the darkness before he could search for Lewis. Moving over to the bar, he bought a beer, then made a tour of the room.

He'd been in here twice this weekend looking for him, but the swine was staying away and Glen knew why. He should never have let Lewis borrow one of his videos.

While Glen had been waiting for the right time to make his move on Dana, Lewis had already been messing around with her. The women always went for Lewis. That's why she'd told Glen to get lost.

In a rage, he wiped the tears from his eyes and slammed the empty beer glass down on the nearest table. He stormed out of the place, intent on a confrontation with Lewis.

He knew he wasn't supposed to show up at Lewis's apartment or his work. But that no longer mattered. Glen had found Dana first. She was his property. Now the scum had gotten to her ahead of him. Lewis was going to be sorry.

Taking off in the truck, Glen headed for the apartment complex on the east end of town. He wound around to every carport. The Harley wasn't there.

Not to be put off, he pulled into the visitors' parking and ran up the steps to the third floor. After pounding on the door with no results, he stomped back to his truck and headed across town to the Jeff Davis Truck Stop where Lewis worked as a mechanic. There was no sign of him or his motorcycle.

Letting out a curse, he got in his truck and made a couple of stops for pipe tobacco and cold beer. Then he drove over to Lewis's apartment once more, turned on the truck radio and kicked back with a Coors.

Lewis had to come home sometime. Glen would be waiting.

AT FIVE AFTER SIX, Dana still hadn't made up her mind whether to go to the café or not. Though her mother had done everything in her power to build her daughter's confidence, all Dana's doubts had crept back once she'd hung up.

She'd stayed in bed most of the afternoon, but her sleep had been fitful. When she couldn't stand it any longer, she threw off the covers and got up, sick to death of this waiting game.

It was her own fault! She shouldn't have made such a ridiculous arrangement with Jace. Even if he did show up, it would probably be out of common courtesy. He was that kind of man. He'd buy her a meal, and then she'd never see him again.

When she really thought about it, the best thing to do was get back to work and avoid the situation altogether. If by any stretch of the imagination he dropped by the café, it wouldn't put him out that much when he couldn't find her. She imagined he'd be greatly relieved to have been let off the hook.

With that decision made, she fastened her hair back with a scarf, then slipped on a clean pair of jeans and a cotton sweater.

"Hi," he said as she opened the door of the trailer a minute later.

"Jace!"

He'd come, just as her mom had predicted. Her heart fluttered crazily.

The Sentra he'd driven to the observatory was pulled right behind her Toyota. He lounged against it with his arms folded. In tan chinos and a dark brown polo shirt he looked so good, she couldn't think, let alone talk.

"I figured you might get cold feet, so I came for you before you headed to the observatory where I'd have trouble breaking down the door."

She sucked in her breath. "You don't have to do this, Jace."

"You mean perform my Boy Scout deed by dining with an ex-felon before I disappear into the sunset?"

Fire scorched her cheeks. "There have to be any number of women you could choose who haven't spent time in prison."

"Millions," he said in a dry tone.

"Why me?" Her voice trembled.

"I could ask you the same question. As I recall, when I invited you to dinner, you volunteered to meet me at the café at six. You didn't have to do that either."

Afraid he'd see the answer in her eyes, she turned

her back on him to lock the trailer door, but she was all thumbs. His presence made her efforts clumsy.

When she faced him again, she found him staring at her with a solemn expression.

"You're a brave woman to live here all alone."

"I'm sure Tony told you I keep a loaded gun inside."

His jaw hardened. "You must have had a good reason to use it on him."

"I did," she admitted in a quiet tone. "My father insisted I have a weapon handy."

"He was right. Is it his?"

"Yes."

"I'm glad he gave you some means of protection."

She shivered. "So am I."

"Does anyone else have a key to this trailer besides you?"

"Ralph Mason said it was the only one."

"Do you believe him?"

Dana knew what he was asking. "Yes, but—"

"But you have no idea what that grandson of his is capable of," he finished the sentence for her.

He could read her mind. "No."

"Yesterday I left an IPS slip on your door. I used it as an excuse to come by and see you."

His admission thrilled her.

"Did you find it?"

"No. It found me."

"You mean Glen took it."

"Yes. He brought it over today."

"That's what I was afraid of. Twice I've caught

him hanging around here when you were gone. I wanted to say something last evening, but I was afraid you wouldn't like me minding your business. But now that he's removed something from your property I left for you, he's made it mine."

He sounded angry.

"It's all right," she assured him. "When I realized what he'd done, I told him I wasn't interested in him and warned him never to come over to my trailer again for any reason. I said that if he as much as showed his face, I would tell his grandfather and there would be trouble. He got the message and left."

Jace moved toward her. "Let's hope you've seen the last of him. However, there's no way of telling how he's going to handle your rejection. He might get it in his head to hide in your trailer while you're at work and surprise you when you're least expecting it. A gun wouldn't do you any good then."

At the scenario he'd just painted, her whole body shook.

"I didn't say that to terrify you needlessly."

"I know."

"The hinges on your trailer door are on the inside, so it can't be removed that way. If you'll let me take out your lock, we'll drive into town right now and have it rekeyed at the hardware store. Then I'll reinstall it and you'll know you're safe."

Dana didn't have to think it over. "Do it!" she urged him.

"On one condition." His half smile turned her heart over.

"What's that?"

"We have dinner after. I'm starving."

"So am I."

"Good. I'll get my tools."

With smooth efficiency, he removed the lock from the trailer. It was over in five minutes. She wished it had taken him longer. While he'd been busy, she'd had a legitimate reason to study his wavy black hair and well-shaped eyebrows, both the same rich color.

Between his straight nose and firm chin lay a mouth she found seductive whether it broke into a smile or tightened with the strength of his feelings. Blessed with a natural olive complexion, he had all the ingredients that made him an irresistible man.

Dana realized she was in trouble to feel this about him. It was no use telling herself she needed to combat the attraction. The damage had already been done.

"We're ready to go, but we'll have to leave the trailer unattended while we're in town. You might want to lock your gun in the trunk of your car until we get back."

It was a new experience for Dana to be taken care of like this. She liked his attention to detail. A woman could get used to this in a hurry.

She handed him her car keys. "I'll be right back."

Once inside the trailer, she removed the clip from the gun, then found her purse. When she carried everything outside, he took the parts from her and packed them in one of the side pockets inside the trunk. After he'd locked it, he handed the keys back to her, then took a few steps to open the passenger door of his car for her.

"Shall we go?"

She hurried to get in, recognizing all the signs of a man who was hungry. Fortunately, the hardware store was only a mile away. Jace got the lock from the trunk, and they walked inside. The sign in the window said the place closed at seven.

"Ten more minutes and we would have been too late," he murmured as he ushered her through to the counter.

The clerk finished waiting on another customer, then turned to them. He smiled at Dana. "I've seen you in here before. How may I help?"

"My friend dismantled the lock on my trailer door. It needs to be rekeyed."

"I can do that, but it'll take me a few minutes. I have to go to my shop in the back. Ring the little bell if anyone comes in while I'm busy."

When he'd disappeared, Jace looked at her. "He's a trusting soul."

"I was that way once," she confessed.

"Being wrongfully imprisoned would change anyone."

"Thanks to Tony Roberts, I'm afraid I lost a measure of trust even before my arrest."

"What did he do to you?"

Jace sounded as if he really wanted to know. "Tony was working on his Ph.D. in astrophysics and taught a lab for the master's candidates. I was put in his section. I was flattered by his attention, and thought his interest was personal. But it became clear in a hurry that his whole purpose in getting close to me was so my father would take notice and offer him an academic opportunity that would boost his career.

"When I realized what was happening, I broke up with him before the quarter was over. It wasn't until I was in prison that Dad informed me he'd dropped Tony from the program and told him to get his degree elsewhere."

Jace's eyes searched hers with restless energy. "When he was here, did he attack you?"

She swallowed hard. "I'm not sure what he was trying to do, but I didn't wait to find out. He threw me down on the couch and started mauling me, so I reached for the gun under the cushion.

"Dad had warned me to keep it loaded and immediately accessible. But I have to tell you, I don't know who was more surprised when I pulled it, me or Tony."

She heard Jace's deep chuckle. "When I picked him up, I can tell you right now he wasn't a happy camper."

"Good." She smiled up at him.

"Here we are." The clerk came out to the counter. "This comes with two keys. Better put them away so you don't lose them."

She tucked the plastic package in her purse, then pulled out her checkbook. "How much do I owe you?"

"That'll be nine dollars and twenty-two cents."

Jace wanted to pay for it, but after hearing about her experience with Tony Roberts, he realized he needed to slow down the pace with Dana. Until he could get this remarkable woman to trust him, he couldn't hope to have a relationship with her.

That's what he was after. He didn't have to think twice about it.

Within five minutes they'd returned to the trailer. He got straight to work. When he realized her eyes were all over him, it felt so good that he took his time getting the job done in order to enjoy the sensation as long as possible.

She was a woman who smelled like a woman should. Every time he was around her, he breathed in the scent of fruit blossoms. This evening he detected apples. But it wasn't just her fragrance that got to him.

Her long, shapely legs and the flare of womanly hips were in his direct line of vision. With the dusky blue sweater draping her curves, she looked warm and inviting. He was close to having heart failure on the spot.

Needing to focus his energy elsewhere for the moment, he asked her to hand him one of the new keys. "Let's see if this works."

"I never had any doubt," she murmured when he proclaimed success.

"You try it, just to make sure."

She opened, closed and locked the door twice. "It's perfect. Thank you, Jace. You'll never know how much I appreciate what you've done." Her voice shook slightly.

"It was a selfish act on my part, Dana. Now I'll feel better about you when you're alone."

With the P.I.'s assigned to tail Glen until further notice, Jace was already breathing a lot easier.

"I'll feel better when you're fed." She flashed him a smile. "Let's go."

Once again they headed for town, but this time there was a difference in her, a subtle breakdown in her defenses. He planned to keep working on that until nothing stood between them.

When they entered the café, a middle-aged woman Jace hadn't seen before brought menus to their table.

"No Millie tonight?" he asked after she'd taken their orders.

"She only works the day shift."

"Do you mind if I ask you a question?"

"Of course not."

"Do you know of a Shelby Norris who lives in Cloud Rim? I tried to deliver a package to that person the other day, but the address was wrong. So far no one's been able to help me."

"I've never heard the name and I've lived here ten years."

"Obviously the sender made a mistake. Thanks for your help."

"You're welcome."

When she walked off, Dana said, "I can see where you would have frustration on the job."

"It happens."

"How long have you worked for IPS?"

He'd wanted to build trust. Now he was going to have to tell her some lies along with the truth.

"Since I graduated from college."

"Where?"

"In Austin. That's where my family lives."

"Do you have siblings?"

He grinned. "Two brothers. Buck is younger by two years. Samson is older by four. They're both married and have children."

"You sound very fond of them."

"We've always been buddies. I couldn't have made it without them after my wife died of cancer. Of course, my parents were there for me too."

Her eyes glistened over. "Mine came to the prison every week. Since my release, they've tried to move mountains for me. What would we do without family?"

"I'm glad neither of us has ever had to find out."

"How did you happen to come here, Jace?"

"I got restless, so the manager changed my assignment. Since moving to West Texas, I've been the relief driver for other regular drivers."

"You mean you won't always be working this route?"

"No."

The way her face fell excited him no end.

"But I'm here for a while longer," he assured her as the waitress brought their dinner.

About nine more days to be exact. If he hadn't found Gibb's killers by then, he'd have to return to Austin and work this case on the side. At that point he'd be able to tell Dana the truth of everything. They'd proceed from there.

By the time they had finished their meal and he'd driven her back to the trailer, it was almost ten o'clock. He'd been enjoying himself so much, he hadn't been aware of anything else.

They stood outside where a chorus of crickets serenaded them. "I hate saying good-night, but work comes early in the morning."

She nodded. "Thank you for dinner, and for making me feel safe."

"It was a pleasure. I'd like to see you again. Do you suppose I could talk the head astronomer around here into letting me look through the telescope tomorrow night?"

Her lips curved in a beguiling smile. "I think that could be arranged. Why don't you come by my trailer after work and I'll fix us tacos before we leave for the observatory. What time are you off?"

"I'll be here at five-thirty."

"That'll be perfect."

"Before I leave, you'd better bring your gun inside."

"Oh! I'd forgotten about it."

"I'm afraid I haven't. In fact, I'd like to take a quick glance around your trailer."

"Please do." She unlocked the door for him.

While she was getting her gun, Jace walked through the interior. Everything looked fine. With the new lock, Glen wouldn't have had time to tear the whole thing apart in order to break in.

"All clear," he said when she came inside. His gaze darted to the gun. "Where do you keep it at night?"

"On the floor right by me."

"As long as it's within reach of your hand."

The last thing he wanted to do was leave, but he'd made progress tonight and didn't want to frighten her off by coming on too strong.

"One more thing. It might be wise if we exchanged cell-phone numbers. I don't anticipate any problems being here on time tomorrow night, but you never know."

"That's a good idea."

After that was accomplished, he said, "Go ahead and lock the door after me."

She followed him to the entrance. "Good night, Jace."

Her smile was the last thing he saw before she shut the door. He waited for the click before he walked to his car.

Glancing toward the ranch house, he noticed the truck was back. That meant Glen had cruised by the trailer on his way home. No telling what he'd made of the strange car in her driveway.

Once Jace had left Cloud Rim, he reached for his cell phone, anxious to hear what the P.I.'s had to report on Glen.

"Pat? What's the latest?"

Jace listened to the rundown.

"Do they know whose apartment it was?"

"They said they'd have that information tomorrow. Apparently Glen was all het up about something. Stayed parked outside in his truck until quarter to nine, then took off for Cloud Rim, leaving a bunch of broken beer bottles behind."

"That figures," Jace murmured. "Glen's angry because he believes this guy is making time with

Dana. While the P.I.'s are at it, tell them to get a list of every employee who works at that truck stop. We'll see if there's a match anywhere, then run a background check.''

''They're working on it now.''

Jace rubbed his forehead. He could feel a headache coming on. What he needed was a good night's sleep, but he couldn't imagine when it was going to happen.

''Pat?''

''I'm right here.''

''I wouldn't blame you if you told me to pack it in and go back to Austin.''

''You know something, Jace? During my career I've been hung up on a case or two that didn't have anything but hope going for them. It kind of reminds me of a time when I was a little kid. My mom told me to say my prayers. I told her I didn't feel like it. She said, 'Then get down on your knees and stay there until you do!'

''That was probably the best advice I was ever given, because it always worked. As I see it, you've got the right instincts. Just keep on doing what you're doing until something happens.''

Jace needed that. ''Thanks, Pat. Tomorrow morning I'm driving straight up here to have a little chat with Ralph Mason while his grandson's at work. Let's hope he tells me something—anything I can use.''

''When more news comes in, I'll let you know.''

BEFORE SUNLIGHT CREPT through the slats of his bedroom blinds, Glen trained his binoculars on the trailer. The black Sentra he'd seen parked behind her car last night wasn't there now. Lewis must have borrowed it from someone at work and taken off for Alpine before dawn.

Glen stood there for another five minutes watching for movement. Sure enough, he saw the Toyota being backed out to the street.

Satisfied she wouldn't return until lunch at least, he hid the field glasses in his duffel bag and put some fresh film for the minicamera in his pocket.

Once he reached the hallway, he said, "I'm leaving for work now, Grandad. There's a frozen macaroni and cheese for your lunch."

"All right. See you later."

Slipping out the back door, he got in the truck and headed for her trailer. But when he inserted the key in the lock of her trailer door, it didn't move. He jimmied it half a dozen times. Nothing happened.

Lewis had changed the lock on him and *she'd* let him! That slimeball had done a lot of things Glen didn't like, but tampering with Glen's private property was something else.

He kicked the door with his boot before stomping back to the truck. In a few minutes he'd reached the grocery store. The owner was getting the cash register ready. He was always there snooping around, watching Glen with his buzzard eyes. Glen hated his guts.

"Mr. Jorgenson?"

"You're late, Glen. The truck is due in shortly and

there'll be a load of boxes to unpack. Before it comes, the produce has to be put out."

"Grandad had another accident this morning. He's been fighting the diapers, but I told him he needed to start wearing them or I'd never be able to get to work on time.

"If you'd let me go to Alpine as soon as I've taken care of the produce, I could be down and back at work by ten o'clock. Just tell the guy unloading the truck to stack the boxes outside the back door. I'll stay late putting everything away."

He studied Glen for a moment before nodding.

"Thanks, Mr. Jorgenson."

Twenty minutes later Glen took off for Alpine, intent on tracking down Lewis to do some real damage. Outside Fort Davis he passed the IPS truck headed for Cloud Rim. It was the same driver who'd been sniffing around Dana the other day.

If Glen didn't have business to take care of, he'd turn and follow the IPS guy to find out what he was up to. He'd never seen him in Cloud Rim so early in the day. It figured he'd driven up early to visit Dana when no one else was around.

He pressed his foot on the accelerator. The sooner he did what he had to do in town, the sooner he could get back to Cloud Rim and give the IPS driver what was coming to him.

Ten minutes later he reached Alpine.

As usual there were a bunch of trucks lined up by the diesel pumps at the Jeff Davis Truck Stop. Glen spotted the Harley around the back of the mart. That meant Lewis was here. Before Glen confronted him, he circled the place several times looking for the black Sentra.

When he couldn't see it, he pulled up to a gas pump and got out of the truck. He purposely walked past one of the open bays where Lewis was working. Once he'd made eye contact with him, he headed for the men's john.

Lewis had warned Glen never to come around his work or his apartment. Any contact would have to happen at the Gray Oak Bar. Since the Christmas holidays, that plan of communication had been working.

But now that Lewis had gotten a look at those videos of Dana, he'd been hiding from Glen, and Glen knew why.

He took a leak and washed his hands while he waited for Lewis to make an appearance. After five minutes he realized he'd been stood up. In a frenzied mood, he stormed out of the bathroom.

Lewis was going to be sorry when he got home from work. He'd discover the lock on his front door had been shot off and the videos were missing. That ought to get his attention in a hurry.

As Glen rounded the end of his truck, Lewis was there checking the pressure in the left front tire. Without looking at Glen, he said, "You'd better have a good reason for turning up here."

"I've got a damn good reason and you know it."

"How many times have I told you we can't make a move until my scheduled vacation in August."

"I'm talking about Dana."

"What about her?"

"I may have let you see those videos, but she's mine, Lewis. You don't have no rights to her."

"I never said I did, you dumb ass."

"The IPS driver said he gave you a ride to her trailer from Fort Davis on Thursday."

Lewis got to his feet, wiping greasy hands on his blue uniform. "Listen to me and listen good. I haven't stepped foot on Mount Luna in two months. What do you think you're doing talking to anyone about me?"

The menace in his voice made Glen a little less sure of himself.

"I caught the driver hanging around her trailer. I told him she was my girlfriend. That's when he told me about the passenger who came up to spend the night with her. I asked him who the guy was. He gave me your description."

Of course it hadn't happened like that. But Lewis would never know.

"Then he was describing someone else. Or else he made it up to give you a hard time because you're so pitiful." His eyes narrowed. "You'd better pray it's one of those reasons. Otherwise it could mean someone's nosing around.

"I warned you to leave that bitch alone. Any mistakes at this point and it's your funeral, not mine."

Lewis walked away without looking back.

Glen wanted to shout that they were both in this together. If *he* went down, so would Lewis!

But he held back because he had a feeling Lewis hadn't lied to him. Something told him it was the IPS driver who'd been having fun at his expense.

With one thing on his mind, Glen got in the truck and headed for Cloud Rim. A half hour later he reached the town and kept his eyes glued for the IPS van.

After checking the main streets, he drove down the alley behind the shops on the north side. There it was, parked at the rear of the drugstore.

As fast as he could, Glen backed out of the alley and parked on the main street far enough away from the grocery store that Mr. Jorgenson couldn't see him. He reached under the seat for his knife with the ten-inch blade and hid it inside his flannel shirt.

He walked to the corner, then hurried across the street and back down the alley. The IPS van was still there. Before anyone could see him, he pulled out the knife and hacked viciously at the right rear tire.

While he was hunkered down at the side of the van, he heard voices. Quickly he hid in the dense shrubbery bordering the alley. Pretty soon the driver came out to load some packages in the van. Then he started up the engine and took off.

When the van turned onto a side street, Glen retraced his steps to the truck. Once he'd put the knife back under the seat, he reported for work.

Half the boxes had already been brought inside. They stood in the aisles waiting for Glen to stack the shelves. Old man Jorgenson acknowledged him between customers.

Glen loaded the dolly and brought the rest of the boxes inside. While he was putting the last row of canned sodas in the fridge next to the checkout counter, he caught sight of the IPS driver who'd come into the grocery store with a package.

While the driver chatted with Mr. Jorgenson, he nodded to Glen. "How's it going?"

They could both go to hell. "Fine."

Much as he hated to admit it, he figured Lewis had spoken the truth. The bastard had something going with Dana and enjoyed making a fool of him. He'd probably figured out that Glen had a key to the trailer, so he changed the lock for her.

Glen didn't think the driver knew about the slashed tire yet. It wouldn't start to fall apart until he'd been traveling on it for a while. Here's hoping it happened while the van was rounding one of those dangerous curves on the mountain road.

"Both of you have a good day," the driver said before he walked out of the grocery store.

"You too," Glen muttered as he envisioned him plunging to his death.

CHAPTER SIX

THE PHONE RANG as Dana was getting out of the shower. Her eyes darted to her watch. It was five-fifteen. She wanted it to be Jace. But if he was calling to cancel…

Throwing a towel around her, she hurried into the kitchen for the cell phone. There was a block on the caller ID. "Hello?"

"Dana? It's Jace."

She'd know his deep voice anywhere. "Jace—I-is everything all right?"

"It is now," came the cryptic response. "When I get there I'll tell you about my experience. I'm at my apartment in Alpine. As soon as I've showered and changed, I'll be on my way. Forgive me for being late to dinner?"

"Of course." She went limp with relief.

"I'm glad you said that. You have no idea how much I've been looking forward to a home-cooked meal."

"It's just tacos and fruit salad."

"Maybe after we've eaten we could take in a movie. I noticed the latest James Bond is playing. Have you seen it?"

"No. I was in prison at the time it was released," she explained in a quiet voice.

"It's actually a pretty good film. Would you like to see it before we head for the observatory?"

"If you don't mind watching it again, I'd love it."

"Good. I'll hurry." He sounded excited.

After they clicked off, she moved to the bedroom to get dressed. Fortunately she'd thought to bring her black sweater and tailored gray wool pants from California. They looked smart without being too dressy.

She wore her hair long from a side part and applied a medium shade of pink frost lipstick. Her eyes and eyebrows didn't need makeup. A touch of lemon splash and she was ready.

When she looked in the full-length mirror behind her bedroom door, she almost didn't recognize herself. It had been a long time since she'd dressed for a man. For a moment her mind slipped back inside Fielding prison where she'd believed she would die without ever tasting freedom again.

You're free now, Dana. Do as the psychiatrist said and put the past behind you. It's over. Have the courage to live the rest of your life. Don't let the pain of that hellish period taint your relationship with Jace. If he thinks you can't get over it, he'll lose interest.

Determined that this evening would be perfect, she walked out to the kitchen to make final preparations. As she started frying the tortillas, she heard a knock on the door.

"Dana? It's Jace!"

"Coming!"

She wiped her hands on some paper toweling before dashing to the door to open it. Though he'd arrived with flowers in one hand and a bottle of wine in the other, it was Jace himself who rocked her foundation to its core.

The black trousers matched with a silky gray sweater molded his powerful physique and underlined his dark curly hair and eyes. Her heart raced as she felt his admiring gaze wander over her with the same thorough scrutiny.

"We match," he murmured at last.

Dana nodded, unable to articulate an answer.

"These are for you."

She took the flowers from him, inhaling their fragrance. "They're beautiful. Thank you. For the wine too. It was very thoughtful of you. Come in."

He did her bidding and locked the door behind him. "Something smells good in here. Did you make bread?"

"That's the tortillas. Do I detect a hungry man?" she teased as she put the flowers in a glass vase and used it as a centerpiece. The yellows, pinks and purples erased the drabness of the trailer.

"Ravenous would be more accurate. I had to miss lunch today."

"Then we'll eat first and talk later."

"A woman after my own heart."

She let out a gentle laugh. "If you'll pour the wine, I'll put dinner on the table."

As she hastened to serve them, she felt an air of unreality about the whole situation with Jace. It was like the way she'd felt on her first day in prison. She couldn't believe what was happening to her then either.

The only difference was that if he was part of some ongoing dream, then she never wanted to wake up.

"Another taco?" she asked awhile later. Judging by the amount he ate, he seemed to enjoy everything.

"How many have I had?"

"I think about seven."

"Make it an even eight. These are the best things I've ever tasted."

"Everyone loves my mom's recipe."

He trapped her gaze. "You forgot to add that you're a fabulous cook. This meal is delicious."

"Thank you. Now, before I die of curiosity, tell me what happened to you today."

He swallowed the last of his wine. "While I was making deliveries this morning, someone slashed one of the rear tires on the van."

"What?"

Jace nodded. "I didn't know about it until another motorist alerted me after I'd pulled out of the alley behind the drugstore. Fortunately, I was still in town and could make it to the filling station without causing any damage to the rim."

"Thank heaven you weren't hurt, Jace! If you'd started down the mountain, you might have—"

"Don't think about it," he broke in on her. "I only told you what happened to explain why I was late. It took more time than I thought to get the spare put on. After that I had to drive at a slower speed to get the deliveries done.

"I should have phoned you earlier to let you know, but I thought I could make up the time as long as I didn't let people detain me to talk."

She shook her head. "I don't mind your being late. What I find so abhorrent is that some teenage criminals are vandalizing property around here in broad daylight."

"It happens." He pushed himself away from the table and stood up. "Let me help you with the dishes so we can get to that movie."

While she put things away, he loaded the dishwasher. Working in such a tiny space, they brushed against each other several times. Every time there was contact, her senses came more alive.

It was a good thing the phone rang when it did or she might have thrown herself at him. As it happened, she'd left the phone on the coffee table.

One look at the caller ID and she recognized the California number.

"Heidi?"

"Dana, I've only got a second before Gideon walks through the door, but I had to tell you first."

"What is it?"

"I just took three different home pregnancy tests to make sure. All of them came out positive. We're going to have a baby!" she cried for joy.

"Oh, Heidi," Dana squealed in delight. "That's so wonderful I can't stand it! This time he'll *know* he's the biological father. I'd give anything to see the look on his face when you tell him."

"Since our wedding night he hasn't talked about my getting pregnant because he's been afraid of putting any pressure on me. But I happen to know it's the news he wants to hear more than anything in the world. Oh—I can hear the key in the lock!'' she cried out again excitedly. ''I'll call you tomorrow.''

''Promise you'll phone the second he leaves for work?''

''I swear.''

Dana clicked off and turned a beaming face to the man who was wiping off the counter.

He stared at her through narrowed eyes. ''I take it your friend is pregnant.''

''Yes!'' She almost shouted the word. ''You can't imagine what this news is going to do to her husband, Gideon. His first marriage failed because his wife was unfaithful, but he didn't find out that their son, Kevin, had been fathered by another man until he went to court to get custody. Her lies really scarred him. Then he met Heidi and everything changed.

''She got off the phone just now because Gideon was coming in the house. Right this minute she's telling him he's going to be a father. He's going to be the happiest man on the planet.''

''I don't doubt it,'' Jace murmured in a solemn voice.

Tears filled Dana's eyes. ''If ever two people deserved that kind of happiness, they do. Heidi's so in love with her husband. As for Gideon, he adores her. To be able to have a baby—to give him his heart's desire and know his child is growing inside her, that's what life is all about. I'm so happy for them I could burst.''

"They're very lucky."

She detected a huskiness in his tone. The conversation must have reminded him of his wife's untimely death. If his marriage had been a love match like Heidi and Gideon's, then she couldn't imagine him ever fully recovering from the loss.

He'd said it was restlessness that had brought him to West Texas for a temporary period. When he told Dana he wouldn't be in the area much longer, had he been cautioning her not to count on anything?

If so, the warning had come too late, because she'd fallen hard for him.

"Thank you for helping me with the dishes. I'm ready for that movie now if you are."

He flashed her an enigmatic glance before escorting her out to his car. Neither of them spoke as he drove them into town. Since Heidi's phone call, there'd been a change in him. Dana was glad they were going to see a film. It would provide a needed distraction.

Dana knew he found her attractive or he wouldn't have asked her out. She imagined he'd dated other attractive women before her, and would do so again after he'd moved on. Dana knew that either he wasn't over his wife yet, or he hadn't met another woman he could love.

Jace drove them to the theater, parked around the corner and paid for their tickets inside. By the time they found their seats, the film had already started.

Once they were settled, the strange tension that had been building on the drive over seemed even more pronounced. Glad for the nonstop action on the screen, Dana pretended to be engrossed in the movie.

At the short intermission, he excused himself for a minute, leaving Dana to her thoughts.

Before tonight, Dana had been afraid he wouldn't want to get to know her better because of her prison record. Now she wondered if the memory of his wife might be an even bigger hurdle.

Dana had no power to fight a ghost like that. She didn't want to. If he asked her out again, she wasn't sure she would say yes.

When the curtain opened for the second half of the film, Jace still hadn't returned. Dana turned in her seat, wondering what could be keeping him.

The sight of Glen Mason staring at her from three rows back sent a shiver of revulsion through her body. He'd come to the theater alone, and Dana felt sure that it was no accident he'd chosen to sit so she was in his direct line of vision.

Though she felt like bolting, she didn't want to give him the satisfaction. Instead, she turned back slowly to look at the screen. To her relief, Jace joined her moments later. When he slid his arm around her shoulders, she felt even better.

"Don't look now but Glen Mason came in while I was on the phone. He's sitting behind us," he whispered into her hair.

"I saw him."

"Did he attempt to talk to you?"

"No. Do you think he followed us here?"

"I wouldn't be surprised. He's seen my car parked next to your trailer. Now he knows who's been visiting you. We'll just stay cozy like this so he gets the point.''

Dana tried to keep her feelings in check. He was only putting on a show to protect her from Glen.

They watched the movie to its conclusion, but Dana had no idea what went on. She was too aware of Jace's warmth, his soapy fragrance, the feel of his hard-muscled body making contact with hers.

As the lights went on, Dana got up from her seat, disengaging Jace's arm in the process. She glanced behind her. "Glen's gone."

Jace rose to his feet with a brooding expression on his face. "Well, he didn't come to see the movie."

When they reached the aisle, Dana made certain she left some distance between them. The last thing she wanted was for Jace to think she'd read anything personal into his playacting.

"How did you like it?"

"I thought the new Bond did a great job."

"Liar," he teased on the way to the car. "With Glen sitting behind us, you didn't have a clue what was going on."

"You're right." *I didn't. However, it wasn't because of Glen.*

"I shouldn't have left you," he said once they were inside the car. "But I needed to make a call to the dispatcher in Alpine about my van. He thinks it'll have a new tire on by morning, but told me not to report to work before ten.

"That means I can camp out up here tonight. Shall we go straight to the observatory, or do you need to go back to the trailer first?"

Jace was an exciting man, but she didn't think that spending any more time with him was a good idea. What she preferred to do was tell him a little white lie. It was a lot better than saying, "I can't handle being a temporary diversion."

"If you don't mind, I'd like to go home. I developed a headache during the film and it seems to be getting worse."

"Why didn't you tell me earlier?" He sounded upset.

"I was hoping it would pass. It's the kind I have to sleep off." She was about to tell him he could look through the telescope on another night, but caught herself in time.

He frowned. "You're frightened about Glen."

"To be honest, I find him more repulsive than frightening, but that's not the reason for my headache."

"No matter the reason, seeing Glen didn't help." On that terse note, Jace drove her home in record time. He got out to open her door, but she jumped out before he could reach the handle.

As she moved past him to open the trailer door, her arm brushed his chest by accident. The tautness of his body surprised her. It appeared he was more concerned over Glen than she was.

"Is there anything I can do for you before I go?" He stood outside the door, eyeing her with concern.

"Nothing, thank you. I had a good time tonight. Thanks again for the wine."

"I'll call you tomorrow," he declared, ignoring her comments.

"That's very nice of you but I'm afraid I won't be here."

His face closed up. "What do you mean?"

"I'm leaving for California in the morning." She hadn't planned to go so soon, but the situation with Jace changed everything. In order to get him out of her system, it meant putting distance between them right now, before she really got hurt.

"When will you be back?"

"In a few days. I've hit a snag in my project only my father can help me with." *Another white lie, but she'd told it in the spirit of self-preservation.* "He does his best thinking when we take long walks in the woods."

After a brief silence, "Since you're leaving on a trip, I'd better let you get to bed so you can sleep off that headache."

She nodded. "Enjoy your campout."

As she started to shut the door, he said, "How am I supposed to enjoy anything when I know in my gut you're lying through your teeth to get rid of me."

Dana averted her eyes. She hadn't been prepared for his comeback.

"Unless you've already canceled, I thought there was a star party planned for a group of children tomorrow night."

Jace reminded her a lot of Gideon, the brilliant detective who'd visited her in prison. A man who never minced words and always got straight to the point. A man whose instincts were so sharp, he knew the moment she'd lied to him too.

"Until the phone call from Heidi, you were with me all the way, so don't deny it."

"I—I won't," she said in a tremulous voice.

"I'm not a vain man, Dana, but I *do* know when a woman is interested. You're not the kind of person to blow hot then cold. I thought we'd gotten past the problem of your prison record. But maybe that was naive of me."

She should never have lied to him.

"Is it possible that despite all your good qualities, you still don't feel worthy of a meaningful relationship? The kind your married friend enjoys with her husband?"

She shook her head, but he didn't seem to notice. Jace was determined to get at the whole truth.

"Are you so afraid of being hurt that you would shut us down before we have a chance to explore what there could be between us?"

"Yes!" she cried, "but not because I've been in prison. There's another reason altogether."

"Then tell me."

Struggling for the right words, she said, "You remind me of an earthgrazer."

"What's that?" he demanded in a soft tone.

"An asteroid that flies close to a heavenly body like Earth. But it can never quite pull free of its own orbit to make contact. After creating a certain amount of havoc, it speeds on into the dark void of space never to be seen again."

"That's a fascinating analogy, but I don't understand how it applies to me."

She lifted her head to face him. "Certain things

happened tonight that made me realize you loved your wife very much.''

"I did." His complete honesty didn't come as any surprise.

"The other night you told me you'd come to Alpine for a temporary period because you've been restless since your loss. You also indicated you'd be relocating soon."

"That's true too."

She had to stifle a groan. "Please don't misunderstand. This isn't some kind of accusation. If the same experience had happened to me and I'd lost my husband, I'm not sure I would have ever gotten over my grief.

"All I'm trying to say is, I know myself too well. It just wouldn't work for me to go on seeing you."

By now he had both hands on either side of the door frame. "I'll admit I've been whipping around the universe licking my wounds for a long time. That is until I grazed by a certain heavenly body named Dana Turner."

As his gaze fused with hers, she felt her legs start to tremble.

"The pull of your gravity knocked me right out of orbit. Since then you and I have been on a collision course, so I'm giving you fair warning. There's going to be contact. It's just a matter of time… Good night."

DUE TO THE STEEPNESS of the terrain, the fenced-off ranches of the northeast quadrant of Cloud Rim didn't have as many outbuildings to search.

After leaving Dana's trailer, Jace spent the rest of the night driving along the fire road to check out the few barns large enough to house a small plane. He found only one, but there was no approach that would allow a plane to land.

Around four-thirty in the morning he called it quits and drove back to Alpine. His frustration lifted the moment he thought of Dana.

The next time he saw her, he intended to do something to move things forward. For now, he required sleep until he had to report to work.

Though he'd set his alarm for nine-thirty, the phone rang before it went off. He reached blindly for the cell phone and put it to his ear.

"Riley," he muttered, still halfway comatose.

"Jace? Sorry to wake you, but I know you're going to want to hear this."

The inflection in Pat's voice brought him to a sitting position. "Go ahead."

"The man at the apartment is named Lewis Burdick. You'll like this part. Through our sources we found out he hired on as a mechanic at the Jeff Davis Truck Stop last December."

Bursting with adrenaline, Jace sat upright. "That puts him and Glen in the Cloud Rim area at the right time."

"The ducks are starting to line up, Jace. His description fits the one that so upset Glen Mason. We got some film of the two of them talking together at the truck stop.

"Burdick drives a black '98 Harley Soft Tail registered to him at that address. There are no outstanding warrants for his arrest, not even a speeding ticket. Like Glen, he's clean as far as the state of Texas is concerned."

Jace's hand tightened on the phone. "Too bad we weren't able to get a good print off the minicamera. We're going to need to lift some fingerprints from the truck and the motorcycle. I'm counting on a computer match to give us a lead."

"I'll get the guys on it."

"Find out if the film of Glen slashing the tire shows him wearing gloves. If he did the job without them, and the knife could be found, it would produce a good set of prints. That may be the only way to track down the information we're looking for."

"What about Ralph Mason?"

"He's in the dark. Yesterday I dropped by on the pretext of asking if he knew the fictitious Shelby Norris. One thing led to another, but he wasn't able to tell me anything concerning Glen's whereabouts before he showed up at Christmas."

"Do you think he was holding back information?"

"No. The man was open in his concern about his grandson. He's grief-stricken over his own son's behavior and despairs of what's going to happen to Glen in the future.

"Get this— He said the only bright spot in his life was the fact that Glen had been dating Dana all month and was in love. Ralph thinks the world of her, and has already given Glen his wife's ring so he can propose. He's praying that marriage to Dana will help straighten out his grandson."

"Oh, boy."

"Oh, boy is right." Jace proceeded to tell him about Glen showing up at the movie theater.

"I'll be heading over to IPS in a little while to get the van. Glen's not going to like it when I show up in Cloud Rim later today, with the van as good as new."

"I guess I don't need to tell you to watch your back, Jace. His jealousy of you has brought out a violent streak that's only going to get worse. Even if the guys are tailing him, he's a loose cannon who'll go off unexpectedly."

Jace couldn't help smiling at Pat's paternalistic concern.

"I'll be careful."

"Good! I take it you didn't have any luck last night."

"None."

"Well, you've still got two more quadrants to explore."

"I'll be doing that this coming weekend. In the meantime, let's put a tail on Burdick."

"It's already taken care of."

"If I haven't told you before, I'm glad it's you I'm working with, Pat."

"You tell me that all the time." His voice sounded suspiciously gruff. "Right back at you. Talk to you later."

Jace hung up and headed for the shower, aware of a growing excitement he hadn't felt in years. The fact that he might be on to something that could lead to Gibb's killers was only a small part of it.

Dana had called him an earthgrazer.

That was a new one on him, but the definition couldn't have been more apt. He *had* been a prisoner of memories. Far longer, in fact, than some of his divorced or widowed friends and colleagues who'd remarried within a couple of years.

Before she'd died, his valiant Cassie had begged him over and over to find someone else and get married again. He'd had to suppress his pain and make her that promise before she found any peace in those last hours before her death.

But when he'd turned away from her flower-laden casket at the cemetery, a blackness had already descended on his soul. In his anger, he raged against God who'd made a beautiful world full of promise, only to snatch all joy away.

As Jace stood beneath the spray, he couldn't relate to that man of seven years ago. He couldn't relate to the man he'd been as recently as a week ago.

In about twelve hours he was going to crash Dana's star party. He just couldn't help himself.

His world was suddenly full of possibilities.

He couldn't believe it.

He felt alive again.

Dana Turner made him feel like a man.

He shuddered to think that if he hadn't given Tony Roberts a lift, he might never have met her.

But for Gibb's murder, Jace would never have come to West Texas, would never have known of her existence.

"Thank God she *does* exist."

When Jace realized he'd said the words out loud,

it shook him. Already her impact was so profound he couldn't imagine his life without her.

She felt the same way about him. He just knew it.

While she'd tried so hard to protect herself from getting hurt, she'd been transparent.

He had plans to erase those fears.

Galvanized into action, he shaved and dressed in record time. The sooner he made his deliveries, the sooner he could come back and get ready for the evening he had in mind.

An evening that would begin after the children had left the observatory...

His heart skipped some beats just thinking about getting her all to himself.

CHAPTER SEVEN

DANA GAZED into the face of each youngster assembled around the platform of the telescope. There were nine of them, an assortment of eager fifth and sixth-graders accompanied by their parents and the directors of the young astronomers program, Bob and Cathy Mitchell.

As Dana was about to begin, there was a knock at the door. Bob told her it was probably a latecomer whose parents had brought their child by car. Dana waited while he unlocked it. When she saw Jace enter the room, she let out a quiet gasp.

All day she'd been hoping he would call. The waiting and wondering had been pure torture.

Tonight he was dressed in a business suit and tie. He was so handsome, she couldn't take her eyes off him. Neither could the other women assembled.

He shook hands with Bob before finding a place at the back with the parents. Then his dark gaze settled on her. The way he was staring at her melted her heart.

"Welcome to the *Starship Luna,* boys and girls." Several of them laughed in delight, but it was Jace's half smile that turned her heart over. "I'm Captain

Turner, your host for our voyage.'' She'd worn her navy blazer over a white skirt to look the part.

"Tonight we'll be traveling through space for a close look at the stars and constellations in our night sky. Before our journey's through, we'll explore the planets of our solar system.

"While we gear up for launch, you'll each get a packet I've prepared for you. It will answer questions like, Why does the moon change its shape at different times in the month? Which planet in our solar system is the coldest? How much do you weigh on the surface of Mars? What are asteroids and comets? What are the rings of Saturn made of?''

She waited until everything was distributed.

"You know, when I was your age, I was lucky enough to look through the telescope all the time.''

"How come?'' one of the boys called out.

"Because my father was an astronomer. At night when most children are supposed to be in bed, my mother would drive me and my baby sister to the observatory where he worked. While he ate the dinner she brought him, he'd let me look at the planets to my heart's content.''

There was a collective outpouring of excited noise from the group, including the parents. Jace's smile had grown broader.

"I knew I was the luckiest girl on this planet, and I never wanted to go home. Because of that experience, I became very spoiled. I remember telling my father that when I grew up, I wanted to live in an observatory the way some people live in a lighthouse.''

The chuckles from the adults were louder than the children's.

"My dreams came true when my father built this small observatory here on Mount Luna. Now that I'm all grown-up, he lets me run this one while he runs the one at Mount Palomar in California. Our computers are linked, so I'm in constant touch with him."

"Do you sleep here?" another child asked.

"Sometimes. There's a kitchen and a bathroom, so I have all the comforts of home."

"I wish we could sleep here and look at the stars," a third child exclaimed.

"Yeah!" the rest joined in.

Dana studied their intent faces. "That's not really possible, but I'll let you do the next best thing and have some good looks tonight for as long as everyone can stay awake. How does that sound?"

The room exploded with enthusiastic cheers. When the din subsided, she asked, "Have any of you looked through a telescope like this before?"

They all shook their heads no.

"Then you're in for a wonderful treat. What's your name?" she asked the boy on the right end.

"Eric."

"Okay, Eric. You come and sit in the chair first. We'll go in turns." Quick as a wink he climbed into it. "I'm going to turn off the lights now, so don't be nervous. The next noise you hear will be the opening of the dome."

She caught another private smile from Jace on her

way over to the wall to flip the switches. Knowing he had come made the evening magical.

Darkness filled the room.

"Ooh…" The children sighed as a heaven full of stars began to appear. Cool night air wafted through the interior.

"Since everyone loves Saturn, we'll start with that planet first." After making some adjustments to the telescope, she lowered it to Eric's level.

"Go ahead and look, Eric."

The boy did, and she waited for his reaction, which wasn't long in coming. "Wow!" he cried out. "Wow!" he shouted a second time. "It's so cool, you guys!" Everyone in the room laughed with excitement.

"That's exactly how I felt my first time, Eric. Okay—who's next?"

"Jennifer."

"Come on, Jennifer."

Dana heard Eric grumble because he had to relinquish his seat. Pretty soon Jennifer was oohing and aahing. By the time each child had taken a look, they clamored to view Jupiter next.

An hour passed by in a flash.

"Come on, parents. It's your turn."

At five to one she decided it was time to call it a night and turned on the lights. The children thought otherwise and protested all the way to the bus.

"Dana?" The Mitchells sought her out. "We'll never forget this night. Thank you for a spectacular evening,"

"I loved it as much as they did. Let me know

when you'd like to bring another group and we'll arrange it."

"You'll be hearing from us soon," they assured her.

She walked to the entrance to wave the children off. When the bus started its downward journey, she locked the door. But she was almost afraid to turn around and face Jace because her heart was pounding too hard.

"I was a very good boy and gave up all my turns for everyone else. How long must I wait for my own star show to begin?" Like a shock wave, his deep, male voice sent a flush through her body.

Dana turned off the lights once more. When she started toward him, she saw that he'd already climbed into the chair. The only illumination in the room came from the reflection of stars overhead.

Though he was all man, she sensed a boyish eagerness in him to see what the others had seen. There was something about looking into space that had that effect on every human, young or old.

"What would you like to see first?" She fought to keep her voice well modulated. But their legs were touching as she made adjustments to the telescope. It was impossible not to be affected by his nearness.

"Surprise me."

"All right. Take a look."

"I have a suggestion that will make this easier."

She felt his hands slide to her hips. Before she knew it, he'd pulled her onto his lap.

"There," he whispered into her hair. "Now I'm ready."

Reaching around both of them, he lowered the eyepiece and took his first look. The rings of Saturn made the view spectacular. Dana felt his well-defined chest expand before any sound came out of him.

"Wow doesn't begin to cover it, does it." His hushed tone of awe, of reverence, matched her own sentiments.

"No. Every time I look, it's like the first time," she admitted. "I'm always humbled by what I see. Let me know when you're ready and I'll focus the telescope on Mars."

"Go ahead. I can see how this could become an addiction."

"It is. When I was in prison and couldn—"

Dana stopped midsentence, wondering how long it would take before she didn't think about the past anymore.

He squeezed the side of her waist. "The only matter of any importance is that you're here now. The rest is history."

"You're right." She knew the death of his wife had put him in a prison of his own for many years. If anyone understood pain, he did.

His hand slid beneath her hair, where he massaged her neck with gentle insistence. Though she assumed it was meant to be comforting, the caress of his fingers only served to fuel her desire.

Fighting the need to get closer to him, she made another adjustment, then invited him to look. "Every planet has its own unique presentation and coloring. There's nothing more glorious than our own solar system."

"Except for your eyes."

The personal remark brought her head around.

He put a hand to her hot cheek. "They don't reflect light. Those perfect twin spheres glow a lustrous gray on their own power. I could look into them forever."

She felt his lips on her eyelids with a sense of wonder. "Jace—" Her voice shook.

"If this is too soon and I'm frightening you, then run for your life because I'm no longer in control of my actions."

His rugged features were as powerful an enticement as his confession. He'd reduced her to a throbbing mass.

"I want you to kiss me," she whispered.

The second the admission left her lips, he covered her mouth with his own. Like a fire that consumed everything in its path, the hunger of his kiss tapped into the wellspring of her passion. It awakened feelings and sensations she'd never experienced before.

Without conscious thought she wrapped her arms around his neck, giving herself up to his embrace.

"*Dana*—" Her name came out sounding ragged with emotion.

By this time she was feverish with longing. All she could do was moan in rapture as one kiss grew into another. Soon his lips roamed her face, her hair, igniting little fires until she was chasing his mouth. Every kiss was ecstasy to her. She couldn't get enough.

"You're so beautiful. I knew if I ever touched you,

it was going to be like this,'' he murmured against her lips.

Her hand stilled against the warmth of his chest. ''I—I didn't know it could be like this,'' she confessed through swollen lips when he allowed her to breathe. ''I didn't know my body had a mind of its own. Look at me!'' she cried in embarrassment, trying to get up. But he held her trapped in the crook of his arm where her hair splayed over his sleeve.

His dark, handsome face floated above hers. ''That's all I've been doing for days. Looking and wanting. Waiting for this moment to happen.''

''I've been waiting too.'' Her voice trembled.

His features tautened. ''You could have fooled me. Tonight I stood in the back terrified you were going to tell the children they could stay and watch the planets until morning.''

Staring up at him through half-veiled eyes, she whispered, ''When I saw you come in the door tonight, I purposely let the program last longer than planned.''

His gaze impaled her. ''Why?'' he demanded.

''Because you didn't call me today. I didn't know what to think. The truth is, I wanted to be alone with you too much and was afraid it showed.''

''Don't ever do that to me again. I couldn't take it.''

''Jace—'' She cried his name before lifting her mouth blindly to his, needing his kiss like she needed air. She strained to get closer to him, but the confines of the chair made it impossible.

He let out a groan of frustration before bringing

them both to their feet. In the next instant their bodies melded as if they were made for each other. Time had no meaning as they clung together with only the stars overhead for witness.

Everything about him was perfect to her. He made her feel safe in his arms. Desirable. She felt every part of her being and body respond to him. *This* was what it meant to be a woman in the very essence of the word.

If Jace hadn't come into her life, she would never have known. She would have missed the whole meaning of existence.

She was so terrified by the thought, she shuddered.

Jace must have felt it because he tore his lips from hers. "What is it, Dana?" His breathing sounded shallow.

"Nothing."

His eyes searched hers relentlessly. "Don't lie to me."

"I'm just overwhelmed by all these new feelings. It's like I've been reborn tonight."

"That makes two of us." He crushed her in his arms. Burying his face in her hair, he said, "There's nothing I want more than to spend the rest of the night with you, but I'd better leave while I still can."

"I wish you didn't have to," she whispered against his neck.

"Don't tell me that now."

Ashamed to have revealed her deepest feelings, she eased herself from his grasp. "Of course you have to go. It's almost four in the morning. You have to be at work in a few hours."

She hurried off the platform and almost ran to the door so she wouldn't be tempted to beg him to stay.

He caught up to her and pulled her back against him. His arms circled her waist from behind. "Don't you know I want to remain locked up in here and make love to you for weeks on end? To hell with everything else...."

Her eyes closed tightly. She wanted the same thing.

"But this isn't the time or the place," he whispered. "Not yet."

His taut body gave a strong indication of the struggle he was having to tear himself away. In her heart of hearts she knew that if she begged him not to leave her, he wouldn't.

The idea that she had this kind of power over him was as thrilling as it was sobering. Much as she couldn't bear to be separated from him, she could hear the nagging voice inside her head. It told her to proceed with caution—he wouldn't always be around.

He swept the hair aside to kiss the back of her neck. "Are you driving to the trailer or staying here for the rest of the night?"

She hadn't thought that far ahead. In her euphoric state, she couldn't think at all.

"Here," she murmured, making an instant decision because he would insist on following her home. Once they arrived, she couldn't trust herself not to invite him inside.

"I'll call you tomorrow," Jace murmured.

She shut her eyes, expecting him to let her go. To

her surprise he spun her around. His eyes were like dark flames.

"It already is tomorrow. Expect to hear from me later this morning."

In a swift movement he cupped her face in his hands, then pressed a hard, hungry kiss to her mouth before relinquishing his hold. When he strode out of the observatory, it took every bit of strength to lock the door after him.

Too keyed up to sleep, she shut the dome and headed for her office. She knew she wouldn't be able to concentrate on work. Until Jace phoned her, she'd be good for absolutely nothing.

The only thing to do was change into a T-shirt and jeans, turn on some music and give the whole place a good housecleaning. After a group like the one she'd had, there were always little papers and candy wrappers left on the floor.

Dana couldn't have been cleaning five minutes before she heard the phone ring. Was it Jace? He knew she was up. No one else would call her in the middle of the night unless there some kind of emergency.

She dashed into her office where she'd left her cell phone.

Clicking the talk button, she said hello.

"Good morning." The vibrancy of Jace's deep voice permeated every particle of her body.

Her heart rate tripled. "Good morning."

"I'm already missing you, so I've come up with a plan."

"I'm all ears." Heavens—she sounded like a love-sick teenager.

"If I don't take a lunch hour today and I hurry, I can finish up by three. How would you like to meet me in the visitors' parking lot of my apartment building at three-thirty. We'll drive from there to the Terlingua Ranch to swim and have dinner. It's a great place to kick back for an evening."

"I've heard about it! There's nothing I'd love more."

"Good. I'll follow you home afterward."

"You don't have to do that, Jace. You do too much driving as it is. I'm a big girl now."

"So I've noticed." His comment sent a wave of heat through her body. "Unfortunately, so has every other man in sight. That's why you're not going back to that isolated trailer alone tonight."

When it came to protecting her, she'd lose any argument with him. It was one of the many reasons she was already so in love with him, she didn't know herself anymore.

"What's your address?"

"I've been living at the Big Bend Apartments."

She groaned inwardly to think how much time they'd wasted because they hadn't met before now. "I've passed them many times."

"Now she tells me." Jace was on the same wavelength. "Drive in the front entrance. I'll be there waiting."

"Take care, Jace."

"I was about to say the same thing to you. See you at three-thirty."

"GLEN? Is that you?"

"Yeah, Grandad. I'm home from work. What do you want for dinner?"

"Soup and sandwiches will be fine."

Soup and sandwiches will be fine, Glen mocked the words as he headed for the kitchen.

Lewis said they couldn't leave until next month, but Glen was ready to get out now and take Dana with them.

Ten minutes later he carried the tray of food to the front room. That's when he saw a huge flower arrangement covered in cellophane sitting on the coffee table.

"Where'd the flowers come from?"

"A florist in Alpine tried to deliver them to Dana, but she wasn't home so they brought them here. They're not from you?"

"Nope. You told me to save my money."

"Maybe her family sent them to her."

Glen had seen the black Sentra parked at the observatory last night after the busload of people left. He figured the flowers were payment for services rendered.

"Maybe."

"You keep doing a good job for Mr. Jorgenson and he'll give you a raise. One day he'll teach you all the tricks of running a grocery store. You can make a reasonable living doing that."

Yeah. When hell freezes over.

"After I get cleaned up, I'll take the flowers to Dana."

Earlier that day, on his way back to the grocery store from lunch, Glen had seen her driving through town. He'd followed her until he was satisfied she was on her way down the mountain. This would be the time for him to make his move.

"Can I use the truck tonight? We're planning to go bowling."

"That means another trip to Alpine. You're spending a lot of money on gas, aren't you?"

"Yeah. Well, there's not that much to do in Cloud Rim. Dana's used to living in a big city like San Diego. You told me you have to court a woman for a while before you pop the question. I'm just taking your advice. Once we're married and have a kid, she won't want to go nowhere."

Glen waited for the old man to finish his food. It took forever.

"Dana will make the prettiest bride this town has ever seen, aside from your grandmother, of course. Don't wait too long to make her yours or someone else will snatch her away."

"What makes you say that?"

"The man who drives the IPS truck stopped by here for a minute yesterday."

Glen gritted his teeth. "I didn't know that."

"He wanted some help finding an address and hoped I might know. I always thought he was a nice fellow. Good-looking too. Found out he's a widower.

"You know, when a man's had a happy marriage, he's likely to marry again. Especially if he's delivering packages to someone like Dana. So you don't want to let any grass grow, Glen. I'm looking forward to dandling your youngster on my knee."

That'll be the day.

When he'd cleaned up, he came back to the front room. The history channel was on TV. Glen reached for the flowers. "See you later, Grandad."

"Remember your curfew."

With you yapping at me, there's no chance of forgetting it.

He stormed out the back door, letting the screen door slam. After he started up the truck, he drove by Dana's trailer. Relieved her Toyota was missing, he took a little detour up to the observatory.

Nope. She wasn't there either. Now was his opportunity to get inside her place.

Lewis could break into anything. They'd done a lot of jobs together and he'd taught Glen everything he knew. No new lock was going to keep him from switching films.

First he put the flowers on the ground next to the trailer, then he got some tools out of the back of the truck. In less than five minutes, he'd taken the lock apart.

Looking around to make sure all was quiet, he slipped inside to the bathroom. The smoke-alarm cover came off with ease, but when he reached for the camera, it wasn't there.

Someone had found it.

Letting out a curse, he pounded the wall with his fist.

It had to be the bastard who was sleeping with her. That's why the door had a new lock.

In less than a minute he shoved the cover back and got the hell out of the trailer. When he'd reassembled the lock, he put the flowers in the truck and

took off for Alpine, laying rubber halfway down the
street.

At Fort Davis he stopped at the service station to
toss the flowers in one of the Dumpsters. By the time
he reached the Gray Oak, the place had started to fill
up. Glen ordered a beer and took it back to his favorite table in the corner.

Two guys he knew sauntered in. They joined him
for a couple of games of pool. Halfway through the
third round, a brown-haired man about six feet tall
and wearing a black motorcycle jacket entered the
Gray Oak and walked straight to the bar. It was
Lewis.

Once he was served a beer, he started looking
around. When his gaze rested on Glen, he slowly
made his way over to the pool table to watch. Glen
finished the round. The others left to get a beer.

Lewis set his empty glass on a nearby table and
grabbed a cue to play. "I've seen that sick look on
your ugly face before. This better not be about you
know who."

Glen averted his eyes.

"Spit it out!"

"A few hours ago I went to exchange the film in
the minicamera in her smoke alarm, but it was missing. I don't know if she was the one who found it."

Lewis froze. "What's that supposed to mean?
Who else has been inside her trailer besides you?"

"The guy she's sleeping with right now."

"You mean the guy you thought was *me?*"

When Lewis's face went all masklike, Glen
quaked in his cowboy boots.

"No. That was another guy."

"You mean to tell me that in the last week she's been in the sack with two different guys?"

"Yeah. If one of them was smoking in the bathroom and set the alarm off, they could have decided to get rid of the battery and found the camera. I figure one of them realized he got lucky and kept it."

"But you don't know if that's what happened." Lewis's eyes had narrowed to slits.

Glen hunched his shoulders.

"Did you make sure you wiped off the cover before you put it back?"

"Yeah."

"Does she smoke?"

"Nope. Her place is cleaner than a hospital. Maybe she took the lid off to get rid of the bugs and found the camera."

"Then she's already contacted the police. Being that your grandfather is her landlord, you'll be the first person they come after," he said in fury. "What else haven't you told me?"

Glen didn't have enough saliva to swallow. "The lock's been changed on the trailer door."

"*When?*"

"Two days ago."

"If she had the lock changed, it doesn't matter who found the camera. She knows someone planted it in there. Since you haven't been arrested yet, that means you're being set up and they're waiting for you to make your next mistake."

"Maybe. Maybe not. The other day she warned

me to stay away or I'd be sorry. She probably had the lock changed then.''

Lewis's rage put the fear in him. ''You'd better start praying the missing camera doesn't have anything to do with the changed lock.''

''No one saw me do nothing. They can't prove that camera's mine.''

''What about the rolls of film?''

''*You* still have them. I want 'em back.''

''I'm talking about unused film, you idiot.''

''There isn't any more.''

''Where are your tools?''

He scuffed his toe against the floor. ''In the truck.''

''As soon as you walk out of here, wipe them off and toss them in the nearest garbage can.''

Glen remembered the knife under the seat. That was something Lewis didn't need to know about. He guessed he'd better get rid of that too.

CHAPTER EIGHT

DANA HAD JUST EXPERIENCED the most wonderful day of her life swimming and sunbathing with Jace. Now that they'd come back to Cloud Rim, she was almost sick with excitement because this was the part she'd been waiting for. The time when they could be absolutely alone.

As she climbed out of her car, he pulled in behind her. For an instant his headlights illuminated her figure clad in shorts and a knit top. To her amusement, she heard a loud wolf whistle.

"You'd better run, little girl."

Laughing with pure happiness, she dashed over to the trailer. He shut his car door.

"If you don't hurry, you know what's going to happen," the devilish male voice followed her.

Dana let out a cry that was part scream, part laughter. She shoved the key in the lock, but she had trouble getting it to turn.

"Gotcha!" Two arms of steel closed around her. Another shriek of delight came out of her as she covered his hands with her own. The key ring dropped to the ground but neither of them noticed.

"You didn't try very hard to get away." He began

kissing the side of her neck. "Could it be you want me as much as I want you?"

Her breath caught. "I'll never tell."

He turned her in his arms. With her back against the door, there was no place to run. When she looked into his eyes, they were focused on her mouth.

"You don't have to. The kind of communication we've both been craving doesn't need words. Ever since you drove in to the parking lot, I've ached to do *this* to you."

She felt his desire like a living thing. When their mouths met this time, it was with primitive need.

A force beyond her control had taken over her body. It didn't feel like her body. She felt a part of his. Oblivious of time and place, they moved and breathed as one flesh.

But no matter how much they gave, it wasn't enough. This striving for more made Dana realize nothing would satisfy until there was a total merging of bodies and souls.

"This is no good," Jace cried after wrenching his lips from hers. He still held her upper arms in his grasp. "I couldn't even wait until we were inside your trailer." His voice shook. "The second I touch you—"

The knowledge that he wanted her this much went a long way to repair the damage he'd done by breaking off their kiss. Heavens, feeling the way she did about him, she never wanted to be apart from him.

"Why are you apologizing?"

His chest heaved. "Because I meant to take this

much slower with you. So help me, Dana, I don't dare to be alone with you tonight. You'd better go in before I change my mind and beg you to come home with me.''

He sounded so intense, she had to take him seriously. But she failed at hiding her disappointment, because he said, ''Don't look at me like that.''

In a euphoric daze, Dana leaned over to pick up her keys. As before, the same problem happened—when she put the trailer key in the lock, it wouldn't turn.

Jace put his hand over hers to help jostle it.

''When did this start happening?''

''Just tonight.''

He grimaced. ''I'll get my tools.''

Within seconds she stood holding his flashlight while he took her lock apart.

''Someone broke into your trailer,'' he murmured.

A shudder racked her body. ''I have a feeling it was Glen.''

''I'm assuming that's who it was. Evidently he was in a hurry. The screws aren't fastened tight, the way I did them.''

She watched him put the lock all back together again.

''In prison I was friends with an inmate who met a guy in a bar,'' she told him. ''She made the mistake of inviting him to her place, but soon had to tell him to leave. He left, but he kept coming back. Pretty soon he was stalking her. She moved to another apartment, then discovered he'd been in there while she was at work.''

Jace turned his head to look at her through shuttered eyes. ''I won't let that happen to you.''

This time she shivered because he sounded deadly serious.

''Now, slip your key in the lock and try it.''

Dana did as he asked. ''It works perfectly.''

''Good. I'll go inside first and have a look around before I put the tools away, then we'll talk.''

Thankful for Jace, she waited while he turned on a few more lights. As soon as he came back out, she entered. How ironic that only minutes ago she'd been wondering how she was going to handle his leaving. But Glen's invasion of her property had changed the tenor of their evening.

As she started to pull her towel and swimsuit from the bag, her cell phone rang. It could be her mom, or Heidi. She put everything on the counter and reached for the phone, but the caller ID said unavailable. A knot of dread formed in her stomach. If it was Glen...

''Hello?''

''Dana? It's Cathy Mitchell.''

Relief swept over her. ''Hi, Cathy!''

''I know it's late to be calling, but I wanted to make sure you got your flowers.''

''You sent me flowers?'' she asked as Jace's well-honed body entered the front room. He looked so good to her, she had to struggle not to fling herself into his arms.

"Oh dear. That means you didn't get them yet. I ordered them early this morning from Hansen's Floral in Alpine. They promised delivery no later than three o'clock this afternoon. After the fabulous treat you gave everyone last night, it was the least we could do to express our gratitude. Darn it!"

Dana's eyes fused with Jace's. "I think I know what happened. I live in a trailer on the edge of another man's property. His house is the only one within a mile of Cloud Rim. People often leave things for me with him.

"Ironically, I was on my way to Alpine this afternoon. That's how I missed the delivery. Please don't worry. I'll go over and get them. That was so thoughtful of you."

"We're the ones who are in your debt. Promise me you'll call me tomorrow and tell me if you got them?"

"Of course! Thanks again, Cathy. Talk to you later." They hung up. Jace moved toward her, resting his hand on the counter. "When Ralph asked Glen to bring the flowers over to you, he must have seen them as a godsend. Where do you keep your waste basket?"

Ill at the thought of Glen being anywhere near her trailer, let alone inside, she closed her eyes for a moment. "In the utility closet," she said in an unsteady voice.

"Let's see if he happened to put them in there." He followed her into the kitchen.

She opened the closet door. "There's no sign of them."

"I'll check your garbage receptacle outside."

When he returned shaking his head, she said, "Maybe the flowers are still at Ralph's."

"If they are, then you can be certain you'll have another visit at some point."

"I don't dare go over there to find out."

"I'm glad you said that, because this has become a police matter."

"I'll phone them now."

"You don't need to. When I took the van into IPS, I had to fill out a report about the slashed tire. My boss called the police in Alpine. They came by and I told them my suspicions, not only about the tire, but the way he's always hanging around your trailer. So the police are already quite interested in Glen Mason.

"Tomorrow I'll phone them about your break-in and the missing flowers. The police will contact the delivery person and find out exactly what happened. If Ralph did receive them for you and asked Glen to bring them over, they'll find that out too."

"But, Jace, what if Glen isn't the person who tampered with my lock? We don't have any proof."

His eyes glittered with a strange light. "True. That's why I think it would be better not to upset Mr. Mason unnecessarily. Let the police run their investigation and see what happens."

Dana lowered her head. "How sad for him. He's such a nice man."

"I know you're frightened, but you don't need to be, because one way or another I won't leave you alone tonight. In the meantime, there might be a temporary solution.'' He pulled a flyer out of his pocket. ''Read this.''

She took it from him and scanned the contents.

''The other day Art Watkins asked me to pass out a bunch of these during my deliveries. I saved one for you in case the situation with Glen reached the crisis stage.

''Now that it has, you mustn't stay here. I don't care if you have a gun. The trailer's too isolated.''

''I agree. Jace—'' she raised hope-filled eyes to his ''—the apartment advertised in this flyer has everything I need, including a garage. Do you think they've rented it yet?''

''I don't know. If you're interested, why don't you call Art now and find out. His phone number is listed there. It's only quarter after ten. When he hears why you're calling, he won't mind being disturbed.''

Dana didn't need any urging. After a short conversation, she hung up and stared at him in shock.

He smiled. ''I take it the place is still vacant.''

''Yes! I can't believe it. Mrs. Watkins says to come now and they'll show it to me.''

''Then grab what you need and let's go.''

She reached for her purse and followed him out the door, locking it behind her.

''If I'd had any idea there was an apartment like that available, I would never have rented the trailer.''

''I don't think it was empty five weeks ago.'' Jace backed the car into the street and they headed for town. ''Even if it's not what you had in mind, tell them you'll take it for a temporary period.''

"At this point I'd do anything to get away from Glen. I can't stand the thought of being near him."

"Amen to that."

Jace drove them to the address listed on the flyer. The Watkinses' ranch-style home turned out to be two streets behind the drugstore. It was situated in the residential area of the town with houses on both sides of the street.

He pulled into their driveway. "Glen will find it difficult breaking into an apartment with all these neighbors around."

She nodded. "That's the first thing I noticed."

As they approached the house, Art and his wife came out of the house to greet them. Their warmth appealed to Dana and so did their furnished one-bedroom apartment. She could see herself living there comfortably.

"Shall I give you a check now?"

"That'll be fine." Art handed her a key. "You can move in anytime."

"I think I'll do it tomorrow. I have friends arriving from California around noon. They'll help me settle in."

Mrs. Watkins beamed. "We're delighted to get a renter like you."

"I'm thankful I heard about the place. If it weren't for Jace, I don't know what I would have done. The trailer is adequate, but it's too far away from town."

"Oh my goodness yes!" the other woman commiserated.

Art darted Jace a meaningful smile. "It looks like I'm really in your debt now."

"Consider it paid in full, Art. Knowing Dana's going to be living here takes a big load of worry off my mind. From day one I didn't like the idea of her being alone in that trailer."

The four of them walked out to Jace's car and the Watkinses waved them off. Jace drove them back to the trailer.

When he pulled behind her car, he said, "I'll give you two choices for tonight. If you want, I'll stay with you in the trailer and use your couch. Or, I can offer you a night out in nature. Tonight, it isn't even cold."

Her heart pounded mercilessly. "If you're asking me to camp with you, the answer is yes. Every time you've gone before, I've been envious."

His right arm lay along the back of her seat. He played with several tendrils of her hair. "You're a woman after my own heart. If I hadn't been afraid of scaring you off, I would have asked you to join me."

I hope that's true, Jace, because I've fallen so deeply in love with you, I'm frightened.

"Where shall we go?"

"I know a grassy spot protected by junipers. It's on a piece of private property about fifty yards from an observatory where we can sneak in for food and drinks."

Her laughter rang inside the car.

"I'll use my bedroll. You can sleep on my air mattress."

"That's very generous of you, but I wouldn't dream of depriving you of your creature comfort when I have a futon."

"This is sounding better and better. I'm warning you now. I have an ulterior motive."

So did Dana. Tonight she wouldn't have to watch him drive away and take the warmth of the night with him. "Am I going to like it?" she prodded.

"Will it be a drag showing me the constellations? I'm a little rusty on that score. This will be a perfect opportunity to learn from my favorite expert."

His comment wasn't the one she'd expected. If she wasn't mistaken, he'd just told her he could spend a night under the stars with her and keep a rein on his emotions. Had he said it for his benefit or hers?

Stop it, Dana.

To read something into every little look or word wasn't fair to him or the situation. Ashamed because she had no control where he was concerned, it made her realize prison had really changed her. Since meeting Jace, she wanted too much, too fast. Somehow she would have to find a way to restrain herself.

"Dana?"

She flashed him a quick smile. "Sorry. You mentioned the constellations and my mind took off for a minute. Mom accuses Dad of the same behavior."

Opening his car door, she said, "I'll just grab some things I need and be right back."

It only took a minute to put her sweats and a few

items in a bag. She gathered her cell phone and turned off all but one light.

Jace was waiting for her outside the door. "Let's go up in both cars. I'm in the mood to protect you. Besides, I don't want Glen to get any ideas about breaking into your Toyota."

"Neither do I," she said as he walked her to her car. Just the mention of his name sent a wave of revulsion through her body. "He's so creepy."

GLEN MASON'S A LOT more than that.

Jace pressed a swift kiss to her lips. "I'll follow you."

He backed out first, then waited for Dana to move ahead of him. Clearly, she had no comprehension of her neighbor's perverted mind, let alone his criminal activities. She didn't need to know about the camera yet. It would only cause her more anxiety.

In Jace's gut he knew Glen had a string of arrests behind him ten miles long. But where? Which states?

About now Jace was ready to put him away for good. But this was a waiting game. Until he had the background he needed on Ralph's grandson and Lewis Burdick, it was too soon to do anything that would make either of them suspicious.

So far there'd been no calls from Pat. When morning came, Jace would learn the status of both Glen's and Lewis's activities. As for the fingerprints, it might be a couple of days before there was any kind of word back.

Jace took a deep breath. For the time being he

planned to put everything away and concentrate on Dana. After a whole week of fantasizing about making love to her, he was finally going to get her in his arms for an entire night.

It would take all the control he could muster, but he would let her set the pace. But by the time they'd set up their little campsite, that was easier said than done.

When she came toward him from the observatory dressed in a pair of gray sweats and a white T-shirt, her hair disheveled by the slight breeze, the effect was almost surreal. Bathed in a sliver of moonlight on top of Mount Luna, she looked like a gorgeous celebrity who'd just walked off the pages of some magazine.

Her body, her mind—everything about her—excited him. She seemed too good to be true. Ever since he'd met her, he felt as if she was part of some fantastic dream that might end at any second. Unfortunately, that kind of paranoia went with the territory when you had to go undercover.

Anything could happen on a manhunt. Much as he craved telling her the whole truth about himself, it was for her safety that he didn't.

There was so much he needed to share with her. Selfishly he wanted her to know what he did for a living. She might not like it. A lot of women didn't. In that case he would have to win her around.

But until he could be honest about everything, he couldn't plead his own case. His only option was to enjoy being with her on a moment-to-moment basis.

Before Dana had come into his life, he would often meet a woman one day and be gone the next. In fact, his mobility had suited his restless lifestyle, especially in a couple of cases where a woman he'd met expected more from him than he'd been willing to give.

Not so with Dana. Upon a first meeting, her feminine beauty had drawn him like a bee to honey.

She'd stunned him with her brilliance and natural teaching ability. The other night she showed she had a way with children that had charmed him. Her charming personality had mesmerized everyone.

Jace had been so proud of her, he'd wanted to shout that he was with *her,* that she belonged to him! It shocked him that she could bring out such a possessive feeling in him.

Maybe that had more to do with Glen than Jace realized. Knowing the creep had been filming her for a month made Jace black with rage.

But he needed to let go of it for tonight.

"I raided the fridge. This is for you." Breaking out in a beguiling smile, she handed him a sack of goodies.

He used his free arm to pull her close. "All this and heaven too."

Her mouth was warm and waiting for him. Ten minutes later he didn't remember dropping the sack. The feel of her body, the taste of her lips had cast their spell.

When she broke off kissing him, he couldn't tell who was trembling the hardest.

"It's almost midnight. Let's see what we can find in the night sky." She bent over and undid her tote bag. "You'll need these."

Jace took the binoculars and stretched out on top of his sleeping bag. "Come here," he urged, patting the spot next to him.

She knelt at his side. When their eyes met, he felt his heart slam against his ribs. "Let me look through the glasses for a moment and I'll find you something interesting."

He handed them back to her. "It will have to be spectacular to compare to what I'm looking at right now."

Even though it was dark, he could tell she was blushing.

"All right—" Her voice sounded a trifle breathless. "I'll give them back. Aim exactly where my finger is pointing."

Enchanted by everything she said and did, he put them to his eyes. "These are powerful!"

"They have to be for fieldwork."

"What exactly am I looking for?"

"A trio of galaxies within the Andromeda constellation."

"Is the largest one a spiral?"

"Yes."

"Then I see it. *Lord,* what a sight!"

"It *is* spectacular because you're also viewing the M31 and M110 elliptical galaxies. From that perspective, you get an idea of the vastness of space."

"I'm ashamed to admit how little I know about

the universe. It's so awesome, I can't find the words.''

"I know what you mean. No matter how many times I look through the telescope, it's always like the first time.''

"A master hand had to be responsible.''

"To me there's no doubt about it,'' she murmured. "Give me the glasses and I'll focus on a portion of Pegasus for you before it's too difficult to see.''

"The winged horse.''

She nodded while she made an adjustment. He marveled at her knowledge. When he looked at the heavens, he saw a glittering canopy of stars. Dana's eyes saw so much more. She understood so much more.

"Okay. Look exactly where I'm pointing. You'll see four stars forming a square.''

Jace found them out almost immediately. "They're brighter than I would have imagined.''

"For most people it's the easiest portion of Pegasus to identify. Look a little to the right to see the rest of the constellation.''

"I'm afraid I can't make it out. Lie down on my shoulder and you can point it out to me.''

He felt her chuckle clear through to his insides. Without any coaxing, she did what he'd been aching for her to do and snuggled up to him. Her warm, soft cheek pressed against his and a wonderful fragrance wafted over him. He pulled her closer and moved the glasses so she could look through them.

Together they gazed up at the shimmering sky and reveled in the closeness of their embrace.

When he couldn't stand it any longer, he put the glasses behind his head and turned on his side to kiss the mouth that had been enticing him forever.

She invited him to drink slowly, deeply. Neither one of them was in a hurry. He could tell she wanted to savor every moment of this incredible night.

After years of mere existence, it felt so good to be touching and loving again. Not only with his body, but his mind and heart. She was everything he craved in a woman.

Her avid mouth clung to his as their passion became inflamed. He pulled her on top of him, the better to feel her long legs and crush her in his arms. Before long he was kissing her into oblivion.

"Dear God, Dana—I want you so much, it's agony. I wanted you to feel safe with me—"

"I do," she cried against his lips. "I want you too. I've never wanted anything so much in my life!"

"No matter how private this seems, anyone could drive up here."

"I know. I'm surprised we haven't seen Glen's truck before now. The thing is, I can't bear to sleep in the trailer again." After a slight hesitation, "Could we go to your apartment?"

There was nothing he would have liked more, but he had too many things around she would question. His cover would be blown. He couldn't afford that.

"The dispatcher at IPS lives near Big Bend Park. With his wife out of town, he asked if he could sleep at my place tonight after he went off duty. If I'd known…'' Damn, how he hated to lie.

"It doesn't matter. Really it doesn't."

"Then you're in a lot better shape than I am." He tightened his arms around her. "Don't you know I'd love to drag you inside the observatory, or take you to a motel? But that isn't the way I want it to be for us.

"I'd prefer to stay right where we are. But you're going to have to help me, Dana."

"What do you want me to do?" Her lips brushed his throat as she asked the question.

"For one thing, you can't do that again tonight."

When she eased her head back to look at him, there was a wicked little smile curving her mouth. "So what *can* I do?" She traced the lines of his lips with her finger.

"Climb onto your futon, you little witch, and I'll cover you with a blanket."

"You're no fun." But she laughed gently before doing as he'd ordered.

Afraid to get close to her again, he gently tossed the blanket at her, then climbed inside his bag and turned away from her.

She was wide awake. He could feel her energy.

"Are we allowed to talk?" she said.

"I'm awfully tired."

"Is that a yes or a no?"

He started to chuckle. "What if I said no."

"Then I wouldn't say another word, of course."

His shoulders shook. "I take it you have something vital on your mind."

"Not vital. I just wondered how long you and your wife were married."

"Three years."

"That wasn't very long."

"No. It passed by in a flash."

"Were you planning on a family before she became ill?"

Jace turned on his back. "We tried to get pregnant on our honeymoon. We kept on trying. Two years later, we consulted a fertility specialist and found out I'm sterile."

Dana had been brutally honest with him about her pain. She deserved no less from him.

"That was the first blow," he said. "The second was the discovery that Cassie had ovarian cancer. After that we tried to live every day to the fullest."

The woman on the futon didn't say anything. He didn't expect her to. After a minute, he resettled on his side and closed his eyes.

Jace didn't remember falling asleep.

The next time he opened his eyes, the sun had come up in the east. A cool flow of air brought the aromatic scent of juniper and pine. There was another scent as well, like wild strawberries.

He was charmed to discover that Dana had moved next to him during the night. She'd flung her arm around him in an embrace. Strands of her fragrant hair fell across the side of his neck.

To his delight she'd snuggled right up against his

back. Her sleep was almost too quiet, but he could feel a strong heart beating and knew she was alive and well.

With the greatest of care he inched around until they were facing each other.

There. The view was much much better.

Waking up to her like this was bliss.

Unable to help himself, he lowered his mouth to her velvet cheek, craving the contact. He kissed the tip of her ear, her eyelids, the corner of her mouth.

This morning he knew a contentment that differed from any previous experience. This went soul deep. She'd transformed his life.

Somehow the impossible had happened.

He was in love.

CHAPTER NINE

"Hey? Wait up!"

"You've got to see this view!"

The sound of voices brought Dana awake. Her heart turned over when she opened her eyes and discovered Jace lying on his side studying her.

In the morning light his black-fringed eyes looked a warmer brown than she'd noticed before. There were crinkle lines at the corners.

"We have visitors," he whispered against her lips.

"I heard."

"A couple of teens on dirt bikes. They'll be gone in a minute."

Dana could have cared less. She'd never seen Jace unshaven. Loving everything about him, she lifted her hand to explore the rasp of his jaw.

"I'm not a pretty sight in the morning."

She moaned inwardly. Jace would have to be a woman to understand how wrong he was.

"You look and feel exactly the way Heidi has described the Texas male."

His lips quirked. "Don't leave me hanging, now."

"Tall, tough and tempting."

Rich laughter poured out of him. He fell back against his sleeping bag.

She leaned over him, loving him. The man had no vanity. "Don't you know men are beautiful in their own unique way?"

"Is that a fact, ma'am."

"That's a fact, sir," she teased, kissing the end of his nose. "When you delivered that package to my trailer, I decided Heidi knew what she was talking about. But first I had to overcome my terror."

His smile faded. "You looked at me like you were ready to faint."

"I almost did," she confessed. "After I was freed from prison, I lived with the constant fear that the judge might change his mind and they'd put me back in there.

"I know it is an irrational fear, but the sight of any police officer terrifies me. You were wearing a uniform. I thought you were one of those Texas Rangers with a warrant for my arrest. I figured I'd fallen for the oldest trick in the book when you shouted, 'Delivery!'"

There was the oddest flicker in the recesses of his eyes, but she was too intent on telling him everything to dwell on it.

"Fortunately I saw your IPS badge before I made a complete fool of myself and passed out at your feet."

"Dana—" came his husky response. "Prison should never have happened to you." His hands slid to both sides of her face. He kissed her long and hard.

When he released her, she buried her face in his neck. "I did my railing against God. When the prison chaplain tried to talk to me, I refused to listen. He left me a pamphlet called *Tragedy or Destiny*. I hated it.''

He smoothed the hair at her temple. ''What did it say?''

''That every human was on an individual journey back to God, that there were certain stumbling blocks placed there especially for us so we'd grow. It said that in time we'd understand their purpose and even be grateful for them.''

He held her tighter.

''I couldn't fathom it then, but I do now.'' She lifted her head to look at him. ''My journey brought me to West Texas. A place I would never have come to otherwise.''

''But the observatory—''

''By the time I was arrested, only the shell had been built. With their world shattered by Amy's tragic death and my incarceration, Mom and Dad gave up their dream to retire here. In fact they were on the verge of having it torn down and the property sold when Heidi and Gideon approached them.

''Gideon told them he was working on my release and needed their input. At that point everything was put on hold while they helped compile information for my case.

''When the judge told me I was free, my parents knew how much I craved privacy and freedom. They spoke to the contractor and he rushed to get the inside of the observatory finished.

''It was Mom who made inquiries and found out · Mr. Mason was renting his trailer. All this was arranged without my knowledge. They've done everything in their power to help me recover.''

His hand stilled on her neck. ''What if you hadn't been imprisoned?''

''I would have gone to England on a fellowship to work on my Ph.D. Then I would have submitted résumés around the U.S. to get a job at a university, hopefully on the East Coast.''

''Instead, the brilliant Ms. Turner is the jewel in Cal-Tech's crown.''

Twice in the last twelve hours Jace had managed to bring a blush to her face. ''Hardly a jewel. But I have to admit, it's made my parents happy to know I'm here guarding the family treasure.''

''I'd like to meet them.''

''I want that more than anything. Speaking of meeting people, Heidi and Gideon will be arriving around noon today. I can't wait to introduce you. Do you think you could arrange your schedule to have lunch with us?''

''I wish I could say yes, but I've already stayed here too long.'' He rolled up his sleeping blanket. ''It's your fault for being such a ravishing creature. As it is, I'll have to work through my lunch hour to get everything done.''

Letting out a sigh of disappointment, Dana reached for the binoculars.

''Hey—'' he cupped her chin ''—you remind me of my little niece, Julia, when she's upset. One troubled look from her can melt your heart. The problem is, IPS doesn't have one.''

Dana laughed before picking up the groceries they

hadn't touched. She followed Jace to his car and put them on the passenger seat. "Enjoy your breakfast en route."

"As soon as I put your futon away, I intend to."

She shook her head. "I'll do it. The sooner you go, the sooner you'll be back." This time she couldn't disguise the tremor in her voice.

He gathered her in his arms. "If you think I want to leave, then you don't have a clue about me."

His mouth—she couldn't get enough of it—of him. To her shame, he had to be the one to eventually break their kiss.

"Where will your friends be staying?"

"I've booked them at the Ponderosa. You know. The *only* motel in town."

"Good. The second I'm through with work, I'll phone you for further instructions." He got in the car and rolled down the window.

"I'm missing you already," she blurted.

"That makes two of us. Come here one more time."

She moved the binoculars out of the way to reach him.

JACE ARRIVED at his apartment in Alpine having wolfed down the contents of the sack. Bananas, granola bars, apple juice. He'd appeased one of his appetites. The other one he couldn't do anything about until tonight when he got Dana to himself.

Thank God she'd be sleeping at the Watkinses' apartment from now on.

While he was shaving, his cell phone rang. He checked the caller ID and picked up.

"Pat, I'm glad you phoned. I was just about to ring you. Tell me you've got some news I can bite into."

"How's this for starters—"

Jace wiped his face while he listened to the rundown on Glen's activities of the night before. The P.I.'s had filmed him tossing the flowers. But it was the part about getting rid of the locksmith's tools and knife in a Dumpster after leaving Burdick in the bar that made Jace's pulse race.

"It was clear to the P.I.'s that Burdick calls all the shots," Pat added.

"That jibes with the testimony of the victim in the armed robbery. He claimed the older of the two gunmen gave the orders. There's no doubt in my mind Glen told Burdick about the missing minicamera and was threatened with holy hell if he didn't stay out of trouble."

"If they're the two we're looking for, then Burdick's paranoia is understandable. He's terrified what Glen's doing could put him in jail."

"We know they're lying low for a reason, Pat. It explains Burdick's attitude toward Glen, who's so obsessed with Dana he's going off the deep end."

"That boy's insanely jealous of your relationship with her. You've got yourself a mortal enemy."

"You're right. But that's not what worries me. Time's running out. After this weekend, I have to report back to Austin."

"I know," the older man muttered.

"All I need is one piece of hard evidence to link them to Gibb's murder and Tom will extend my leave of absence. I've got to find it, Pat!" His voice shook.

"The lab in Austin is working overtime because they want Gibb's killers nailed too. I was promised some results on the fingerprints by the end of the day."

Jace let out a deep sigh. "We can't ask for more than that. I'm moving up my timetable. Dana has friends coming from California. After I've met them for dinner tonight, I'll camp out and check the third quadrant. I know in my gut that plane's around here somewhere.

"Do me a favor and get me a forest service truck. Have one of your officers park it in front of my apartment and leave the keys on the kitchen counter. Tell them to bring a uniform for me too. After I leave Dana's, I'll drive back to Alpine for it.

"So far I've been lucky and no one's caught me doing surveillance. But things are heating up now. I'll feel better if I look like I'm on official business."

"Good idea. I'll get right on it."

"Thanks. Before we hang up, you need to know Dana is moving to the Watkinses' basement apartment in Cloud Rim." He gave him the address. "I drove her over there last night and she paid the first month's rent. Today she'll be moving in."

"It's about time!"

"I agree. After the flower incident, she didn't need a push. Let the P.I.'s know so they won't wonder what's happening when they drive by."

"Hey, Jace, you remember what I told you about the hair standing on the back of my neck when I can feel we've locked on target?"

"Yes?"

"It's standing on end now."

"I had the same reaction when you told me Glen dumped the tools and knife. He wouldn't have done that unless Burdick was running scared. Something big's about to happen. I've just got to figure out the time and the place."

"You'll do it. Talk to you tonight."

AT ONE O'CLOCK, Dana left the observatory and drove to the Ponderosa. She sat in her car outside the lobby entrance keeping an eye out for Gideon's Acura. Hopefully she'd see the IPS van as well.

She didn't know if Jace had arrived in Cloud Rim yet. For that matter he might have already come and gone. But her heart raced at the possibility of seeing him for even a few minutes while he made his deliveries in town.

All of a sudden a car turned at the corner. Dana saw the flash of familiar red-gold hair before recognizing the Acura. She jumped out of her car and started running toward them.

"Heidi!" she screamed in excitement.

"Dana!"

Gideon had to brake so his wife could get out. She ran toward her friend. When they reached each other, they hugged. That in turn set off their tears.

"You have no idea how happy I am to see you," Dana said.

"Me too."

"There's so much to tell you I hardly know where to begin. If I'd had to wait a minute longer—"

Heidi's eyes gave her a thorough scrutiny. They'd always been able to read each other's thoughts. "Dana Turner? You're glowing!"

"So are you."

"No—I mean it. There's a light in your eyes. Something earthshaking has happened. If I don't miss my guess, it's brown eyes himself, the IPS man. Hmm? Fess up."

"Yes!" She nodded. "I'm in love with the most wonderful man alive! Present husband excepted, of course. Oh, Heidi, I'm so crazy about him, I can hardly stand it. He'll be here after work. The second you meet him, you'll understand. You're going to love him the way I love Gideon.

"Speaking of the famous father-to-be, let's take a look at what he's done to you. Stand still."

Heidi blushed as Dana walked all the way around her. She was so happy it shone from her whole being.

"I do believe your figure has become more voluptuous since the last time I saw you. I bet hubby likes that."

"Dana!"

"Isn't that right, Gideon?" she teased as he and Kevin emerged from the car with Pokey at their heels. The adorable beagle ran over to Dana and sniffed her sandals. She reached down and scratched his head.

Gideon grinned at her. "I'm afraid I didn't hear the question, so I'll take a hug and a kiss first."

Dana flung herself into his arms. "I hear you're going to be a daddy for the second time. I'm glad you're here so I can congratulate you in person. You must be ecstatic." She kissed his cheek before he swung her around.

"That's putting it lightly," he whispered before setting her down. His blue eyes searched hers. "You've grown even more beautiful in the last month. I didn't think that was possible."

"That's what I told Heidi after she met you." Her gaze switched to Kevin. The teenager seemed taller than last time.

"Are you too old for a hug from your aunty Dana?"

Kevin's smile widened. "No. It's okay."

"I'm glad you said that, because I was going to do it anyway." When she grabbed him, Pokey tried to get in on the act. Everyone laughed.

Suddenly Dana's eyes filled. "I can't tell you what it means to see all of you again. Why don't you get registered and settled in, then we'll go to lunch at the café, unless you've already eaten."

"I'm afraid the guys ate a couple of brownies your mom made for you," Heidi said. "But take it from me, those were just a couple of drops in the ocean. Frankly, we're starving."

"No morning sickness yet?"

"No. Just constant hunger. I can't believe it."

"Oh, Heidi. It's so exciting. You're going to have a little baby. Has it sunk in yet?"

"No."

"I hope it's a girl, because it's probably going to have red hair," Kevin interjected.

Dana saw the secret smile that passed between Gideon and his wife. "Then she'll break a lot of hearts."

"I know one man with red hair who is extremely handsome," Dana said.

"Who?"

"Dr. James McDermitt, a very famous astronomer from England."

"That's where Heidi's ancestors come from, huh?"

Heidi nodded.

"Do most English people have red hair?"

Gideon's shoulders were shaking with silent laughter. "No. I think my other half is a throwback to some unknown Irish ancestor."

"Just think, Kevin," Dana said when the chuckles subsided, "you might get a little brother or sister with dark hair like your dad's."

"That would be cool."

"You know what? You'll adore him or her no matter what they look like."

"I know."

Gideon threw an arm around his son. "Come on, Kev. Help me sign in. The girls want to gab."

"Stay, Pokey!" Kevin ordered.

The dog sat at Heidi's feet while the men disappeared.

"I'd say you and Kevin have made a lot of progress. Otherwise he wouldn't feel free talking about red hair around you."

"He's wonderful."

"What about his mother? How are things going with her?"

"Better. I think she's stopped feeling so threatened. Now that Kevin has the freedom to be with both parents, he spends a lot of time with her when Gideon is working a case. That's the way it should be. All I can do is be a good friend."

"Whatever you're doing, it's working. I'm proud of you, Heidi. I don't care what anyone says. Taking on a child who isn't yours can't be easy."

"Gideon makes it easy for me. I love him more than ever. If I have any concern, it's that Kevin might think his father loves the new baby more than him. Gideon and I have talked a lot about it, and how to handle it so Kevin feels totally secure."

"As long as you're both aware of his needs, you can't fail."

"I hope not."

Heidi took a deep breath. "It's heavenly up here with all that sun and blue sky."

"I know. I'm spoiled, because it's been like this going on two weeks. One of these days there has to be a storm, but I can wait." She stared at her friend. "How does it feel to be a full-time housewife?"

"Incredible. I'm disgustingly lazy. After I fix Gideon a big breakfast and see him off to work, I take Pokey for a walk along the beach. Then I go home, do a little housecleaning and start planning dinner for my husband.

"I found out from his sister that he was raised on meat and potatoes. So I've been doing that. He always says I shouldn't go to the trouble, but I notice he walks in the back door right on time every night and asks what we're having.''

''Marrying you was like dying and going to heaven.''

''Oh, stop!''

''Now, tell me, what did you decide about teaching?''

''I gave my notice.''

''Gideon must be thrilled.''

''Deep down he is, but I think he's worried I'll be bored staying home. The scars from his first marriage run deep.''

''Then he's still got a lot to learn about you.''

''That's what I'm counting on. We're going to convert the spare bedroom into a nursery, but he doesn't know about the baby quilt I've started. Kevin helped me pick out the different fabrics.''

''Including him was inspired on your part.''

''He's a remarkable person. Oh, here they come, and I haven't even emptied the car yet.''

Together they made swift work of carrying their things into the adjoining rooms. After Kevin filled Pokey's water dish, the four of them walked around the corner to the café.

Gideon linked his arm through Dana's. ''I know you've been dying to ask me about Consuela, so let me put you out of your misery. I'm waiting for one more crucial piece of evidence. When I've got it, I'll contact her attorney and we'll ask the judge to look at her case again.''

"Just the way you did mine. What do you think her chances are?"

"Right now? As good as yours at this stage."

"Gideon—" she squeezed his hand "—because of you she'll probably get her little daughter back, and have a chance to start a new life. How am I going to repay you for everything you've done?"

"I was paid in full when Heidi joined my night school criminology class to help you. Because of your friendship, I've found the kind of happiness I never expected to experience."

"I have news for you. She feels the same way."

When they entered the café, Dana introduced everyone to the owner, who took their orders. Once they'd eaten lunch, and dessert had been served, Gideon asked what everyone wanted to do with the rest of the afternoon. His eyes were at half-mast. He'd been driving for a couple of days.

Dana took one look at Heidi, who needed more sleep these days, and made a decision.

"Hey, Kevin, how would you and Pokey like to help me with a project while your dad and Heidi take a nap?"

"Sure."

"Come on. We'll go in my car." She paid the bill for everyone before Gideon could, and got up from the table. "See you around six."

"Now I'm in *your* debt." Gideon looked like a happy man. Heidi mouthed her own thank-you.

Dana flashed them a mischievous smile before following Kevin out of the café. After they'd put Pokey in the car, they took off.

''What are we going to do?'' Kevin said.

''First of all, you don't have to do anything. I just wanted the company. But if you'd like to help, I'll pay you fifteen dollars an hour.''

''That's a lot more than I can make mowing lawns. What is it?''

''I need to move my things from the trailer to my new apartment.''

''Heidi didn't tell me or Dad about that.''

Dana pulled alongside the trailer and stopped the car. ''She doesn't know. I only paid the rent last night.'' They got out. Kevin called to Pokey, who started sniffing around.

''How come you're moving? I think this is a cool place to live.''

The lock didn't give her any trouble today, thank heaven. ''Remember that guy who lives next door?''

''You mean the one Heidi calls Little Custer?''

She laughed. ''Yes.'' They went inside. ''He's gone from being a nuisance to breaking into my trailer when I'm not home.''

''Whoa.''

''Whoa is right. Because of that, Jace helped me find a new place to live.''

''Who's Jace?''

''Jace Riley, the man I've been seeing.''

Kevin cocked his head. ''You've got a boyfriend?''

She nodded. ''You're going to meet him tonight.''

''Do you love him?''

''Yes.''

''Are you going to marry him?''

"If he asks me."

"Then I hope he does."

"Thanks, Kevin... Okay, where shall I start?"

"Have you got those big plastic green garbage bags?"

"You're reading my mind."

"You don't have a lot of stuff in here. It won't take us very long."

"I love your attitude," she said. "While I look for them, would you mind going back out to the car and opening the trunk? You just push the lever on the side of the seat."

"Sure."

The second he disappeared with Pokey, Dana grabbed the gun from under the cushion and pulled out the clip. She hurried to the bedroom, where she shoved the weapon into the pillowcase. After piling more bedding on top, she carried everything to the car.

In about two hours they'd emptied the trailer, and there was still enough room in the car for Kevin to sit with Pokey in the front seat.

"We do good work." She put three ten dollar bills in his hand.

"Thanks."

"You earned it. I'll come back and clean the place next week. Let's go." Later tonight she'd let Mr. Mason know she'd moved out. She'd tell him she would pay extra for not giving him advance warning.

On their way to the apartment, her cell phone rang. Her pulse quickened as she reached for it.

"Hello?"

"Dana—"

Every time she heard Jace's voice, she melted like a Popsicle in the sun. "How are you?"

"Fine now that I'm talking to you, but I'm running a half hour late. What's the plan?"

"Why don't you meet us outside the Ponderosa at six-thirty and we'll decide from there."

"I'll hurry."

Kevin was watching her as she hung up. "What are we going to do now?"

"If you don't mind, I'd like to drive over to the new apartment. I need a shower and change of clothes. While I'm busy, you can take Pokey for a walk around my new neighborhood, or I can drive you back to the motel right now."

He rubbed the dog's head. "You'd like a walk, wouldn't you, Pokey."

She patted Kevin's arm. "Do you have any idea what a great guy you are? You've made this fun for me. I really appreciate it."

"I had fun too."

"Heidi said she adores you. Now I know why."

"She's really cool."

Wouldn't Heidi love to hear that!

After spending about an hour at her new apartment, they drove back to the motel.

Kevin started to get out of the car. "Aren't you coming in?"

Dana shook her head. "I'll stay out here until they're ready."

"Okay. I'll wave to you when it's safe."

Gideon may not have fathered Kevin in the biological sense, but he'd reared a wonderful son who was all the things a parent could wish for. When he opened the door to let Kevin and the dog in, he motioned to Dana to join them.

She climbed out of the car and locked it. The sum total of the worldly goods she'd brought to West Texas were inside.

The nap must have done them a lot of good. They both looked refreshed and had changed clothes. Heidi put some cold drinks on the table.

"Come and sit with us while Kevin's taking his shower. I understand Jace Riley will be here at six-thirty. We want to hear all about him."

Gideon pushed an icy-cold Coke her way. "Kevin says you want to marry him."

"I—I hope he asks me."

"You're ready to marry a man you only met a week ago?"

Heidi covered her husband's hand. "I knew you were the one I wanted the first time I sat in on your class."

"I knew the same thing." He kissed her hand before looking at Dana. "Don't mind me. I guess your news has taken us by complete surprise."

"We're both in the habit of feeling very protective of you," Heidi confided.

Dana felt her throat tighten. "I love you for it."

"Tell us everything."

"Well, he's from Austin and went to college there. His wife died of cancer about seven years ago. It's taken him a long time to recover. He thought a change of location would help. IPS transferred him to the West Texas area some time ago.

"He's the backup driver when the other drivers go on vacation. Right now he rents an apartment in Alpine to cover the Alpine-to-Cloud Rim route. Pretty soon he'll be assigned somewhere else, but I'm trying not to think about that."

"Have you met his family?"

"Not yet. His parents and two brothers live in Austin. They're both married and have children."

Heidi scrutinized her. "You used to call me every day, but after you met old brown eyes, the phone's been silent. What have you two been up to?"

Heat crept into Dana's cheeks. "Lots of things."

Kevin chose that moment to enter the room with Pokey. He was still drying his wet hair with a towel. "Did you tell them Little Custer broke into your trailer?"

"What?" Heidi cried out.

Gideon's face darkened. "When did this happen?"

"It's a long story.

"We want to hear. All of it!" Gideon demanded. Like quicksilver, he'd changed into his serious interrogation mode. Dana supposed it was as natural to him as breathing.

"Jace was the first to discover that Glen had been hanging around my trailer when I wasn't there. He checked my lock, and decided it wasn't safe. The other night he took me to buy a new one and installed it for me.

"But then we discovered Glen had broken in

again. At least we assume it was he. On that same night I found out some flowers the Mitchells— they're the directors of the young astronomers club— had sent to thank me for a star party had been delivered to the Mason house. Somehow they never made it to my trailer.

"Jace likes Glen's grandfather, Ralph Mason, as much as I do. He thought it best not to ask questions that could upset him where Glen's concerned and I agreed with him. His solution was to find me an apartment to rent."

"She's going to sleep there tonight," Kevin interjected.

"Thanks to your wonderful son who helped load everything in my car, I'm free of Glen."

"She paid me thirty dollars!"

"Did you call the police about the break-in?" Gideon persisted, oblivious to his son's comment.

"No. Jace told me he'd tell them."

Gideon's face broke out in a frown. "An officer should have come to your trailer to investigate."

"I forgot to tell you someone slashed a tire on his IPS van. Their company phoned in a report to the police. Jace told them he thought it was Glen who'd been responsible for everything, so they're looking into it."

"That isn't the point, Dana. You should have called the police at the first sign of trouble. Jace was wrong to have decided against it. He was wrong to tell you not to talk to Mr. Mason about his grandson. You shouldn't have listened to him. I know you're in love, but it sounds like he's already taken control of your life. I don't like it.''

By this time Heidi had gotten to her feet. She put her hands on Gideon's shoulders to massage them. ''Sweetheart? We're on vacation, remember?''

She flashed Dana a signal of distress, trying to let her know she was sorry her husband had gotten so exercised over a problem that had nothing to do with him.

Dana darted her a response that said she didn't mind. On the contrary, it was wonderful Gideon cared enough to come on like a protective older brother. Between him and Jace, she felt totally safe.

She glanced at her watch. ''It's almost six-thirty. I'll go outside and watch for him. There's a fabulous buffet at the Pride Ranch in Fort Davis. Would you like to go there for dinner? Afterward we can walk around and see the sights.''

''That sounds terrific, doesn't it, Kevin?'' Heidi said.

''Yeah. I wanted to go the last time we were here.''

''Then it's settled.''

CHAPTER TEN

JACE HAD BEEN PREPARED to like Dana's friends, sight unseen. He wasn't disappointed. Heidi Poletti was a total sweetheart. Kevin turned out to be one of the nicest, most well-behaved teens he'd ever met. As for Gideon, he was the kind of person any man would want to claim for a friend.

There was only one problem. For some reason, the detective didn't seem to like Jace.

The other man didn't do anything overt or tangible to give Jace that impression. It was just something he sensed. He could tell Dana noticed it too. She tried to protect him by keeping up a lively conversation with Kevin and Heidi throughout dinner.

But he'd been with Dana enough to know she was talking too fast. Her topics touched on everything but the personal. Gideon, on the other hand, only offered a comment here and there. Finally Jace decided to end the evening.

He put his arm behind her chair. "It's getting late. Why don't I drive you home so I can help you unload your car."

"I was about to suggest the same thing," Gideon muttered. "With five of us, we'll make short work of it."

"I thought we were going to walk around here and sightsee."

"We'll do that tomorrow, Kevin. Let's go."

Jace pulled out his wallet and put six twenties on the tray the waitress had placed on their table. Gideon scooped them up and handed them back to him. "This is my treat tonight."

Dana's eyes entreated him not to argue.

"Thanks, Gideon. Just remember that tomorrow night is on me. See you all back at the motel." He put his hand behind Dana's waist and escorted her to his car.

After they turned onto the highway headed for Cloud Rim, he reached for her hand. "Are you all right?"

She clutched it hard. "No."

"Tell me what's wrong."

"It's Gideon. He was acting strangely at dinner."

"Maybe he's worried about his wife's pregnancy."

"That's not it."

"Then it's about me." He waited for her to deny it. "What did he do? Warn you off me?"

"No. But he thinks I should have called the police when I found out someone had broken into the trailer."

Gideon's right. I wouldn't think much of him as an officer of the law if he hadn't said something.

"When I told him the reason why I didn't, he got upset. Usually he's so much fun and laid-back. Tonight I hardly recognized him."

Jace cleared his throat. "I noticed he was kind of

quiet. But that's understandable. He was just giving you girls a chance to catch up.''

"Don't make excuses for him, Jace. He was cold to you. It's simply not like him. I don't understand the drastic change in his behavior.''

"It seems to me he's just looking out for your welfare. I'm the new guy on the block and he's sizing me up. After all, he's the one who obtained your release from prison. Knowing his wife loves you like a sister, I would imagine his protective instincts are on full alert.''

Dana's head turned toward him. He could feel her gaze upon him. "You're an amazing man. If only Gideon knew you the way I do.''

"Give it time. This is only the first day.''

"But it shouldn't be like this,'' she blurted. "Here I've been so excited for all of you to meet. Now I wish they hadn't come.''

"You don't mean that.''

"Yes, I do. Everything was perfect be-before—''

"Dana, nothing's changed for us.''

"I hope it hasn't.'' A slight wobble betrayed her anxiety.

They'd come to the first stop sign in Cloud Rim. Instead of driving on, he pulled her close and kissed her with a thoroughness that made him forget where they were. Until Gideon's Acura and several other cars pulled past them, he hadn't realized he'd been holding up traffic.

"Are you convinced yet?''

"Yes.'' Her eyes rivaled the stars for their luster.

"Please promise me you won't let his attitude bother you?"

"How could it? My only concern is that this is painful for you."

"Just because I wanted you and Gideon to like each other."

"I do like him." *A lot. He's got all the right instincts.*

"I don't see how. Even Heidi's bewildered."

"You're making too much of it. By tomorrow this will all have blown over." The motel came into view. "I'll drop you off at your car and meet you at the apartment."

"See you in a minute." She leaned over to kiss his cheek before climbing out of the car.

GIDEON STOOD next to her packed Toyota. "If you'll allow me, I'll drive you over to your new place. Heidi's going to follow in our car."

Her spirits plunged. He was determined to have a private talk with her. If she didn't want to make a scene, she had no choice but to get in the passenger seat of her car without protest.

After she shut the door, he said, "Tell me where to go."

No sooner had she given him directions than he pulled out of the parking space. "Don't hate me, Dana. I think you know how much I love you. How important you are to me."

Tears stung her eyes. "I do."

"Then trust me. I have to ask you a few more

questions. The cop in me is telling me something's not right here.''

Dear God. Now she was getting nervous. She loved Gideon. She trusted him with her life. Because of him she *had* a life. If his instincts were telling him something was wrong, then she needed to listen.

''Have you ever met this man's friends?''

''No.''

''Do you think he has any?''

She exhaled a deep sigh. ''He told me about a colleague who slept over at his apartment last night. I didn't meet him because Jace and I camped out.''

His expression turned grim.

''It isn't what you think, Gideon. We're not lovers. I didn't want to stay in the trailer, so we slept out by the observatory last night.''

''Tell me again why he changed your lock the first time.''

Dana smoothed the hair away from her face. ''It was right after the ordeal with Tony Roberts. Jace wanted to know if I had the only key to the trailer. I told him I wasn't sure, so he suggested changing the lock to keep me safe.''

''You say he gave Tony a lift to your place?''

''Yes. He also found him hitchhiking down the mountain after Tony left the trailer, so he gave him a ride back to Fort Davis.''

''In my mind that's almost too convenient.''

''You think the two of them knew each other before or something?'' she cried out, aghast.

''I don't know. Tony was very angry when your father let him go. It's not inconceivable that he had some sort of plan to get back at you and used Jace to find you.''

''I can't believe that of Jace. I won't!''

''This is killing me almost as much as it is you, but I have to ask. Do you know positively that he's from Austin?''

Her eyes closed tightly. ''No. Everything he's told me I've taken on faith because he's never done anything to make me doubt him.''

''Weren't you suspicious when he didn't want you to call the police? Especially with Glen's past history of bothering you whenever he felt like it?''

''Not at the time, no.''

''Think about it. Whoever broke in had a damn good reason. They would have left fingerprints. Glen would have been brought in for questioning. The police would have checked his prints against the ones found at the crime scene. If he's breaking and entering, he needs to be put behind bars.

''But what if Glen's not the culprit? What if Tony hired Jace to become friendly with you so he could steal your disks with all of your projects?''

Dana gasped.

''I know it sounds ugly, but if there's any possibility it's true, then Jace wouldn't want the police finding any prints that didn't belong to Glen. It would also explain why he's pinning all the blame on your neighbor.''

''I feel sick.''

''So do I. But if you're in trouble, something has to be done. Did you see the slashed tire on the van?''

She let out a shuddering breath. ''No.''

"So you only have Jace's word that his company called the police to investigate. Don't you see, Jace could have made it up to cast more suspicion on Glen?

"For all we know, Glen's simply a tragic loner who has a terrible crush on you, nothing more."

Dana felt sick in the pit of her stomach. She wished he'd stop talking. The more he explained his suspicions, the more alarmed she grew.

"Something else disturbs me. How did Jace know Glen had been hanging around your trailer when no one was there?"

"I can't answer that question."

"If he drives an IPS truck all day long, there's no way he could make an assumption like that. Maybe he and Tony knew each other in California. Jace could have hired on as a temp for IPS."

"A temp?" At this point Dana was horrified.

"I have to be honest and tell you that I've never heard of a regular driver being allowed to move from route to route filling shifts for his colleagues on vacation."

She buried her face in her hands.

"Has he been in your office at the observatory?"

"Several times."

"What kind of interest has he shown in your work?"

Wiping her eyes, she said, "A lot."

"Has he pushed?"

"No."

"Whose idea was it to camp by the observatory?"

A sharp pain pierced her heart. "His."

"Does he have a habit of coming up to the observatory?"

"Not exactly. He's driven up there several times. There was the star party. And the day after we met, I found him on the road to Mount Luna. I thought he was delivering a package to me at the observatory. I guess I assumed he knew I worked there from his conversations with Mr. Mason."

"So what excuse did he proffer?"

Her body felt like ice. "He said he was looking for an address and wondered if I could help him."

"Did you?"

"No. I'd never heard of the person. I told him to ask the café owner in town because she'd lived here for years."

"How long has he been working this route?"

"I don't know. He said he'd come to Alpine recently and wouldn't be in the area much longer."

"That was probably the truth."

She clutched the armrests. "If Jace isn't who I think he is, what am I going to do? Help me, Gideon!"

"I know this isn't going to be easy, but when we pull up to your apartment, try to act as natural as you can. Don't let him think that anything has changed.

"Later tonight, when the family goes to bed, I'll run a background check on him and see what comes up. When I've got the information, we'll go from there."

Dana groaned. "I've known betrayal in my life from Tony—my sister— But if it turns out Jace has been using me, I might as well not go on living."

"Don't say that, Dana. Don't even think it. Maybe I'm wrong."

She shook her head. "You're never wrong. That's what's killing me."

"I could be this time. It's because of *you* that I want to play this extra safe, just to be sure."

He started to slow down the car. "We've arrived. Remember who you are. You walked through fire before and came out whole. You can do it again if you have to."

"KEVIN? Do you remember seeing one of my astronomy journals when we were loading the car?"

"No. Where was it?"

"I thought on the kitche—no, wait—on the couch."

Jace could hear their voices coming from the hallway. He carried a laundry basket full of kitchen items into the apartment kitchen where Heidi was busy putting silverware in the drawer.

"This is the last thing to come in."

"You're kidding. With everybody helping, it's taken only five minutes to get her moved in. Incredible!"

"What would you like me to do now?"

"I think we're through."

Since Gideon had driven Dana over to the apartment, there'd been no opportunity to talk to her alone. She'd smiled at Jace coming and going. She'd said all the appropriate things with a bright friendliness, but she treated him the way she treated Kevin.

Dana was no longer the woman who'd reached for him in the night.

Gideon was no fool. The cop inside him had been putting two and two together all evening and had come up with several sums, none of which added to four. He'd said enough to Dana on the drive over from the motel to turn her inside out.

Instinct told him Heidi's husband wasn't about to leave things alone. Something had to be done before he ran a little investigation of his own and jeopardized the operation.

Jace walked down the hall. Gideon was in the bedroom with Kevin making Dana's bed. He found her in the bathroom putting things away in the cabinet.

"Your car has been emptied."

"Already?" she cried, but she concentrated on her task and refused to look him in the eye. "You've all been wonderful."

"If you'll give me the key to the trailer, I'll drive over there for a final inspection. If I see your journal, I'll bring it back."

"I'll go with you."

Jace had hoped Gideon would pick up on the plan, and the other man didn't disappoint him. But his offer seemed to cause Dana more grief. There was a big clatter as she dropped half a dozen items in the sink by accident.

"My key ring is on the kitchen counter."

He put his hands on her shoulders and kissed the side of her neck. "I'll find it."

Her tense body wounded him, but there wasn't a thing he could do about it yet.

"Can I come?"

"I'd rather you'd stayed here with Heidi and Dana, Kevin. We won't be long."

Jace found her key ring and put it in his pocket. Gideon gave his wife a hug and told her they'd be back in a minute. She didn't look any happier about it than Dana.

Jace slipped out of the apartment and got in his car. Gideon was right behind him and climbed in the other side.

Once they were on their way, Jace waited for the inevitable interrogation. It wasn't long in coming.

"Dana tells me you're the driver IPS hires when their regular men go on vacation. That must be quite a challenge, learning the ins and outs of every route in such a short period of time."

"It takes a fair amount of concentration."

"With such mobility in a job, it would be hard to put down roots."

"Up until recently the idea of settling into anything permanent hasn't interested me."

"But now that you've met Dana, you're considering it."

Anger and sarcasm dripped from Gideon's tongue. Jace rejoiced that Dana had a man like Gideon for a friend.

"I'm planning on it."

A few minutes later he slowed down and pulled alongside the trailer. He was glad Dana had left a light on. Before long, Glen would discover she'd moved out. No telling what alarm bells that would trigger.

As Gideon got out of the car, Jace reached under the seat for a certain item and joined him at the door. He reached for her key ring and unlocked the trailer.

"After you," Gideon muttered.

Jace went inside. The first thing he did was move the cushions from the couch. Sure enough, he found the missing journal. While he repositioned them, Gideon made a tour of the trailer.

"The place is clean," he said after checking the drawers and cupboards in the kitchen.

"Kevin was a great help to Dana. You must be proud of him."

Gideon walked toward him with a brooding expression. They faced each other like adversaries. It was time for that to change.

"I can read your mind, Detective Poletti. You smell a rat. A big fat one. And you'd be right."

He reached inside his trouser pocket and pulled out his official identification and badge. Gideon took it from him.

During the long, satisfying silence, he watched the other man's face undergo a complete transformation. Gideon finally lifted his head. They stared at each other with a new understanding.

A smile curved Jace's mouth. "Why don't we start all over again. I'm Captain Jace Riley of the Texas Rangers out of Austin, Texas."

"Thank God."

The two men shook hands. Their mutual love for Dana, plus the fact that they were fellow officers of the law, produced an instant camaraderie that was almost tangible.

"You've stumbled onto a manhunt for two criminals who committed armed robbery in Austin last Christmas. They killed three people. One of them was a retired ranger, Gibb Barton, a virtual legend in Texas.

"The killers disappeared in a small plane over the Davis Mountains. They haven't been seen since. I'm here undercover to pick up their trail."

Gideon groaned. "You don't even want to know the scenario I imagined in my mind about you and Tony Roberts being in league together against Dana. I'm afraid I expressed my fears to her."

"Don't worry about it." Jace chuckled. "If you want to swap horror stories, listen to this— I imagined Roberts was one of the killers. When Dana let him inside her trailer, I had visions of the next ax murder being committed. At one point I got so nervous, I broke in expecting to see body parts all over the floor."

Eyeing him ruefully, Gideon said, "We both know too damn much about the dark side."

"Agreed. It's an occupational hazard." Jace put his ID back in his pocket. "Let me explain how Dana's world and mine happened to collide."

Gideon took the chair opposite the couch, eyeing him with grave concern. Jace knew exactly what the other man was thinking.

"To answer your question, I'm in love with Dana." He reached in his pocket and pulled out a gold wedding band. "Before my wife died, she begged me to find someone else to marry. At the time, I didn't think I'd ever be able to fall in love again. Then I met Dana. Today I took this off my finger.''

"That's all I needed to hear," Gideon said in a relieved tone of voice.

He put the ring back in his pocket. "Unfortunately, there isn't a thing in hell I can do about it while I'm still undercover. Until I'm free to be honest with her, I can't even tell her I love her."

The other man nodded. "Understood. My best friend, Max Calder, was with the FBI for a long time. He went undercover to infiltrate the Russian mob and fell in love with an immigration attorney he thought was one of them.

"I provided backup for him at the time, and believe me—it was hell for both of them until she unwittingly helped Max bring them down. Now they're happily married and he's gone back to being a detective in my department."

"Thanks for telling me that. It all helps. However, I may not be so lucky with Dana."

Gideon blinked. "Why do you say that?"

"For one thing, I found out during my marriage that I can't give a woman children. When I mentioned this to Dana, she didn't say anything. I happen to know she's crazy about kids. I was there when Heidi told her the news about your baby. You should have seen her reaction."

"There's always adoption, Jace."

"Some women can't handle the idea. Dana could be one of them. Then there's the added problem of my profession, which might be a real turnoff."

"It's early days yet. Don't borrow trouble," he

urged in a commiserating tone. "Tell me about the case you're working on."

"Gladly." Jace leaned forward, clasping his hands between his legs. "I could use a mind like yours to give me some input."

A half hour went by while he filled in the holes to paint the whole picture for Gideon. "The problem is, I'm working against a short time frame. If I don't come up with hard evidence by Sunday night, it's back to Austin on Monday."

Gideon rose to his feet. "I'm going to help you look for that plane. Let's get started. If we move fast, we can have both quadrants covered by morning."

Jace shook his head. "I couldn't ask that of you. You're on vacation. I know what it means to your family to get you away from your work. Needless to say, Dana's been waiting for you to come."

"Let's get something straight. Dana's family to me. When I think about that minicamera..." He sounded as savage as Jace felt.

Getting up from the couch, Jace grabbed the journal she'd been looking for and followed Gideon out the door. Once it was locked, he joined the other man and started up the car.

"When we get to the apartment, just play along with me," Gideon murmured. "I'll think of something to tell Heidi and Dana that will be reassuring yet won't blow your cover.

"When I get my wife alone, I'll explain that you need to confide in me about Dana, so we're going to camp out and have a man-to-man talk. She'll be fine with it."

"You don't have to do this."

Gideon turned his head toward Jace. "What if our positions were reversed and it was Heidi who was in danger?"

"Touché. I'll pick you up at the motel after I've said good-night to Dana."

"Good luck keeping it short."

Jace smiled. "I can see you've been there."

"I solved the problem by asking Heidi to live with me for a week while we hunted for evidence to free Dana."

"I hear it was a whirlwind courtship."

"It's the only way to fly."

"I'll remember that."

"WHERE ARE YOU GOING, Glen?"

"To say good-night to Dana. She had to work late at the observatory. Now she's back. I saw her headlights. We'll drive around town for a little while."

"You tell that young woman to come over and visit me tomorrow."

"I will. Do you want the TV on or off?"

"Leave it on. It's almost eleven. Time for that mystery show."

"Okay. See you later, Grandad."

Glen disappeared into his grandfather's bedroom and removed his hunting rifle from the closet shelf. In the dresser he found a box of ammo and took it.

Once out the back door, he put everything in the truck. It was packed and ready to go. All except for Dana's clothes.

She'd slept out with that bastard IPS driver last

night. If she was up at the observatory with him again tonight, she could plan to kiss him goodbye.

He drove over to the trailer and pulled alongside it. Before climbing down from the cab, he took a moment to load the rifle. He didn't give a crap if anyone saw him using his own trailer for target practice. The house, the property…it would all belong to him when the old man died.

Taking careful aim, he fired once at the lock.

Bingo.

After putting the rifle back in the truck, he reached for the empty duffel bag. It excited him just thinking about packing her clothes, especially all that lacy underwear.

The impact of the bullet had ripped the door clear off the hinges. He pushed it back and went inside.

His eyes narrowed to slits.

The place was empty!

He charged through to the bedroom. Nothing was in the drawers or closets. When he checked the bathroom, it was completely bare.

The bitch had moved out!

Because of the light she'd left on in the living room, it had led him to believe she still lived here.

Damn her to hell!

With hair flying, he retraced his steps to the truck and took off for the observatory. He kept his hand on the rifle as he rounded the summit to the top of Mount Luna.

Neither car was there.

The bastard had talked her into moving in with him. Glen's plan—to go away with her tonight and get married—would have to be postponed until he could find her.

Tomorrow he'd beg off sick from work and follow the IPS van. When he discovered where the driver lived, that's where he'd find Dana.

Lewis wouldn't like it, but Glen was tired of not getting his own way in anything. Besides, his grandfather approved of Dana. In fact, she was about the only thing he *did* approve of where Glen was concerned.

He'd be happy when Glen brought Dana home on Sunday as his bride. With his grandfather so sweet on her, she was his insurance to get all that was coming to him.

There was no reason to tell Lewis anything until after the wedding. This was one time he wasn't going to let him screw things up.

Satisfied with his plan, he drove back to the house. Leaving the duffel bag on the seat, he grasped the rifle and ammo and walked around to the back of the truck. He climbed over the tailgate to bury the weapon between the blankets and sleeping bags, where it would be safe.

He'd thought of everything. Cooler, water, rope, flashlights, butane lanterns. She'd have all the comforts of home.

When he slipped inside the house, the clock was chiming midnight.

"Glen? Is that you?"

"I'm back, Grandad."

"Is Dana going to come over tomorrow?"

"Either tomorrow or Sunday. She says she's looking forward to seeing you."

"That's what I like to hear."

"Is there anything you need before I go to bed?"

"No. I'm going to sleep now."

"Okay. Good night, Grandad."

"Good night."

CHAPTER ELEVEN

"Mom?"

"Dana, honey—"

"Did I wake you up?"

"Heavens no. Your father and I are watching a movie. Did Heidi and Gideon get there all right?"

"They arrived around one. It's so good to see them. Thanks for the brownies. You know how much I crave a taste of home. I've eaten three already."

"Good. You need to put on more weight."

"It's coming on fast now. Listen, Mom, tonight I moved from the trailer to a nice apartment in town. It even has a garage. Everyone helped and now I'm all settled in."

"That's music to my ears. Wait till I tell your father. He'll be as relieved as I am you won't have to be around the Mason boy Heidi said has been making a nuisance."

Dana shuddered just thinking of Glen. "The trailer served a purpose, but it was too isolated. If you've got a pen handy I'll give you the address."

"Just a minute."

While she waited for her mother to come back on the line, she heard voices coming from the front room. Jace and Gideon were back. There'd been so much tension before, the knot in her stomach tightened.

"Okay, honey, go ahead." When she'd written down the details, she said, "Now, tell me about Jace."

"He's in the living room waiting for me. I'll have to call you back."

"All right. But I expect to hear from you in the morning."

"I promise. Give Dad a kiss for me."

"I will. Good night, honey."

"Good night." She hung up.

Now was the moment she'd been dreading. With her heart sinking to her feet, she walked into the front room.

"We've been waiting for you," Gideon said as soon as she appeared.

Jace stood next to him. His dark brown gaze sent her a private greeting.

"I found the magazine under the cushions on the couch," he said. "You didn't tell me you had an article published in anything as prestigious as the *Royal Astrophysical Journal.* I'm very impressed."

"Thank you." What was going on? She looked at Heidi, who was curled up on the couch. "Where's Kevin?"

"The Watkinses came down to see if there was anything they could do. When they saw him, they asked if he'd like to go upstairs and play on the Playstation they bought for their grandchildren. He'll be back in a few minutes with Pokey."

Gideon cleared his throat. "I'm glad you're all

here because I have an announcement to make. Actually, it's an apology.''

Dana flashed a questioning glance to Heidi, who didn't seem to know what was going on either.

''I spoke out of turn when I criticized Jace for not calling the police about the break-in. While we were at the trailer, he let me in on a few facts that made me feel like a fool.

''For one thing, he knew about your fear of the law since your release from prison. In an effort to protect you, he contacted the police without your knowledge. I was wrong to jump to so many conclusions.

''Chalk it up to my love for you, Dana. I've already asked for Jace's forgiveness. Now what I need is yours.''

The relief of knowing he no longer had any doubts about Jace sent her flying into his arms. ''Of course I forgive you,'' she whispered. ''I love you for caring so much.''

Beyond his shoulder she could see Heidi smiling with happiness again. Thank heaven today's nightmare was over.

''My love,'' he addressed his wife, ''I think it's time we all got to bed. Tomorrow we'll have the whole day to spend with each other. I'll go upstairs and drag Kevin out of there.''

''I'll come with you.'' She jumped up from the couch. After hugging Dana and Jace good-night, she joined her husband. ''Dana?'' she called over her shoulder. ''I'll phone you first thing in the morning.''

Dana followed them to the door. ''Remember, this

is supposed to be a vacation. Don't worry about getting up early. You're pregnant and need your sleep. Take care.''

"I will.''

"Finally,'' Jace whispered as she shut the door. She turned in his arms. ''It seems like we're always waiting to be alone, doesn't it.''

"Yes.'' Her arms twined around his neck. ''Kiss me, Jace,'' she cried softly.

His mouth descended. It was life to her.

The turmoil Gideon had created had been resolved, but Dana still felt its effect.

With her emotions so near the surface, she felt out of control, but she didn't care. She loved this man. Tonight she wanted, needed to hear the words from him. She wanted to tell him what was in her heart.

"Dana—'' his voice sounded ragged ''—right now there's nothing I want to do more than concentrate on you for the rest of the night, but I'm afraid I have to go.''

The dreaded words.

"If I get my work done early, then we'll have the whole weekend together.''

"I know,'' she murmured, fighting every instinct to beg him to stay. ''I guess camping out with you last night spoiled me.''

"I loved every moment too. Never doubt it.'' He took her mouth in a fiery kiss, then eased her away from him. ''Lock the door after me.''

She nodded.

"I'll phone you tomorrow.''

When his footsteps faded, she turned out the lights and got ready for bed. But it was with a heavy heart.

Though she sensed Jace wanted her, he always had a reason to walk away. She'd thought tonight would be different. It wasn't.

Jace seemed content to live for the moment without looking ahead. Was there something wrong with her that she wanted more than he could give right now?

Had prison changed her capacity to be patient?

If she didn't get a grip, she was going to ruin what they had.

A woman who had to beg a man for what she wanted would be throwing away her best chance of success.

WHILE JACE DROVE THEM to Alpine, Gideon used a flashlight to study the forest service maps. "I take it you've already canvassed the crossed-out portions."

Jace nodded. "As you can see, there's still a lot of territory to cover. Probably more than we can get done tonight."

"Maybe, maybe not. Why don't we start with the northwest quadrant. I'll do one half, you do the other. Then we'll drive to the northeast section and see how much we can get done by first light. Whatever's left we'll do tomorrow night."

"Sounds like a good plan. My compliments on the way you handled everything with the girls."

Gideon folded the map and put it on the back seat. "Dana's so crazy about you, she swallowed the story hook, line and sinker. As for my wife, she's been living with a cop and has learned to read between the lines. When she kissed me and told me to have fun out camping, she gave me one of those looks that said she didn't believe a word of it."

"You're lucky to be married to an understanding woman who doesn't give you grief when you have to keep everything to yourself. Some of my colleagues' wives—"

"Don't go there, Jace," Gideon broke in. "You don't know how Dana will or won't feel. It's too soon."

Jace rubbed his forehead. "You're right. I want answers when I haven't even asked the questions yet."

"That's only normal. If I'd met Heidi while I was undercover, I probably would have been as paranoid as you. It's true not every woman is cut out to live with a cop. But most of them learn to adapt.

"When Gaby found out Max was FBI instead of a Russian immigrant, she ran home to her family in New Jersey. That had to be the worst month of his life. I wasn't too happy about it either." They exchanged smiles. "To be honest, I wasn't sure she would come back. But she did.

"To his joy, she told him that when she thought about it, she liked his living on the edge. She said it made their life more exciting. It made her appreciate him more. Needless to say, they have a fantastic marriage."

"You mean one like yours."

"Yes."

"Like I told you before. You're a lucky man."

"So are you, Captain Riley. You've met an extraordinary woman."

"You think I don't know that?"

"What's so great is, she thinks you're extraordinary too, but she's got a little paranoia of her own going."

"Like what?"

"She said something to Heidi about your being an earthgrazer. Does that ring any bells?"

Jace let out a groan.

"If I've touched on a sore point, just tell me to mind my own business."

He shook his head. "No. I'm glad you brought it up. What surprises me is that she's still not convinced I'm over my grieving for Cassie."

"Who was your wife."

"Yes. To be honest, I don't know at what point I let her go. But I guess seven years without remarrying has sent Dana the wrong message."

"After my divorce, I went longer than that. It takes the right woman to come along. *If* she comes along."

"*If*'s the operative word all right. There I was, delivering a package to some woman who might or might not be the person Tony Roberts was looking for, and there she was. This beautiful brunette who looked so frightened, every instinct in me wanted to reach out and comfort her."

"I know the feeling. When my boss asked me to take over his criminology class, it was the last thing I wanted to do. I was knee deep in a new case and didn't know how I was going to explain to Kevin that it would interfere with his visitation.

"And then this gorgeous redhead appears around the door, desperate to become part of the class and afraid I wouldn't let her in."

"Their devotion to each other is amazing."

"I couldn't agree more."

Jace pulled into his parking space at the apartment. His gaze darted to the visitors' parking, where he spotted the forest service truck.

"If I don't get a lead and have to report back to Austin on Monday, I'll tell Dana the truth before I leave. What scares the hell out of me is that everything's going to change."

"Better for it to come out than for both of you to remain in limbo knowing your relationship can't go anywhere."

"You're right," Jace muttered. "Come on. Let's go inside while I change."

No sooner had they walked in the door than his cell phone rang. He checked the called ID. "It's Pat, my backup man. Let's pray the computer found a match on those fingerprints."

He clicked on. "Pat? What's happening?"

"Nothing in the fingerprint department yet, but Glen broke into the trailer and found it empty."

Jace listened to Pat's report. When he was through, he said, "Tell the officers not to interfere unless they feel her life is in danger. I'm leaving in the truck right now to search for the plane. If you need to talk, call me any time. I don't care if it's four in the morning."

"Got ya."

After hanging up, Jace put on the forest service

uniform and they were out the door. Once they climbed in the truck, he told Gideon the latest news.

The other man's jaw clenched. "Sounds like he's lost it."

"The pervert's starting to make big mistakes now. That's what I'm counting on. If it turns out he'd not linked to Gibb's murder, at least we'll have enough evidence of another kind to put him away."

"THOSE WERE GOOD WAFFLES," Kevin commented.

Gideon smiled at his son. "So was my Denver omelette."

"I'm lucky the only café in town has such a great chef. I've never been served a bad meal. Jace says he usually grabs a bite of lunch here."

But not today. Today he was hurrying so he could finish up early to be with her.

The three of them watched Heidi who was working on her second helping of pancakes and blueberries. Dana loved it. The new mother-to-be was eating for two.

When she'd chased the last blueberry around on her plate, she raised her head. "I'm finished."

Gideon's eyes danced. "You're sure?"

Heidi blushed on cue and everyone laughed.

"Okay," her husband said, "what shall we do with this beautiful day?"

"I want to see Fort Davis."

"We will," Dana assured Kevin. "But first I need to run by Mr. Mason's house and tell him I've moved out. It won't take me more than a minute."

"I'll come with you," Gideon offered, getting to his feet.

"Stay with your family. I'll swing by the motel as soon as I'm through."

Heidi waved her hands. "I have a better idea. Let Gideon go with you while Kevin and I return to the motel and take Pokey for a walk. Glen might not have left for work. I don't want you to have to face him alone."

"I don't want that either. Thanks, Gideon."

"Kevin and I will meet you at your apartment in a half hour," Heidi said. "Since we're going to Fort Davis in our car, you might as well put yours away."

"Sounds good," Gideon murmured. He paid the bill before walking her out to the car. "Have you forgiven me for casting unfounded aspersions on Jace?"

"Of course. How can you doubt it?" She started up the car and they took off.

"Because I know how much you care for Jace and it makes me feel badly I upset you."

"It's all right. I know you did it out of love."

"I was wrong about him. When I understood the lengths he'd gone in order to protect you, I realized he's an exceptional man."

"He is," she retorted in an emotional tone. "When I told him I'd been sent to prison and then was freed, he accepted everything I told him without question."

"You know why, don't you? Your innocence shines through you. The first time I talked to you at the prison, I knew you couldn't have committed a crime. Jace knows it too.''

"Now you're going to make me cry all over again.''

"Do it later," he teased. "In case you didn't notice, we've arrived. With the truck gone, we can get this over in a hurry.''

"I'm so glad Glen's not here.''

Gideon helped her out of the car and they walked up to the front door of the house. After she rang the bell, she could hear Mr. Mason call out that he was coming. It took time with his walker.

"Well, Dana," he said when he opened the door. "I've been hoping you'd drop by. Come in.''

"I've brought Gideon with me. You met him before, when he and his family helped me move in.''

"I remember. Come on in, Gideon.''

"Thank you, Mr. Mason.''

They entered the house and followed him into the living room. "Sit down." He used his hand to gesture at the chairs across from the couch. They waited while he lowered himself onto the cushion.

"I've kept at Glen to invite you over, but he says you're so busy at that observatory, you haven't had the time.''

She flashed Gideon a distress signal. "It's true. I'm working on my Ph.D., and it requires a lot of hours.''

"Well, you're here now. I'm glad you came while Glen was at work. I've been meaning to talk to you about him.''

"You have?" Dana couldn't imagine.

"Ever since he met you he's talked of nothing else. I've encouraged him to be worthy of you. If he can get on track and stay there, I'll give him the piece of ranch property I own northeast of town below Mount Luna."

The news about his other property was a surprise to her.

"There's a barn that's big enough to be turned into a real nice house. I was saving it for my son who used to take Glen out there when we were clearing out all the trees. Mother would make a picnic and we'd work till dark. But that was all a long time ago before my son disappeared..."

There was a brief silence while tears moistened his eyes. After clearing his throat, he said, "I'd like Glen to have it. He's been out there a lot since his arrival and has plans for it.

"I would will him this house, but I've already promised it to a nephew from my wife's family after I'm gone."

Dana averted her eyes, not daring to look at Gideon. If she'd heard Ralph correctly, he had the idea she and Glen were going to get married. Dear God.

"That's wonderful for Glen." She tried to stop her voice from shaking.

"Well, he knows how I feel about you, Dana. You're a lovely lady, just like my wife."

"Thank you for the compliment."

Gideon sent her a signal that he'd handle this.

"Mr. Mason? As you know, Dana's been running the observatory by herself. But now the time has come for her to hire a graduate student to help operate the computers when she can't.

"When she told me this, my wife and I found a place for her to rent in town. She needs more room to entertain her colleagues from Cal-Tech who'll be coming out here from time to time. We wondered if it will be all right if this person rents your trailer. Dana has several candidates in mind. They'll be dedicated and hardworking."

Dana couldn't quite stifle her gasp.

Ralph's white head lifted. "Well, yes. Of course. But I'm surprised Glen didn't tell me."

"He didn't know," Dana rushed to assure him. She hated lying like this, but she had to play along with Gideon, who had some agenda of his own. She'd learned he never did anything without a very good reason.

"My friends only arrived yesterday," she added. "That's when we got to talking. What I'd like to do is pay you for the second month's rent. When this person moves in, they'll reimburse me. In the meantime, I'll get the place cleaned so it looks the way it did when you rented it to me."

"Don't you worry about that. Glen says you keep a perfect house. Nice and neat the way my wife did. He'll give it a brush up for you. In fact, he'll be hurt if you don't let him. I guess I don't have to tell you how crazy he is about you."

She bit her lip. "No. He's been a constant visitor, always wanting to help."

"Well, when you've met the right woman, you

don't want to be anywhere else. Isn't that so, Gideon?''

''You can say that again.''

''I'm writing out a check for the rent and the light over the sink.'' Her hands trembled so much, she could hardly read her own signature. ''There. I've put it on the coffee table. Glen will deposit it in the bank for you.''

''I'm expecting you for Sunday dinner.''

''I'd like that very much, Mr. Mason, but my friends are here on vacation. Tomorrow I'll probably go to Big Bend Park with them for a few days.''

''Glen's going to miss you then, but there's always next Sunday. Say—how did you like the flowers that were delivered here?''

The flowers. Dana had forgotten all about them.

''They were lovely.''

''At first I thought Glen had sent them, but he assured me he's saving up his money. I guess I don't have to tell you why.'' He chuckled.

''No.''

Gideon got to his feet. ''It was a pleasure seeing you again, Mr. Mason. Now, if you'll excuse us, my wife and son are waiting for us so we can start sightseeing in Fort Davis.''

''That place is full of history. You'll enjoy it.''

''We're looking forward to it.''

''Don't get up, Mr. Mason,'' Dana said. ''We'll see ourselves out. Is there anything we can do for you before we leave?''

''Now that you've visited me, not a thing.''

''Take care.''

She fairly ran all the way out to the car. When Gideon got in his side, she took one look at him and broke down in tears. "Poor Mr. Mason. Do you have any idea how much I hated lying to him?"

"I didn't like it any better, but his grandson is up to no good. Until the police have completed their investigation, it's wisest to let Ralph keep his dreams. One day, when things are different, he'll need consoling. Then you can be his friend."

She backed out of the driveway and headed for town. "I know you're right, but it's so terrible to think of Glen, taking advantage of his grandfather's immobility and bad eyesight."

"The very fact that he has no regard for the old gentleman reveals Glen's sick nature."

"Jace didn't trust him from day one."

"I had a bad feeling about him when we moved you in the trailer, but I kept quiet because you were so happy to be in Cloud Rim. Knowing your father gave you his gun was the only reason I didn't urge you to stay at the motel until you found another place."

"Thank heaven you didn't," she blurted. "If I'd lived anywhere else, I might never have met Jace."

Gideon smiled at her. "It always comes down to Jace. You have a serious case of lovesickitis."

She chuckled. "I know I'm pathetic. I try hard not to let it show around Jace. Last night I came close to begging him not to leave."

"I'm sure he didn't want to go."

"Maybe he did…" Her voice trailed off.

"Perhaps he wanted to be begged."

"No. That turns a man off faster than anything."

"It depends on who's doing the begging."

"Maybe if I knew he loved me, I'd get brave."

"How many days has it been?"

"Nine. Well, eight, if you don't count the first day. I didn't know his name then."

Gideon burst out laughing. Pretty soon she joined him. By the time they reached the motel she was in better spirits. Gideon had a way of making everything all right.

JACE HAD BARELY ARRIVED in Fort Davis to start his deliveries when he saw that Pat was ringing him. There'd been no sign of the plane last night. With Gideon's help they'd covered a lot of ground. If he didn't get some good news pretty soon...

"Pat? What's up?"

"How would you like an early Christmas present?"

On cue his adrenaline kicked in. "You already know the answer to that question."

"I'm still waiting for word on Burdick, but we got a match on Glen's prints. He's being sought as a prison escapee by the Spalding County Sheriff's Office in Atlanta, Georgia, for armed robbery, aggravated assault, aggravated battery, kidnapping, feticide."

Feticide? Jace's eyes closed tightly for a moment.

"These are his aliases—Mason Sherwood, Mason Sturges, Glen Sturges, Glen Sherwood, Sherwood Mason. He was last seen wearing a dark buzz, no facial hair."

Jace took a shuddering breath. "Call in all the officers Tom will give us now."

"I've already taken care of it."

"Tonight Gideon and I will finish our search. If nothing shows up, we'll close in on him tomorrow morning and put him away. Do me a favor and phone me again around five-fifteen. I'll be at dinner with Dana and her friends. When I answer, I'll pretend that you're my boss at IPS and I have to go in to the office."

"I'll do it. Talk to you then."

For the next forty-five minutes Jace worked like a madman so he wouldn't think about that jerk having anything to do with Dana. As soon as he'd heard about Glen using a rifle to break down the trailer door, he knew in his gut the pervert had plans to kidnap her.

No way.

This was Jace's last run with IPS. Anxious to get to Cloud Rim and finish the job, he didn't realize four people were waiting by his van until he walked out of the Overland Trail Museum and Pokey ran up to him, sniffing at his legs.

He lifted his head to meet a pair of translucent gray eyes smiling at him with their own special luster. After what he'd found out about Glen, he didn't care if he had an audience. Like a heat-seeking missile, he started toward her.

Dana must have felt the same way, because she ran straight into his arms. "Gideon spotted your van. I was hoping we might see you."

"Some dreams do come true," he whispered

against her cheek, then pressed a hard kiss to her mouth.

"Long time no see." Gideon's teasing remark brought Jace's head around. "Such a hard worker deserves a break. Step to the rear of my car and you can have the drink of your choice from the cooler."

Attuned as he was to the other man at this point, Jace realized it was no casual offer. He looked down at Dana. "What would you like?"

"A lemonade?"

He squeezed her shoulder before joining Gideon, who'd opened the trunk.

"Here's your root beer, Kevin."

"Thanks, Dad."

"You bet. Will you please take this cream soda to Heidi?"

"Sure."

Gideon's eyes swerved to Jace. "What will it be for you?"

"Two lemonades."

"I hope we've got two in here."

They both started searching around in the ice. "In ten minutes I'll find a rest room and call you on your cell phone," Gideon whispered.

Something important had happened or he wouldn't have gone to this much trouble to be certain Jace would get his call.

"It looks like you packed half a dozen. Thanks." Jace walked over to Dana, who was standing next to Heidi. He handed her a drink, then slid his arm around her waist.

In a second, Gideon joined them holding a Coke.

His gaze flicked to Jace. "We knew you couldn't take time out for lunch, but we figured you could spare five minutes for this."

"I *could* go to lunch with you. There's nothing I'd like more. But I'd rather finish early to be with you guys."

"Is there a good steak house in Alpine?"

"If that's what you're in the mood for, I know of two places," Jace said.

"How soon will you be able to join us?"

"Four-thirty?"

"Then we'll meet you at four-thirty in front of your apartment."

"I know where it is," Dana asserted.

Everyone chuckled before Gideon said, "Perfect."

"Come and say goodbye to me," Jace murmured against her temple. They walked to the front of his van. "I'm counting the hours."

"So am I."

"Enjoy the rest of your day."

"I will now that I've seen you."

"If you had any idea how much I'd like to kiss you senseless right this second..."

"I dare you to say that to me tonight."

"You *are* a little witch. Tonight you won't need to dare me, and that's a promise." He brushed his lips against hers before climbing in the van.

With a wave of his hand, he pulled away from the museum and headed toward the highway leading to Cloud Rim. Gideon was the only reason he could leave Dana right now and feel good about it.

Not long after he began the climb out of Fort Davis his cell phone rang. It had been exactly ten minutes. He picked up.

"Gideon?"

"I've got incredible news. Just listen."

Jace almost lost control of the van as Gideon told him everything that had transpired at Ralph Mason's house.

"That barn has to be it!"

"Everything seems to fit."

"I've got some news of my own. It came in from Pat Hardy a little while ago." In the next breath Jace told him about Glen's criminal record.

Gideon whistled. "That's one of the breaks you were looking for. If we find that plane, you've got them."

"Even if we don't find it, we've still got Glen."

"Amen. See you later."

CHAPTER TWELVE

"Is that you, Glen?"

Who else would it be. "I'm home, Grandad!"

"You're early."

Damn that speed trap to hell! There must have been ten cars pulled over outside Alpine. By the time the officer wrote him a ticket, he'd lost track of the van.

After he stopped at a pay phone to look up the address of IPS, he drove by the place. There were three trucks parked in the back. No sign of the black Sentra. Where the hell was Dana?

"Mr. Jorgenson said I'd been doing a good job. He let me come home an hour early because it's the weekend."

"Good for you. I told Dana I was proud of the way you've been handling yourself lately."

He stopped in his tracks. "When did you see Dana?"

"She and her friend Gideon dropped by this morning. Come in the living room and I'll tell you about our visit. I like her better every time I see her."

Bristling with fury, he marched through to the front of the house. "Are you talking about the man who helped her move in the trailer?"

"That's the one. She brought the rent, but I found out it's not for her."

"What do you mean?"

"She's hired a person to work at the observatory so she doesn't have to run the whole place herself. A graduate student is going to be renting the trailer from now on."

The conniving little bitch. "I told her she'd been working too hard. I'm glad she listened to me and decided to get some help. That means we'll have more time together in the evenings."

"I think you're winning her over. Last night her friends from California helped her move into an apartment in town. She said she could entertain there better. Sounds like she's thinking it would be a nice starter place for you two."

"Yup."

"After we eat, I'd like you to go over to the trailer and give it a good housecleaning so she won't have to. It'll be a nice surprise for her when she gets home from Fort Davis with her friends."

Glen tossed his head back. "I knew they were coming some time this weekend. We were going to show them the sights. She probably came by the grocery store while I was around back stacking boxes. Dana knows Mr. Jorgenson doesn't approve of my talking to her on the job. I figure when she couldn't see me, she left."

"I'm sorry you missed each other."

"If I hurry and get the trailer cleaned now, could I take the truck to Fort Davis later? It won't be hard to find her."

"You can try, but don't be too disappointed if you don't catch up with her."

"What do you mean?"

"She said something about visiting Big Bend Park. I don't know if her friends will come back to the motel tonight, or just go on from Fort Davis."

"There's an easy way to find out. I'll drive over to the motel and ask if they're still registered. If they are, that'll save me a trip down the mountain. Do you want meatballs and pasta, or chicken and rice for dinner?"

"The meatballs sound good."

"Do you want some watermelon to go with it?"

"That sounds good. You're getting to be a real expert at picking out produce. The melons you've been bringing home are as sweet and juicy as anything I've tasted in a long time."

While his grandfather was still chatting away, Glen started to leave the room.

"When you were just a little fellow, you loved watermelon. Those picnics your grandmother made were really something, but you'd always go for the fruit first.

"Is that right."

"Just this morning I was telling Dana about the good times we all used to have out on the property. I let her know that with some work, the barn could be converted into a real nice house."

Glen froze.

"Thanks, Grandad."

"You bet. Anything I can do to help. Like I said, someone else will grab her if you don't."

"There's no way I'll let her marry anybody else."

"I'm glad to hear it."

A few minutes later he brought a tray to his grand-father. "I'll go clean the trailer now, then I'll drive over to the motel."

"Hope you catch up with her."

"Don't worry. I will."

He left the house and climbed in the truck. He figured he could do this alone, but it would be better if he had Lewis's help.

"THIS PLACE MAKES a great steak. How's yours, dar-ling?"

Heidi nodded to her husband because she was in the middle of swallowing a bite.

"What about you, sport?"

"I prefer hamburgers, but this is pretty good. I'll save the bone for Pokey."

Dana was so happy to be with Jace, she had no idea what the food tasted like.

His arm tightened around her. "I ate here the first night I came to Alpine. But I must admit, the best restaurant in West Texas is your kitchen. Those tacos were to die for."

"I'm not surprised." Heidi finally spoke. "Her mom is probably the greatest coo—"

Dana didn't hear the rest because Jace's cell phone rang.

"Excuse me, everyone."

He edged away from Dana to answer it. As soon as she heard him say *now,* her heart took a plunge.

"What is it?" she asked when he'd hung up.

His penetrating eyes searched hers for a moment. She could tell that whatever it was he had to say, she wasn't going to like it.

Not now, she groaned inside.

The evening was still young. She'd been counting the hours until they could be alone. A whole weekend lay ahead of them.

"I have to run over to the office. It appears the regular driver is back. My boss says the regional manager of IPS wants to discuss my new assignment."

No!

Swallowing her anguish, she said, "Does this mean you'll be leaving Alpine?"

"I'm afraid so."

"You warned me." Dana fought to hold back the tears. "How long do you think you'll be?"

"You never can tell. Maybe you'd better drive back to Cloud Rim with your friends."

"We'll take care of her."

"Thanks, Gideon." He turned back to her. "I'll call you the minute I know anything. If it's not too late, I'll drive up and join you."

She struggled for breath. No matter how he couched his words, she sensed she wouldn't be seeing him for the rest of the night.

It killed her that he hadn't asked her to go with him. But no matter what Gideon had said about the right woman being able to beg, she didn't have the temerity. They hadn't spent enough time together for her to feel that confident with him.

He pushed himself away from the table and stood

up. "Sorry I have to bow out like this. Just so you know, I've already given my credit card number to the waitress. This dinner is on me."

In a lightning move he leaned over to kiss Dana's neck. "I'll phone you as soon as I can. I swear it."

She believed him. He always followed through. But she could feel him distancing himself from her. Not just physically, but emotionally. It looked as if he was still holding to his pattern.

Dana couldn't watch him walk away. It was too painful.

"After dessert, can we go to that new movie Jace said was playing?"

"You know what, Kevin?" Gideon said. "I think Heidi is tired from so much walking around Fort Davis. What do you say we all trek back to Cloud Rim and I'll take you to that Sylvester Stallone film."

"I thought you didn't like him."

Gideon smiled at his son. "I said a lot of the police stunts were phony, but I think he's an entertaining actor."

As it turned out, everyone was too full to order dessert. They ended up leaving a few minutes after Jace. Dana never remembered the ride home.

When they arrived, Heidi insisted Dana keep her and Pokey company while Kevin and his father went to the movie. The second they disappeared out the door, Dana broke down sobbing.

After a little while she pulled herself together and sat up on the bed, where Heidi was propped with her back against the headboard.

"I'm sorry." She wiped her eyes. "I used to do

this to you in prison. The minute I saw you through the glass, I'd break down and force you to sit there while I poured out my grief.

"You must be so sick of me and my problems you could scream. I wouldn't blame you if you gathered up your family tonight and drove away for good."

Heidi stared at her for a long time. "Remember what your doctor told you in counseling? That because of what happened to you, you'd have a tendency at first to turn every concern that came along into a soul-destroying catastrophe?"

Dana remembered. "It's called having issues with loss."

"You haven't lost Jace."

"You're right. To lose something implies ownership. I don't own Jace. His dead wife does."

"Dana—"

"No, Heidi," she cut in on her. "When he told me he was being reassigned, I felt that he was relieved."

Heidi shook her head. "I don't believe it."

"That's because you love me and want to shield me from pain, but it's true. He can't commit to anyone. Seven years of being single is mute testimony."

She got up from the bed. "Don't worry. I'm not going to go off the deep end. After the miracle of gaining my freedom from prison, that would be unconscionable to me, to you and God.

"Let's face it. I'll never forget Jace."

"I can see why."

Dana averted her eyes. "What I am going to do is concentrate on the work I came here for. If I can be thankful for one thing about our brief association, he got me away from Glen by finding me an apartment with people I can trust.''

''It's the perfect place for you.''

''I agree. Knowing I can come and go without worry, I'll have breakfast with you in the morning, then follow you as far as Alpine. While you go on to Big Bend, I'm going to take a commuter flight to El Paso. From there I'll fly to California.

''I want to spend a day with Rosita and Consuela. Then I'll visit Mom and Dad. There's no one I want to see when I get back, so I don't have to keep to any deadline.''

''When you and your dad talk shop, you always come away rejuvenated. Much as I'd hoped you come to Big Bend with us, I'm glad you're going home for a few days. It'll do you a world of good.''

''I think so too. Excuse me while I go wash my face.''

While she was rinsing off the soap at the bathroom sink, she heard a phone ring.

''It's yours.'' Heidi called out.

''I'm coming!''

She grabbed a hand towel and wiped her face, then hurried into the other room. The phone was in her purse. She pulled it out and said hello.

''Dana?''

Every time she heard his deep male voice, she went weak all over. She supposed that was one reaction she'd never conquer.

''Are you still in Alpine?''

''Yes.''

"I see."

"It looks like I'm going to be stuck here for a few more hours while they iron out schedules. You don't know how sorry I am. I'll meet you for breakfast first thing in the morning. You name the place."

Did he honestly think she could eat?

"Just a minute. I'll check with Heidi."

She turned to her friend, who was eyeing her with too much compassion. "What time do you think you'll want to eat in the morning?"

"Probably eight."

Dana put the phone to her ear once more. "Eight o'clock at the café."

"I'll be there."

"See you then."

As she was hanging up, she thought he called her name. But it was probably her imagination. No more wishful thinking. She'd already had her miracle in this life. To want another one was greedy.

The Bible had been her constant companion in prison. She knew what it said about the sin of ingratitude.

"Dana? When Gideon gets back, do you want me to come over and spend the night with you? I'll sleep on the couch. Kevin will love it if he and his dad can have a whole boys' night out together."

Dana smiled in spite of her pain. "Kevin might love it, but I saw the way your husband was looking at you at dinner. He can't wait for bedtime. To be honest, neither can I. Suddenly I'm very tired."

"Then I'll run you home now."

"No. You know how Gideon feels about you going anywhere at night alone. The cop in him worries about your safety, so we'll wait.''

In the stillness, Dana's cell phone rang again. She didn't dare look at the caller ID or pick up. She'd had all the pain she could handle for one night.

Heidi stared at her, but bless her heart, she didn't say anything.

After ten rings, it stopped.

"Care if I look?''

"Go ahead.''

As she watched Heidi reach for the phone, her heart pounded in her ears.

Their gazes met. "It says R. Mitchell.''

So it wasn't Jace calling after all.

"I forgot to phone Cathy about the flowers she sent. I'd better call her right now.''

She purposely turned her back on Heidi so she wouldn't fall apart.

GLEN EYED every person who walked into the Gray Oak. If Lewis didn't show up soon, he'd drive over to his apartment.

After going one more round of pool and a beer, it was a no-show. He tossed the cue on the table and cut a straight line through the crowd to the door, hell-bent on finding Lewis.

Just as he was backing out of the parking lot, he saw the Harley streak by. When he realized Lewis wasn't about to turn in the parking lot, he took off after him. At the next light he slammed the heel of his hand on the horn until the bastard turned around shaking a fist.

When the light changed, he roared away. At first Glen thought he was trying to ignore him. But three streets farther, Lewis turned the corner into a shopping-center parking lot and came to a full stop. Glen pulled up alongside him.

"Are you still set on waiting till your vacation?"

"Why?" Lewis demanded. He'd stepped off his Harley and was walking up to the truck with an expression in his eyes that always scared the hell out of Glen.

"'Cause I'm leaving with Dana this weekend."

"She's not going anywhere with you. You're a loser."

Glen swallowed hard. "She won't feel that way when she sees my half of the money."

Lewis's hand closed around his throat so fast, he didn't see it coming. "Let's get something straight. No one's touching that money until I say so. It had better still be where we left it."

"It is, but I'm just saying I want what's mine now."

"What's the big hurry?"

"She started sleeping with that IPS driver. Now she's moved out of the trailer."

"So what? We don't need her."

"I want her, Lewis, and I'm taking her with me as soon as I can find her. The truck's all packed with everything we need."

"How far do you think you'd get? As soon as your grandfather can't find you, he'll sic the cops on you and you're history. Then they'll come after me!"

"I don't give a crap anymore. And I'm tired of waiting around till you're ready."

For once Lewis didn't have a ready comeback. "Where does the guy she's shacking up with live?"

"I would have found out if it hadn't been for that damn speed trap coming into Alpine today. I got pulled over with a bunch of other cars and lost his trail."

Lewis's eyes looked as if they were about to bulge from their sockets. "You got a ticket?" He hissed the question.

"Yeah." He hunched his shoulders to hide the shivers. "Everybody did. It wasn't any big deal."

"You couldn't let that broad alone, could you," he muttered. "Because of that mistake, the police have your driver's license on record. It's your funeral now."

"I've got blond hair. There's no way they'll match me with any of my old mug shots."

"I'm talking about fingerprints, you ass. They could have lifted them right off your license."

When Glen remembered the officer taking his license back to the patrol car with him, the moisture in his mouth dried up.

Lewis wasn't saying anything. As the silence lengthened, Glen's skin broke out in a cold sweat till he was wringing wet.

"This is what you're going to do," he finally spoke. "Get the hell out of here and go home. *Now.* When it's dark, you slip away without anyone seeing you and head for the cave on foot."

"Hell."

"Just shut up and do it! I'll meet you there."

"What about Dana? I told you, Lewis. I'm not leaving without her."

"I heard you the first time. You let me take care of her."

"How?"

"She runs that damn observatory. No matter where she is or what she's doing, she'll show up there at some point. *Right?*"

Glen hadn't thought of that.

"Right."

"We've got enough stuff stored in the cave to last a week. We'll keep a watch out for her with the binoculars, then nab her. Now get the hell out of my sight while I figure out how I'm going to disappear. If you're busted before you get there, that's *your* problem!"

GIDEON WENT INSIDE the apartment with Dana and checked everything out.

She smiled. "I'm perfectly safe here."

He winked. "It's a habit I can't shake."

"Go home to Heidi and Kevin. I'll see you in the morning."

He put his finger under her chin so she couldn't look away. "Things aren't always what they seem."

"You're talking to the woman who found that out the day the judge said, 'You're free.'"

"I'm not referring to your case."

"I know."

He pressed a kiss to her forehead. When he walked away, she shut the door and turned the dead bolt.

After moving to the center of the room, she looked all around.

This is your life, Dana Turner. Get used to it.

Except the more she thought about it, the more she realized she couldn't. With or without Jace in her world, she hadn't lived in a place that reflected her personality and taste since her apartment in Pasadena.

She'd planned on running the observatory until her father retired. But that probably wouldn't happen for another three to four years. It was too long a time to live with whatever was available.

Though this apartment was a vast improvement over the trailer, it wasn't home. Not in any sense of the word.

When she'd first come to West Texas, she'd been in a rush to separate herself from the past. Her only priority had been to escape the demons plaguing her. To her chagrin, she hadn't considered that she'd brought a lifetime of habits and interests with her, integral parts of her that were being ignored or stifled here.

If she really expected to take hold and make a life, she needed to entrench herself as a member of the community. One way to do that was to become a home owner.

An inheritance from her grandmother Howard remained untouched in a money-bearing account. Once upon a time Dana had imagined saving it for her retirement. But she could just as easily invest part of it in a house.

When she got back from California, she'd contact

a Realtor and find out what was available. It might be wiser to buy something in Alpine where she could expect good resale value when it came time to leave. She loved the drive to Cloud Rim, so that wasn't a factor.

Her parents had put all her treasures in storage. They were still there. If she had a place of her own, she could send for them. How would it be to have her piano again? And all her sheet music, favorite books, paintings and the furniture she'd bought over the years from working at the furniture store Heidi's family owned.

She'd acquired some wonderful pieces on her trip around the world with Heidi. Being in this apartment made her miss her things. An armoire from France, a wood-and-tile table with hand-carved chairs from Italy. Oriental rugs for hardwood floors. A fabulous inlaid mother-of-pearl Japanese screen. Handblown Venetian glass goblets, a set of Sevres china from Paris, an Alençon-lace banquet cloth.

She climbed into bed still cataloging the many happy associations with the past.

Of course, her favorite things could never replace a broken heart. But they would help her to feel a stronger sense of who she'd been, and who she still was.

She'd lost her sense of self in prison.

It was time to get it back. If she didn't, she'd remain needy. Too many women fell into that category. She refused to let that happen, otherwise she would never meet the right man.

A man whose heart hadn't been permanently buried with his wife.

Jace—

She turned on her stomach and sobbed quietly into the pillow.

IT WAS THREE in the morning. So far, Jace and Gideon had come across half a dozen ranches with barns, but they'd found nothing else. Twice they had to leap a fence when someone's guard dog came after them.

There hadn't been time to delve into the land records to pinpoint Ralph Mason's exact ranch location. Hunkering under a pine tree, they consulted the map using a flashlight. Jace crossed out the section they'd just covered with a pen. That left one more small area to explore over the hill on their right. He drew a circle around it.

"X marks the spot," Gideon muttered.

"Wouldn't it be nice if it were true. Let's go."

A few minutes later they came to the crest.

Jace's breath caught. "Do you see what I see?" Below them lay a long stretch of grassy meadow with a barn at one end.

Gideon nodded. "You're looking at Ralph Mason's legacy to Glen. A good pilot could land a plane there with little problem."

By tacit agreement they made their way down the hill clustered with trees, then raced unhampered across the grass toward the barn.

The windows on the sides were boarded up tight.

Gideon shone his flashlight on the barn doors. The handles had been secured with a heavy chain and lock. It gleamed in the moonlight. "This hasn't been on here long."

"And it's not going to be!" Jace insisted as he reached in his backpack for the silencer. Then he drew his gun and screwed the silencer on the end of the barrel. They both stood back. One well-aimed shot and the lock was useless.

Gideon went in with the flashlight. Jace followed. The strong smell of airplane-fuel fumes met their nostrils. That's when they both came to a standstill.

There sat the twin-engine Beech Craft that seemed to have eluded Jace forever. Several large fuel drums stood next to the side of the barn. He climbed inside and looked around the interior. When he emerged, he said, "They've stashed the money somewhere else."

"You'll find it, just like you've found your evidence *and* your connection to Glen Mason. How does it feel, Captain?"

Jace jumped down and clamped Gideon on the shoulder. "If anyone knows, *you* do. I'm indebted to you."

"For very personal reasons this has been my pleasure, believe me."

Elation swept through Jace. As soon as he could wrap up this case, he could start over again with Dana. No more secrets.

"I've got a phone call to make."

"Go ahead." Gideon directed the beam of the flashlight while Jace punched the programmed button.

A groggy-sounding Pat answered the phone. "Jace?"

"We found the plane on Mason property. It's sitting here fueled and ready to take off."

His colleague made a whooping sound.

"I'm returning to Cloud Rim to bring Glen in. I should be there within forty-five minutes. Tell backup to surround the Mason house. Have helicopters and ambulances standing by.

"We'll wait till Glen comes out of the house, to cut down on the trauma for Ralph Mason. You'll be the one giving all orders through me."

"Understood."

"Call Tom Haster and tell him what's happened. We're going to need more officers to round up Burdick at his apartment. If it turns out he isn't Glen's partner, we'll worry about that later."

"You've been on the money so far. I ought to be getting a report on his prints any time now." There was a pause. "Jace?"

"Yes?"

"Take care."

"Don't worry."

After he hung up, he pulled out a flash camera from his pack and took pictures of the plane and the barn's interior. He snapped a few more pictures of the exterior, then turned to Gideon. "Let's get out of here."

Now that he could go in pursuit of Glen, Jace found his second wind. Gideon kept pace with him till they reached the truck.

"I know what you're going to say," Jace blurted

as soon they were lumbering along the rutted fire road. "But I'll have a lot more peace of mind if you go to Big Bend with your family and Dana as you'd planned."

"I'll stay with them," Gideon murmured. "However, I want you to know we're not leaving Cloud Rim until this is all over."

Jace couldn't argue with that. During the drive back to the motel, they talked strategy. He lamented that Ralph had to be anywhere around. "No matter how it goes down, it's going to be ugly. He could suffer a heart attack."

"I know. That's always the tough part. No matter how you call it, there are always complications because of the innocent."

"If the shock doesn't kill him, the news that his grandson is a wanted felon will. He shouldn't be alone after this ordeal."

"That's where my family and I can be of help. Dana will want to comfort him too. Ask one of the officers to contact us when we're needed. You've got my cell phone number."

Jace nodded. "Thanks, Gideon. I'll take you up on that."

He drove the truck into the parking lot of the motel. Gideon climbed out and walked around to the driver's side. The two men communicated in silence for a moment.

Gideon spoke first. "After you've nailed that vermin, Dana will be here waiting for you. We all will."

"I like the sound of that," he said in a husky tone.

"I thought you would. Watch your back."

CHAPTER THIRTEEN

DANA DRESSED in a pair of white cotton pants and her favorite pale orange cotton top. It would be a comfortable outfit to wear on the plane, and perfect for the warm weather in Southern California. Deep down she wanted to look her best for Jace when he joined them at the café.

If he joined them.

Where a change of job location was involved, Jace might not have the choice of when he'd have to leave. It would be foolish to count on anything. She knew he'd phone her if he couldn't make it. No matter how it pained her, she would handle the bad news with grace—even if it killed her.

The alarm had gone off at six, but she'd been awake long before that. After a shower and shampoo, she blow-dried her hair. It contained enough natural curl so she could brush it until it fell into soft waves.

She packed what she'd need in her overnight bag and made sure everything was turned off before she left the apartment.

If she decided to stay in California longer than a few days, she didn't want to have to rush back because of something she'd forgotten to take care of.

With a half hour to spare, she could run up to the observatory and turn off the main computer.

A gust of wind whipped her hair as she stepped out the door to the garage. When she looked up, there were clouds gathering in the western sky. After a long spell of beautiful weather, it came as a surprise to see a storm brewing.

How ironic she'd picked today of all days to fly. She hoped there wouldn't be too much turbulence.

By the time she rounded the summit to the observatory, the wind was buffeting the car. She parked close to the building. Not bothering to lock it, she hurried inside so she wouldn't get blown away.

She made a beeline for her office and e-mailed the latest project she'd been working on to her father. With that accomplished she turned off all the machines. Now she was ready to join everyone at the café.

Be there, Jace. Please be there.

The wind played havoc with her hair, blinding her as she stepped outside with the remote to set the electronic lock. Then she retraced the few steps to the car.

She'd just fastened her seat belt when an arm grabbed her around the neck from behind in a headlock, almost cutting off her windpipe. She felt something hard pressed to the back of her skull. Then she heard the unmistakable click of a gun hammer.

"Give me any trouble and I'll kill you."

Oh dear God.

"W-what do you want?" She was so terrified she could hardly form words.

He reached in front for her purse. "We're going to take a little ride. If you so much as look at anybody or cry out, I'll blow everyone away. Let's get going. I'll tell you when to turn."

She was trembling uncontrollably. It took her a minute to start the car, let alone put it in gear.

"Quit stalling!" He shoved the barrel of the gun harder against her head.

"I—I'm not."

The whole time she descended the summit, a vision of the horrors awaiting her filled her mind.

Why had she left her gun at the apartment?

Why hadn't she thought to tell Heidi her plans?

No one knew she'd come up here. No one would know where this monster was taking her. She started praying.

"Turn left at the next road."

What choice did she have?

It was a fire-lane road that ran through the mountainous terrain beyond the ranches. One afternoon she'd followed it for a little while before turning around because it was too isolated.

Why didn't some rancher or forest service employee come along who would at least remember passing her car?

Maybe her assailant wouldn't notice if she turned on her headlights. In case there was someone out there, she could flash them on and off to get their attention. But the second her left hand moved off the wheel, she felt the nudge of the gun.

"Both hands where I can see them."

She tried to get a good look at him in the rearview

mirror. Though he stayed out of her line of vision, she had the impression of dark hair and an unshaven face. His voice was unfamiliar.

In prison she'd listened to the other inmates talk about the ways they defended themselves against abusive husbands and boyfriends. The one thing they were unanimous about was that they'd rather take the chance of getting stabbed or shot than lie down and submit to whatever was going to happen.

Dana felt the same way. At the first opportunity she would do whatever it took to escape, or die trying.

She heard her cell phone ring, but he had her purse. It was after eight. It could be Jace or Heidi wondering where she was.

A mile farther and he told her to pull off the road. "Wind around the back of that clump of trees."

"My car's going to high center."

"Do it!"

She geared down and left the road to drive through the underbrush. The underside of the car mired down two or three times, killing the engine. She had to keep starting it up again.

"Don't stop till I tell you when."

He wouldn't let up until he'd made sure her car was hidden from the road. Her body broke out in a cold sweat.

"This'll do."

She applied the brakes.

"Turn it off."

Please God. Help me.

"That's it. Now slowly undo your seat belt."

When she was free of the straps, she decided it was now or never. Taking several deep breaths, she fell sideways against the passenger seat to reach the other door. By the time he got out of the back, she'd rolled out on the low-growing vegetation and had begun to run.

"You little bitch."

As she raced to the next clump of trees, she could hear his footsteps gaining on her. He should have fired by now. The fact that he hadn't meant he was afraid someone would hear gunshots and come to investigate.

Encouraged, she scrambled up the steep terrain. At one point her lungs were ready to burst, but she didn't dare stop. Ahead she could see an outcropping of rocks. If she could reach them before he did, she could throw a small slab at his head to slow him down.

It wasn't much farther now, but she had a pain in her side. Gasping for breath, she pressed on. Then like a miracle, she saw movement. Someone was standing on the rocks above her.

"Help me!" she cried out. "There's a killer after me! Please help me!"

A head appeared over the edge. A head with long blond hair parted in the center and a pathetic goatee. She grew icy cold.

"I got her here," came the voice behind her. "Now let's get the hell inside."

"Inside where?" she whispered, conscious of a ringing in her ears.

"You'll find out."

Her assailant grabbed hold of her arms and dragged her around the rocks until they reached the ledge. Behind him was a yawning black hole.

"Welcome to your home away from home. Glen's been waiting for you."

"Don't make me go in that cave. I can't!" she screamed.

"Better shut her up, Glen, or I will," she heard him say before she wasn't cognizant of anything else.

THE STAKEOUT had been in place three hours, but nothing was happening. Jace got on the forest service truck's speakerphone, which was patched in to Pat.

"It's already eight-fifteen. Glen doesn't work weekends and could be sleeping in, but this is taking too long. I'm going to wait five more minutes for him to come out of the house. If he doesn't, I'll ring the bell and wait for someone to answer. When the guys see me go inside, tell them to close in."

"Understood. While you're waiting, I thought you'd like to hear this. The info on Burdick came in an hour ago. He's been on the FBI's ten most wanted list for over a year."

"I *knew* it."

"He has a string of aliases. Was doing time in a Florida prison for murder when he escaped. Get this—he was born in Nebraska. Among his occupations as a mechanic and construction worker, he's been a crop duster."

Jace let out a cry of satisfaction. "He and Glen met up somewhere and planned that robbery. With the ability to fly a plane, and a place to land it, they must have thought all their ships had come in.''

''Wait it out a year, stay clean, then fly over the border and live it up in good old Mexico.''

''Not this time,'' Jace vowed.

''I got on the phone to Austin. They've sent more manpower and they're rounding up Burdick at his apartment as we speak.''

''Why does this seem too easy, Pat?''

''What are you talking about? It's taken two months for you to break this case with only a hope and a prayer. I'm proud of you. Now go get Mason, and every Ranger in Texas will be celebrating to-night.''

I hope you're right. But for some reason, Jace had an unaccountable sense of foreboding. It had come over him while he'd been waiting for Glen to make an appearance. Another one of those gut instincts that told him something was wrong. He just didn't know what.

''I'm getting out of the truck now. Tell the guys to be ready.''

HEIDI HUNG UP the phone and glanced anxiously at her husband. ''Mr. Watkins said Dana left the apartment in her car around seven-thirty this morning and hasn't come back.''

Gideon rubbed the lower half of his face with his hand. ''She never showed up at the café. Neither did Jace. We've been to the observatory. She's not there, and she's not answering her cell phone.''

''Do you think Jace was able to drive up here after

all? Maybe at the last minute he asked her to meet him halfway?''

After a hesitation he said, ''It's possible, but one of them would have called to let us know.''

Kevin sat on the end of their motel-room bed with Pokey. ''She was really upset last night about Jace. Maybe she felt so bad she just decided to fly home to California as soon as she got up this morning. She knows we're on vacation and probably didn't want to wake you up.''

Heidi's gaze met her husband's. ''Kevin could be right. Shall we call the commuter airline in Alpine?''

Gideon nodded. ''I'll do that right now.''

Her body tensed while she waited for him to get the number. When he finally reached someone, she saw lines darken his face. Her heart dropped to her feet. Kevin's face mirrored her concern.

She got up from the chair. ''What did you find out?''

''Dana hasn't been there. In any case, all planes in the West Texas area are grounded because of an incoming storm. Two tornadoes have already touched down near Odessa and Marfa.''

At this point Heidi was beside herself with anxiety. Her husband's grim expression wasn't reassuring.

''Why don't you call her folks. Maybe she talked to them last night or early this morning and they know something we don't.''

''You must be worried or you wouldn't want me to alarm them when it's only a little after 7:00 a.m. in California.''

He gathered her in his arms. "I'm only trying to narrow the field."

"You're thinking what I'm thinking!" she cried out. "That horrible Glen's been stalking her. What if he found out where she lived and waited by the garage. He could have overpowered her when she was in there and she would have been helpless to—"

"Hush, darling." He crushed her against him. "I'm sure there's a reasonable explanation." Just then Heidi's cell phone rang. "That's probably Dana now."

"Oh I hope so!" She dashed over to the dresser to pick it up. "The caller ID says out of area." She pressed the talk button. "Hello?"

"Is that you, Rose Red?"

"Dr. Turner, hi!"

"A few minutes ago I was checking my e-mail and saw that my daughter has decided to pay us a surprise visit today. We thought she was planning to vacation with you this weekend."

"We were all going to go to Big Bend Park, but something came up and Dana changed her mind."

"Well, since she's not answering her phone, we thought maybe you knew the details so we could meet her plane. She didn't give us the name of an airline or a flight number."

Heidi flashed her husband a distress signal. "There's bad weather here and all flights have been grounded. She probably didn't know that when she sent you the e-mail."

"Let me handle this," Gideon murmured.

"Just a minute. My husband's right here and wants to talk to you." She handed him the phone.

"Dr. Turner? Gideon here. I've been following your conversation with Heidi. Could you tell us the time Dana sent her message?"

"It's on the screen in front of me. Here we are. It came in at seven-forty Texas time."

"That explains why she didn't know about the planes being grounded. When she finds out, she'll drive back to Cloud Rim. I'm sure she'll phone you as soon as she can. If we hear from her first, we'll call you so you won't worry."

"I'd appreciate that. Say, just between you and me, how come she wanted to come home while you're there? Is she having a hard time?"

"Not in the way you think. She's met a man."

"Jace Riley."

"Yes. Maybe she just wanted to talk to you about him in person."

"That sounds like my Snow White. Thanks, Gideon. Enjoy the rest of your trip."

"We will. Talk to you later." He hung up.

Heidi grasped his arms. "Dana must have gone to Alpine straight from the observatory. She's probably on her way back now. If her cell phone died, that could be the reason why she's not answering. Let's drive to Alpine. Maybe we'll see her on the highway coming home."

Gideon's instincts told him that finding Dana wasn't going to be that simple. If she was missing, and Jace didn't know about it, then all hell was about to break loose.

"Let's go." He ushered his family out to the car. Raindrops carried by the wind hit the car with surprising force. They rushed to get inside and took off. When they reached the outskirts of Cloud Rim, Kevin cried, "Whoa, Dad, what are all those police cars doing there?"

"Oh please don't let Dana have been in an accident—"

Gideon's hand slid to his wife's thigh. "It a roadblock, darling." He pulled the car over to the side and stopped. "Stay here while I find out what's going on." He climbed out and started walking toward the barricades.

The rain was coming down hard now. With his back to his family, he phoned the number Jace had given him to reach Pat Hardy. When the other man picked up, he said, "Sheriff? This is Detective Poletti."

"Jace said you'd be calling about Ralph Mason. He's going to be all right, but it looks like Glen eluded surveillance and escaped on foot during the night. We've got police swarming these mountains looking for him."

Dear Lord. "How long has the road been blocked out of Cloud Rim?"

"Since five this morning."

"I have more bad news for Jace, Sheriff. Dana Turner's missing."

"Oh boy."

"We know she was at the observatory at quarter to eight this morning. If she tried to drive her white

Toyota to Alpine around that time, did any of your officers see her?''

"One minute and I'll check.''

He rubbed his eyes while he waited. His wife's deepest fear might be closer to the truth than she knew.

"The guys have made a notation of every vehicle trying to get in or out of Cloud Rim. There's been no sign of her or her car.''

Gideon felt as though a thirty-foot wave had just pounded him into the ocean floor. "Glen's obsessed with her. I'm thinking he kidnapped her at the observatory and has taken her somewhere in her car. It wasn't there when I drove up earlier.''

"At least you've given us a point of reference to concentrate our search. Trust a big storm like this to blow in now. We can't send the helicopters for a look yet.''

"They might not be able to fly all day,'' Gideon surmised. "I'm going to help with the search.'' He gave Pat the information on his Acura and his license plate number.

"If you're going to join in, you need to know Lewis Burdick, Glen's partner, also turned up missing from his apartment this morning. The FBI's been looking for him for over a year now. He's a murderer with an arsenal of handguns and assault rifles.''

His jaw hardened. "Thanks for the info, Sheriff.''

"Be careful.''

Gideon hung up and raced back to the car. By the time he got in, he was soaking wet.

"Darling?" she cried in panic. "Did you find out anything about Dana?"

"I've been talking to the police. We believe Glen kidnapped her at the observatory. There's a manhunt on for him."

She broke down sobbing.

"Jace is out there looking for her. You better believe he won't rest until he's found her. I'm going to help with the search."

"Can I come?" Kevin asked.

"Thanks, son, but I'd rather you and Pokey kept Heidi company until I return."

Her head reared back. "I don't want you to go, but since it's Dana—" Tears gushed from her eyes.

"Do you think I want to leave you?" he asked urgently. "Tell me not to go and I won't."

"I can't do that. She's in trouble. I've got to call her parents and tell them what's happened."

His wife was right, but he groaned because he knew what the news would do to them.

In a few minutes she handed him the phone. "Dana's mom wants to talk to you."

He took it from her. "Mrs. Turner?"

"Gideon, my husband and I are on our way. Before we hang up, there's something you should know. When I was a youngster and visited my grandparents, my cousins and I used to play on the property up there. That part of the ridge near the top to the west has a lot of caves. I—I'm afraid the kidnapper might know about them. If he's taken her to one—"

They all knew about Dana's claustrophobia. Yet

no matter how shaken she was, Dana's mother must have been inspired just now.

"God willing, we'll find her, Mrs. Turner. Stay in close touch. I have to go now."

Before handing his wife the phone, he called Pat.

"Sheriff? It's Detective Poletti. I've been given a tip you and Jace should know about."

"Hold on. I've got him on the other line. We'll make this a three-way." After a moment, "Go ahead, Gideon."

"Jace?"

"I'm here." The man's voice sounded haunted.

"Dana's mother told me something that could be vital." Without preamble he repeated her words.

"You just told me what I needed to hear," Jace said.

"Jace? I'll start a search along the first firebreak road below the observatory. It's the one that cuts through the terrain in a westerly direction."

"Sounds good. Pat? Give him backup and tell the patrol division to send their K-9 handlers to that area. Without helicopters, we'll need the dogs to track."

"We're going to find her," Gideon said.

He heard a harsh intake of breath. "In what condition?"

"Don't think like that, Jace. I'm hanging up now."

TWO HOURS LATER the thunder had passed over, but the weather still resembled a monsoon. Despite the impossible conditions, the guys behind him were relentless and methodical in their search. Jace had nothing but praise for them, but so far nothing had turned up.

He made his way between the huge clumps of junipers, keeping his eyes poised on the ground for anything that might give him a lead. Suddenly he heard something that made him stop in his tracks.

It had to be one of the officer's cell phones ringing.

He pressed on, then halted again. Wait a minute—the ringing was coming from a cluster of trees ahead of him.

Jace broke into a run and circled the junipers. There stood the Toyota.

"Up here!"

A dozen officers hurried to join him.

The left rear door and the front passenger door were open. He spotted Dana's remote and purse lying in the wet grass. Her phone had stopped ringing.

The keys were still in the ignition. There was no sign of blood or a struggle, thank God.

Her overnight bag lay on the back seat. He opened it. Several changes of clothes had been neatly packed. He grabbed one of her sandals and walked over to the dog handler.

"Rudy? See what Fritz can do with this."

"Hey, Fritz—" He let his German shepherd grab hold of the sandal. "You like shoes better than anything, don't you, boy. That's right. Get that smell in your nose. Go ahead. Play with it."

While Rudy helped the dog to become familiar with Dana's scent, Jace gave Pat an update. Finding the car had narrowed the search to an area where all their manpower could be focused.

"Hand me her purse," Rudy said.

Jace gave it to him.

As soon as Rudy put it under the dog's nose, Fritz got excited. "Good boy." He handed the purse back to Jace. "Okay, let's see what you can find."

Fritz sniffed the front seat of the car and ground where Dana's things had fallen. Then the excited dog took off at an angle up the mountain.

Signaling for the guys to spread out and follow, Jace stayed a few paces behind Rudy to give him and the dog space as they began their trek up to the ridge.

Though the rain wasn't coming down as hard as before, it was still difficult to see. Yet miracle of miracles, the dog seemed to know exactly where he was going.

They'd been climbing a few minutes when Fritz began to strain at the leash. Rudy held him back and waited for Jace to catch up.

"See those rocks above us?"

Jace nodded. "Fritz found our cave."

A fresh spurt of adrenaline filled his body as he opened his backpack and pulled out a pair of night-vision goggles. After putting his pack back on, he said, "You men know the drill. Let's go."

DANA HAD BEEN Glen's prisoner since she'd awakened in the smothering dark of the cave. She'd glimpsed firearms and camping gear when they'd used the flashlight. Without light, they were entombed in thick, heavy blackness. The cave reeked of the awful cologne he wore. Everything was closing in on her.

Glen had made her sit down between his legs. "This is nice and warm, now, isn't it."

He'd wrapped his arms around her waist. Most of the time he rested his chin on her shoulder and kissed her neck. Every once in a while his hands roamed, but so far he hadn't tried to rape her. She knew he was waiting for Lewis to leave them alone.

"Please let me go outside. I'll be quiet and do what you say. Just don't make me stay in here. I can't breathe!"

"It's raining out. You might catch a cold. Can't have my bride-to-be getting sick before the wedding. We'll stay in here where it's dry. You sure smell sweet."

"I'm feeling sick, Glen. I need to get out of here."

"You'd better shut her up or I'll do it for you."

Glen smoothed the hair away from her ear and kissed it. "You don't want Lewis to get mad," he whispered. "We'll get out of here as soon as it stops raining and fly away to Mexico. I got money, Dana. So much money we'll never be able to spend it all. I'm going to buy you a white Mexican wedding dress. No woman'll look prettier than you in one of those."

"You can't go to Mexico and leave your grandfather. What will he do without your help?"

"The same thing he done before I got here."

"He loves you a lot, Glen. Your dad broke his

heart. Are you going to run away and break it again?"

"Grandad don't love me."

"Then how come he's going to give you the property with the barn you can turn into a house?"

"How does she know about that property?" Lewis demanded.

Dana had already figured out Lewis was older than Glen. He saw himself as the one with the brains and abused Glen unmercifully.

"I went to see your grandfather yesterday morning to give him the next month's rent. He bragged about what a good job you're doing at the grocery store, how dependable you'd become. That's when he told me he was giving you the land and the barn for a wedding present."

"I told him I was marrying you. He's sweet on you too."

"Do you know how lucky you are to have a grandfather who's looking out after you and your future? If you run away to Mexico and take all that money you say you have, he can't help you."

"If you don't believe me, I'll show it to you. I'm sitting against one of the bags right now."

"You show her anything and I'll blow both your heads off."

Ignoring Lewis, she said, "I don't want to see the money, Glen. It's not yours. You didn't earn it, and you know the police are going to get it back one way or another. Why risk going to prison when you're already earning your grandfather's respect?"

"'Cause I know you won't marry me if I don't take you to Mexico."

"Glen, you don't want to marry me. For one thing, I'm older than you, and I'm a scientist who studies the stars. My world is inside that observatory.

"You need to find a younger woman who will love you and look up to you to protect her. Think what a wonderful life you could have here in Cloud Rim as a rancher with a wife and family. Everything respectable."

"I don't want no other woman."

"But I'm in love with someone else."

"It's that IPS driver, isn't it?"

"Yes."

"Did he ask you to marry him yet?"

"No."

"Why not?"

"Because he's in love with his dead wife. But when he finds out I'm missing, he's going to come looking for me."

"Don't make no difference. He's never going to find you."

"You mean you'll lock me up somewhere in Mexico and force yourself on me."

"If I have to."

"The law calls that kidnapping and rape. If you'll leave this cave with me and go back to your grandfather's, I'll tell the police it was Lewis who dragged me up here. He'll be the one in trouble, not you."

"That's where you're wrong, bitch," Lewis muttered. "Glen's a wanted man. He's got nowhere else to run but Mexico, and I'm the only one who can fly the plane to get him there. So shut your mouth and leave him alone.''

''You haven't thought this through,'' she persisted, sensing that Lewis wasn't as sure of Glen as he thought. ''You can't take me over the border without a birth certificate. The Mexican authorities won't let me in.''

''I know you think I'm dumb, but I'm not that dumb, Dana. I took the passport out of your bedroom drawer the second day you moved in to the trailer.''

Glen had been coming and going from her trailer the whole time she'd rented it?

Ice filled her veins.

Jace had never trusted Glen. She recalled him asking her if she had the only key.

''You sure wear some pretty underthings,'' he murmured against her ear. ''But you're even prettier without them.''

Had he hidden in her closet to watch her?

Bile rose in her throat.

She had to do something. She couldn't just sit here and hope to be rescued.

The moisture had all but gone from her mouth. ''Glen—we've been in here for hours. I need to relieve myself.''

''Hey, Lewis…?''

''I heard.''

''Where should I take her?''

''Nowhere. In a few minutes I'll go to the front of the cave and see if it's stopped raining. If it has, then we'll get out of here and she can go outside on the way to the plane.''

"Did you hear that, Dana?"

Lewis chose that moment to shine the flashlight in their faces. "You better not let her con you into doing anything while I'm gone. I don't need you to help me fly, and I sure as hell will enjoy spending your half of the money."

CHAPTER FOURTEEN

THE CAVE SEPARATED into two tunnels after a distance of about two hundred yards. Glen and Lewis were in the right tunnel about a hundred yards from the split.

Officers and FBI were positioned throughout the cave from the opening to the place where the tunnel separated, awaiting Jace's instructions.

For the last half hour he and three men had remained hidden in a recess of the cave wall in the right tunnel. With their night-vision goggles, they'd been able to see Dana and her assailants.

He'd heard their conversation. He knew she was frightened, but she was being so brave and using her head to survive. The old divide-and-conquer theory was working well for her.

Burdick was nervous. He didn't trust Glen now that Dana was working on him to give himself up.

She'd survived prison. It had made her strong. This courageous woman was doing everything in her power to survive this nightmare. Most women would have fallen apart by now. Especially someone who suffered from severe claustrophobia.

Lord, how he loved her.

Now he knew she loved him. In front of everyone, visible or hidden, she'd declared her love for him. He felt his heart expand.

This was the hard part. Waiting for everything to go down so he could crush her in his arms.

Five more minutes and Lewis got up. He was going to make the biggest mistake of his life leaving Dana and Glen alone. The break they'd been waiting for had come. He got on his walkie-talkie.

"Burdick's just passed us on his way out of the cave. He'll be rounding the curve in the tunnel before long. There's a semiautomatic in his left hand and a flashlight in his right. Give him two minutes, starting your count now."

In his own mind, Jace began the countdown.

"Hey, Dana. Lewis is gone. How about a little kiss. I won't force ya unless you make me."

"I have to go to the bathroom so bad it hurts. How can I think of kissing you?"

The need to strangle Glen with his bare hands sent the adrenaline surging through Jace until he was jumping out of his skin. Then his ears picked up unmistakable scuffling noises. Everything went silent.

"Hey, Lewis?"

It was too much to hope Glen wouldn't have heard any sound. No matter how well the men might handle Burdick, even if they could disarm him without a shot being fired, everything resonated inside the cave.

"I don't think I can wai—"

"Shh."

Jace watched him muffle her. When that wasn't enough, he slapped her. Her whimpering sounds devastated him.

"I don't like doing that to you, Dana, but you got to shut up like Lewis said."

Agonizing minutes passed while Jace waited for Glen to make his next move. The sight of him holding her between his legs was enough to tear him apart. But with that gun at Glen's side, Jace and the other officers couldn't go in until there was a minimum risk of injury to Dana.

"Please let me up for a minute, Glen," she begged.

Good, Dana. Make him do it. At this point he removed his goggles.

"Hold on."

"I don't think he's coming. Maybe he took his money and left you."

"He wouldn't do that."

"Turn on the flashlight and see."

Jace heard the click and saw light before it was shut off again.

"The money's still here."

"Maybe he decided to leave anyway."

"Not without his share."

"Then why hasn't he returned?"

"He's probably looking at the sky, trying to decide how soon we can take off."

"I've got to relieve myself."

"I'm not moving from here."

"So you want me to go where I'm sitting?"

"All right. You can get up and walk over there a couple of steps. No funny stuff or I'll have to use this." He turned on the flashlight. In his other hand he pointed a gun at her.

Jace saw her rise to her feet.

"I'd like my privacy, Glen. Turn off the light."

"Forget it."

"If you're going to keep that light on, *you* can forget it."

In the next second he saw her spin around and kick the flashlight out of his hand.

"You bitch!" he yelled. In that second of confusion Jace lunged for him, knocking the gun away. It went off, the bullet striking the wall.

While Dana's screams reverberated throughout the cave, Jace wrestled Glen to the ground. The pervert let out a vile curse and scrounged for his weapon.

Dana's cries grew faint. It meant one of the officers was leading her outside into the fresh air. Knowing she was safe gave Jace the latitude he needed. Summoning his strength, he rolled Glen across the cave floor like a crocodile with his victim.

Their bodies slammed against unyielding rock. Glen let out a groan.

"Cuff him!" Jace ordered, taking advantage of his weakness. In a matter of seconds the men had rushed to Jace's assistance, securing Glen's wrists and ankles.

At that point light filled the tunnel. The whole

team rushed in to begin their investigation of the crime scene.

The men set Glen on his feet. His head reared back when he saw who'd tackled him.

"You!"

"That's right, Mason. Your friendly IPS man."

"You ain't no delivery-truck driver!"

"Right again. I've been on to you since the day I saw you letting yourself out of Dana's trailer. Too bad you didn't take her advice and let her go while you had the chance. Now you'll be sent up for life."

"I never killed no one. It was Lewis who gunned down the driver and that cop. He was the one who cut the pilot's oxygen. All I did was shove him out after he was dead."

"Save it for the judge." Jace nodded to one of the men. "Read him his rights."

"Captain Riley?" An officer walked over to him. "I found this inside his personal things." He handed him Dana's passport.

Jace opened it to her picture. She'd been twenty when it was taken. Anyone might think she wasn't that much older now. But he could see the difference. The sunny smile of the woman in the photo was that of a happy girl without a worry in the world.

The smile of the woman Jace had come to know didn't have that carefree look anymore. Wretches like Glen were a big part of the reason her joie de vivre had been extinguished.

"Get him out of my sight."

Jace put the passport in his pocket. He would give

it back to its owner just as soon as he could wrap up this case.

"DANA?"

She'd been praying Jace would be standing there when the police officers brought her out of the cave. Instead, it was Gideon's voice she heard calling to her. But she wasn't complaining.

After thanking the officers profusely for saving her life, she made a dash for his outstretched arms. At this point, she was so grateful to be free of those monsters, she couldn't find words.

He held her tight. "The nightmare's over, Dana. Glen's been taken into custody. He's no longer a threat to anyone."

She shivered. "I didn't think I'd ever see my loved ones again."

"You're safe now."

"Gideon? I've got to talk to Jace. Where is he?"

"Giving information to the FBI. He'll come by the apartment as soon as he can."

"The FBI's involved?"

"Yes. As it turns out, both Glen and Lewis have outstanding warrants for their arrest in Georgia and Florida, so the feds were called in."

"Mr. Mason's going to be devastated."

"Life's dealt some serious blows to that poor man. Maybe tomorrow we'll visit him and see how we can help. Right now I have a wife who told me not to come home unless I brought you with me."

"I'm beginning to think *you're* the poor man."
She made a sound between a laugh and a cry.

"Why do you say that?"

"Because ever since you met Heidi, you've been
rescuing me from one disaster after another."

He eyed her narrowly. "Am I complaining?"

"No." Tears spilled down her cheeks. "But you
must be sick of it."

"It's not your fault you've had a run of particularly bad luck, kiddo. However, I have it on good
authority that's all going to change. Come on. I was
talking to the sheriff a minute ago. Sometime later
they'll send an officer to return your car and take
your statement. For now, you're in my care. How
does that sound?"

"You *know* how that sounds." Her voice trembled.

They made their way down the sodden slope to
his car. While she'd been in the cave, there'd been
a downpour. Now it had stopped. So had the wind.
But it was still dismal out.

The area near the firebreak road looked like a disaster scene after a bomb explosion, with all the ambulances, police cars and vans, officers on walkie-
talkies, even a K-9 unit.

After Gideon had helped her in to his car, she noticed the time. "It's almost six o'clock!"

"You must be starving," he said as he backed
around so they could reach the main road.

"I guess I am. But I was running on adrenaline in
there, praying Jace would come.

"Trouble seems to follow me around. I've started thinking of it as the Turner syndrome. I should have some signs made up. Stay away. Disaster lurks. Proceed at your own peril."

Gideon made no comment as he pulled into the Watkinses' driveway. By the time she got out of the car, Heidi had rushed from the apartment. She threw her arms around Dana.

"I swear, if anything had happened to you—"

Suddenly it was Dana comforting her friend, who'd broken down sobbing.

"LOOKS LIKE they brought everything in here but a TV set."

"They had enough food stashed for at least two weeks!"

Jace listened to bits and pieces of conversation floating around him while he opened the bags containing the money. For a minute he almost lost it imagining what might have happened to Dana if he'd never come to Cloud Rim.

What if Tony Roberts hadn't asked for a lift? Then Jace probably wouldn't have met her. She would have been kidnapped from her trailer and brought here with no hope of rescue.

"Jace?" a familiar voice called to him. "*Jace?*"

He blinked, then turned his head. It was Pat.

"The news has gone out all over the department. I hear they're whooping it up in Austin. The partying has already started. Your name's going to be in every top news story tonight. So how come the grim face?"

Jace let out the breath he didn't realize he'd been holding. "If I hadn't come to West Texas, Dana—"

"But you *did* come," Pat broke in. "She's safe and well. Your friend, Detective Poletti, has already taken her back to her apartment."

Those were the words he'd needed to hear.

"It's over, Jace. You did it!"

"*We* did it, Pat. I couldn't have accomplished anything without your backup."

"We made a good team."

They gave each other a heartfelt hug.

"What do you bet old Gibb is smiling down right now. He's saying, 'I knew I could count on you, Riley.'"

"You think?" Jace said in a husky voice, feeling his eyes smart.

"Don't you?" Pat asked in surprise.

He gazed at the older man. "I guess I wasn't certain until just now."

"Let me help wrap things up here. The sooner we finish, the sooner you can drive over to Dana's and get her statement." He winked after he said it.

"Has anyone told her I'm not an IPS driver?"

Pat shook his head. "Gideon said you wanted to be the one. So far she doesn't have a clue you were part of the stakeout, let alone directing it."

His chest heaved. "That's good."

"Why do I get the idea you're worried?"

After a brief silence, he said, "Dana's had her fill of the law. When she finds out—"

"Wait a minute, Jace. Let me tell you something

for you to cogitate on for a while. You never saw anyone so glad to be rescued in your life. She was practically gushing over every officer out there.''

''That's just the point, Pat. I allowed her to remain in harm's way too long.''

''No,'' he said in a stern voice. ''You were doing your duty, and took every precaution to protect her at the same time.''

''Despite all our safeguards, Glen and Lewis got the slip on us during the night. That mistake resulted in her being kidnapped. She might never want to see me again once she learns the truth.''

He eyed Jace with concern. ''I think Dana Turner is a much stronger woman than you give her credit for.''

''I know she's a fighter, Pat. If you'd seen her attack Glen—''

''I heard about it. But I'm not referring to anything physical. Let's talk about the time she spent in prison. Innocent though she was, she didn't emerge unscathed. Her experience has given her depths you haven't plumbed yet. How could you when you were working undercover?

''Now it's time for the mask to come off. Instead of being afraid of it, be glad she's going to get acquainted with the real you.''

Pat always saw the glass half-full. For the most part, so did Jace. But this was different.

''You know what you need—a *real* vacation. Tom has authorized me to tell you he's giving you three weeks off. In fact, you've been ordered *not* to report back to work until the latter part of August.''

''I'm not expecting favors. Did you have something to do with his decision?''

The other man's face sobered. ''No, Jace. He confided that you'd never used any of the vacation time coming to you since the year your wife died. I could only agree with him that it's long overdue.''

Jace was vastly relieved Gibb's killers had finally been caught. But there was something else at stake now. The next time he saw Dana it would be under totally different circumstances. He had to admit he was scared out of his gourd, as his nephew Ricky liked to say.

BY QUARTER TO SEVEN the team was able to finish their initial investigation and everyone left the cave. Jace headed straight for Alpine in the forest service truck for a much-needed shower and change of clothes.

He debated whether to appear at Dana's apartment wearing his Ranger's uniform. In the end, he opted for jeans and a sweater. When she opened her door, the last thing he wanted to do was frighten her again. That woman had undergone more than her share of pain for one lifetime.

On the way out of Alpine he stopped at a drive-in to grab himself a hamburger and a malt. After being awake for fifty hours, he needed fuel to support his adrenaline attack. Later on he'd pass out. First he had to see Dana.

He pulled his car behind Gideon's, which was parked in front of the Watkinses' home. Ever since he'd arrived in Cloud Rim, Detective Poletti had been on first watch where Dana was concerned. After two nights without sleep, Jace figured the other man was ready to crash. Some vacation this had been for their family!

It was Jace's turn to take over. Raking an unsteady hand through his hair, he climbed out of the car and walked around the back to her apartment. He could hear the TV. His pulse rate tripled as he rang the bell.

Before he could take a breath, Dana opened the door.

Lord. She looked so beautiful, he couldn't do anything but stare at her for a moment.

She was wearing a blue flower-print dress he hadn't seen before. Her hair had been freshly washed. If he hadn't been inside that cave to witness her charging at Glen in dirt-stained clothes earlier, he would never have known she'd lived through such a harrowing ordeal. Not seeing her like this.

"Jace—"

He pulled her into his arms.

"Dana—" was all he could manage to say before desire took over. Their mouths and bodies locked in mutual hunger. Her close escape had brought their emotions to the surface. They both trembled with longing.

"Thank God you're alive!" he cried, crushing her more tightly against him.

''Gideon said you joined in the search. You were the first person I looked for when the officers walked me out of the cave. But then I couldn't see you anywhere and—''

''I'm here now,'' he murmured against her lips. Explanations would have to come later. ''Just let me kiss you, feel you, hold you for a little while so I can believe I'm not dreaming.''

In such a euphoric state, Jace didn't realize a car had pulled into the driveway. It wasn't until the beam of headlights outlined their entwined bodies that he had any cognizance of his surroundings.

She tore her lips from his. ''It's Mom and Dad.''

Jace groaned. Of course they would come, but what a hell of a time for introductions. He'd been well and truly caught in the act of kissing the daylights out of their daughter. Taking a deep breath, he relinquished his hold of her so she could greet them.

Soon pandemonium reigned as Gideon and his family came out to greet the Turners. Pokey pranced around, jumping up and down on everyone.

Jace stood in the background listening to the laughter and the tears. All of it happy sounds. A daughter who'd been feared lost was back home with family and friends where she belonged.

So many questions forced Dana to relive her traumatic ordeal. It was cathartic for her and should have gone on much longer. But he saw that she was looking around for him.

''Come and meet my parents, Jace. Mom and Dad? This is Jace Riley, the man I've been telling you about. He's the IPS driver who delivered those photographs you sent.''

Jace recognized her parents from the snaps in her office. "It's a real privilege to meet you.''

"We've been wanting to meet you, Jace," her mother assured him.

After shaking both their hands, he said, "Dana's told me a great deal about you. But through no fault of your daughter's, she's been laboring under a misconception about my line of work.''

Dana's eyes widened in surprise.

"Why don't we all go inside the apartment and I'll explain.''

Her parents had come to bring comfort and hear exactly what had happened to her. Now seemed the best time for the truth to come out. As long as Dana didn't eye him with loathing after he'd unburdened himself, he might be able to take a deep breath again.

While a confused-looking Dana sat on the edge of the couch next to her father, who held her hand, Heidi rushed around playing hostess, getting drinks and treats for everyone.

As people settled, his glance met Gideon's across the room. The other man flashed him a look of compassion followed by a smile of encouragement.

Jace stood near the door, his legs slightly apart. "This is going to take a while." His eyes swerved to Dana's.

"You told me that when you opened the trailer door and saw me in uniform the first time we met, you thought I was a Texas Ranger with a warrant for your arrest."

Her mother sat forward on the couch. "Why, darling?"

"Because I'm still paranoid."

"Honey..." Her dad patted her hand.

After a slight pause, Jace continued. "*You were partly right*, Dana. I'm Captain Riley of the Texas Rangers working in the field office out of Austin."

He could tell his revelation had shaken her. She rose to her feet with a look of incredulity stamped on her features. He pulled the ID from his pocket and walked over to hand it to her.

She studied it for a moment, then lifted her head, comparing the face in the photo with the real thing.

"I did have a warrant with me. Two, in fact, for the arrest of the men who killed three people in Austin last Christmas. One of the victims, Gibb Barton, was a retired Ranger who was a legend with the department and a very close friend of mine.

"The killers escaped in a plane that was last spotted flying over the Davis Mountains. My colleagues believed they made it to Mexico. However, the Mexican authorities never turned up any evidence to corroborate that theory.

"I couldn't abide the idea of them getting away. At one point my boss put me in charge of a manhunt to find them. I had to go undercover. When I came out to West Texas two months ago, I had nothing going for me but a hunch that they were still somewhere in the area.

"It wasn't until Tony Roberts asked me for a lift to Cloud Rim because his car had broken down that everything started to come together."

"I knew something was up the second Gideon changed his tune about you so fast!" Heidi cried.

"Yeah, Dad!" Kevin piped up. "I never saw you act like that before."

"Your dad's not named *Detective* Poletti for nothing, Kevin. He was ready to grind me up for hash, so I had to tell him the truth. But putting levity aside for a moment, I'd like to explain about the case, with this caveat.

"If I'd had any idea Glen was a wanted felon who'd been plotting to kidnap Dana and take her to Mexico with him, I would have sent her home to California a week ago!"

"A felon?" she asked in a shaky voice.

He nodded. "Unfortunately, you have to take the evidence as it comes. Gideon will tell you it's like putting a patchwork quilt together."

"Except my husband said it's like painting with numbers," Heidi said.

"Gideon's right. One item or number at a time. You keep trying to make sense of it. With each new addition, a pattern begins to form. In Glen's case, I didn't know what he was up to, so I had a twenty-hour tail put on him."

At Dana's stunned expression, he said, "It was as much for your protection as my need to monitor his activities. Little did I know it would lead to Lewis

Burdick, another felon who'd escaped from prison while serving a lengthy sentence for murder.''

DANA STOOD THERE in fascinated silence, which slowly changed to horror as Jace outlined the chilling scenario. It might have been something right out of a psycho thriller, yet she'd lived it. So had Jace.

When she realized it was he who'd tackled Glen to the ground in the cave, she cried, "I heard him fire the gun. You could have been killed!"

"No. With our equipment, we could see you. Once Burdick left you two alone, we knew how to approach Glen." His eyes smiled. "That mighty kick you gave him couldn't have worked out better for us if we'd planned it."

Dana felt his warmth in every particle of her being.

"Burdick's going to get the death penalty. Glen will probably get life."

Dana's mother got up from the couch and reached for Jace to give him a hug. "Thank you for saving our daughter's life."

Her father wasn't far behind. He grabbed Jace's hand and shook it hard. "How can we ever repay you?"

"Don't be too hasty in thanking me. We don't know why, but for some reason Glen and Lewis knew they were being set up and gave our men the slip at the last hour. In that short window of time, Lewis kidnapped Dana."

"I know what happened, Jace!" He looked at her expectantly. "Lewis baited Glen mercilessly for getting a ticket after he was caught in a speed trap outside Alpine."

"When?" he demanded.

"Sometime yesterday."

Jace let out a groan. "That explains Burdick's paranoia. Fear of Glen's driver's license being traced must have set off the alarm bells. Those are the kinds of details I need to get in a statement from you for the record."

Gideon rose to his feet. "You'll probably want to do that tonight while Dana's memory is still fresh. Come on, family. Let's all go home to bed."

"We'll leave for the motel too," Dr. Turner said. "It's been a long day. But it has had the most wonderful outcome." Dana's parents hugged and kissed her.

Heidi waited to take her aside. "Shall we try for breakfast at the café again—say at nine?"

"Make it eleven," Gideon amended before kissing her cheek.

Kevin gave her a hug. "I'm glad you're okay, Dana."

"Me too."

Pokey barked as if to put in his two cents. Everyone laughed before going out the door. But inwardly Dana's heart was doing a wild tattoo because she was finally alone with Jace.

"You have wonderful parents," he said.

"I do. Thank you."

She turned toward him, wanting to run straight into his arms. To her surprise, he invited her into the kitchen and put a tape recorder on the table. "Why don't you sit down and we'll get your debriefing out of the way."

"Right now?"

"There's no better time."

He pulled out a chair for her, then seated himself at an angle. Again he reminded her of Gideon when he was all business. This was a fascinating new side of Jace. Only now was it starting to sink in he was Captain Riley.

"When I turn this on, just start talking in a natural voice about where you went and what you did after you left your apartment this morning. I may interrupt from time to time. Ready?"

After she nodded, he pressed the tab and indicated she should go ahead.

"I made a last-minute decision to fly to California for a few days. Since I didn't know the precise moment of my return, I thought I'd better drive up to the observatory before breakfast and turn off the main computer."

He stopped the machine. His brown eyes searched hers with a fierce intensity. "Last night at dinner you didn't say anything about leaving for California. Why would you do that when your friends came expressly to vacation with you?"

"B-because I felt Gideon needed some time alone with his family. Also, I hadn't been to see Rosita for a while and didn't want her to think I had forgotten her."

His face darkened with lines before he turned the

machine on again. She tried to pick up where she'd left off, but his change of mood distracted her. After averting her eyes, she was able to concentrate and told him everything she could think of.

"So," she summarized, "except for threats, Lewis didn't talk to me. It was Glen who spoke about an eight-seater plane hidden in his grandfather's garage. He said Lewis had plans to land on someone's rancho in Guadalajara, Mexico, where they had friends waiting for them and—well, that part doesn't matter."

He turned off the machine again. "What part?"

She shuddered. "Glen had delusions about marrying me there. He's such a revolting person, I can't bear to think about it."

"Then you don't have to." He pocketed the recorder.

"You mean I'm through?"

"Yes. You gave us more than enough information. Thank you."

He was being so formal.

"Does this mean you have to leave now?" She fought to quash the tremor in her voice, but failed miserably.

CHAPTER FIFTEEN

"DO YOU WANT me to go?"

"No!" she cried. "How can you ask me that after the way we were kissing each other a little while ago? It's just that now I know what you really do for a living, I imagine you're anxious to get back to Austin."

Suddenly he pushed his chair away from the table and stood up. She rose to her feet in response.

Beneath the kitchen light she noticed him waver. This close she detected fatigue lines marring his features. There was a weariness to his movements, and no wonder. The man hadn't been to bed for two nights.

"Come over to the couch." She reached for his hand and pulled him after her. "Stretch out."

"You're sure—"

"Jace—lie down before you collapse."

"Just for a minute. Then we have to talk."

He was asleep the moment he'd lowered his powerful body to the cushions.

There was a blanket on the end of her bed. She ran to get it and the extra pillow. Within seconds she'd covered him and propped his dark, curly head.

After darting around turning off lights, she pulled the chair close to the couch.

The knowledge that Jace was under her roof safe and sound filled her with inexpressible joy. At last she could relax. She lifted the remote from the coffee table and turned on the TV.

It was too late for the ten o'clock news. She grazed the channels. When she came to the cable news she saw the words Breaking News, and paused.

"There's word out of Austin, Texas, that two wanted felons responsible for three murders during an armored car robbery last Christmas are in custody tonight.

"The manhunt, led by Ranger Captain Jace Riley, apprehended the two men in the mountains of West Texas where they'd kidnapped a woman whose name has not been disclosed. She was released unhurt.

"Lewis Burdick was on the FBI's ten most wanted list. Glen Mason was a prison escapee wanted in the state of Georgia. Both the stolen plane and a million dollars were recovered.

"Now, turning our attention to Spokane, Washington, a child—"

Dana switched off the remote and disappeared into the bedroom to slip on her sweats. Once she was ready for bed and her teeth were brushed, she dragged her bedding into the living room and set up a makeshift sleeping bag next to the couch.

This was the closest she could get to Jace right now without disturbing him. For the rest of the night she would keep watch over this heroic man who'd risked his life again and again to save her from Glen.

His exhaustion was so complete, he never moved while she was still awake to see to his needs.

Dana didn't know at what point she fell asleep, but oblivion must have taken over. The next time she was aware of her surroundings, she opened her eyes to a living room filled with daylight.

As she lifted her arm to check her watch, it brushed against Jace's right hand, which dangled to the floor. The contact brought both their heads around.

The second he saw her he grasped her hand, threading his fingers through hers. It made her heart leap.

She looked up at him. "Good morning."

"Good morning," he whispered back. "You slept by me all night?"

"Yes. When I led you to the couch, you passed out. After what you'd been through, I wanted to stay close by in case you needed anything."

His thumb rubbed her flesh. "You were kidnapped yesterday. I should have been the one watching over you in case you had nightmares."

Dana smiled, enjoying this moment more than he would ever know. His five o'clock shadow was back, and his black curls were disheveled. With dark brown eyes gleaming from thick black lashes, he reminded her of a modern-day pirate.

"My sleep was dreamless," she assured him. "The last nightmare I had was about prison, and they hardly ever happen anymore. As for the kidnapping incident, that was different. Lewis dragged me to the cave for Glen's sake. When I realized he wanted me alive, not dead, I was more sickened and angry than anything else.''

His jaw hardened. ''You shouldn't have had to go through either experience.''

She decided it was time to act on Gideon's advice about a man not minding a little begging if it was from the right woman.

''We've had this conversation before.'' She gazed directly into his eyes. ''Our orbits would never have crossed otherwise. How could I ever be sorry about that?

''Do you know they talked about you on the news last night? It was my fantasy come true,'' she confessed with great daring.

He leaned closer. ''What fantasy?''

''Ever since Heidi caught herself a detective, I've been jealous. We go back to childhood, remember. She and I did everything together. And then she went and found herself this big, gorgeous wonderful hero who'd take bullets for her because he was so crazy in love with her.

''He was willing to do anything she wanted. She even managed to drag him to the prison in order to save me, if you can imagine.

''After his first visit, I'd lie on my cot and pretend the same thing had happened to me. This fantasy cop would come into my life. He'd take me away and protect me and love me the way Gideon loved Heidi.''

Jace held her hand tighter without realizing it. ''I thought you hated the law.''

''That was an hysterical reaction to being on the

wrong side of it. Last night the anchorwoman talked about *you* saving *me*. It hit me then that a real live Texas Ranger had come to my rescue, just like I'd imagined in my dreams.

"This big, gorgeous hunk of a hero with the most beautiful brown eyes I've ever seen had put his life in jeopardy. Not just for me, but for all the people Glen and Lewis had destroyed with their evil."

She turned on her side and kissed his arm. "Do you have any idea how amazing you are to me, Jace Riley? This wasn't a one-time deal for you. Next week, next month, next year you'll be out there saving more lives, putting yourself in harm's way, protecting the innocent."

Tears filled her eyes as she continued to look at him. "I'm so proud of what you did, what you do. I saw the same awe in my parents' eyes last night."

"Dana, there's a difference in admiring what I do, and being able to live with it on a twenty-four-hour basis."

If he'd just said what she'd thought he'd said...

She sat up.

"The only thing I couldn't live with is a ghost."

"Do you feel a ring on my finger?"

Her gaze flicked to their hands. The gold band was gone. Breathless, she looked back at him. A faint smile lifted the corner of his mouth.

"I told you before. Your gravity pulled me out of my orbit. When we collided the other night, it felt like a hundred thousand hydrogen bombs had gone off."

"How did you know about that?" she cried in

surprised delight at his reference to the measure of an earthgrazer's impact on the rare occasion it did escape its orbit.

"I have my sources." Then he sobered once more. "I also happen to know how you feel about having a baby."

"Of course I want one. Maybe even three or four. Don't you?" she asked gently.

"I can't give them to you." She heard a world of pain in his voice.

"Do you have a problem considering adoption? Because I don't. Consuela and I have already talked it over. If it turns out Gideon can't get her freed from prison, then I've told her I'll raise Rosita on my own. If Consuela never gets out, I plan to adopt her little girl. She's so adorable, Jace. I love her."

Quick as lightning he sat up. His gaze seemed to search her soul. "You really mean that, don't you?"

"Yes. I've never been pregnant, so I don't know what it's like. But I have to tell you, I'm all for avoiding nine months of morning sickness, serious weight gain and fifty years of worrying about birth control."

"*Dana—*"

Desperate to convince him his sterility meant nothing to her, she pressed a kiss to his lips. "The important thing is to have a child to love."

Just then her cell phone rang. The timing couldn't have been worse, yet she didn't dare ignore it. "That's probably my mom or Heidi calling. I'll be right back. Don't you dare move." She kissed him again before running into the kitchen to pick up.

"Hello?"

"Dana? It's Gideon."

"Good morning!" Heavens, it had to be the most wonderful morning of her life! "Did you get a good sleep?"

"Yes, but a I need a couple more nights just like it." Dana could well imagine. "We decided to drop in on Ralph Mason on our way to breakfast. He'd like to talk to you. Afterward, your parents will meet us at the café."

"Jace and I will be right there."

"You sound happy," he teased.

"I'm afraid you don't know the half of it, Detective Poletti."

"Do you want to bet?" he murmured before ringing off.

"Where are we going?" Jace asked as she put down the phone.

"To see Glen's grandfather. He's asked for me. While I get dressed, why don't you freshen up in the bathroom. There's a new toothbrush in the cabinet you can use."

"I thought you told me not to move."

The man was irresistible. "I did, but—"

"First we have to get everything else out of the way." By now he was on his feet, all two hundred pounds of hard male muscle. "Keep in mind our time's going to come," he vowed before disappearing down the hall.

A MAN WHO TURNED OUT to be Ralph's nephew answered the door. Dana was glad Mr. Mason wasn't alone. The minute she entered the house with Jace, she could hear the old man weeping in the living room. It tore her heart out. She couldn't bear to see him so unhappy.

Heidi's solemn expression said it all. The sadness was hard on everyone, even Pokey, who'd settled himself next to the couch and plopped his head on Ralph's slippered feet.

After squeezing Jace's hand, Dana left him to go over on the couch next to Ralph.

"Mr. Mason?"

"Ah—" He lifted his head. "It's good of you and Jace to come. Glen did such a terrible thing to you, I can hardly find the strength to speak of it."

"Then don't try. It's over, Mr. Mason. I'm fine. Jace rescued me. You need to know Glen never wanted to hurt me, and he didn't."

"My son abandoned him. It turned him into a criminal."

"Glen's mother also shares the blame. He became a victim who craved love. I know he would have protected me from Lewis."

"You're a sweet person to try and make me feel better, but nothing can do that. Where did my wife and I go wrong?"

"My parents used to ask themselves that same question about my sister, Amy."

"You have a sister?"

"She's dead now." In the next breath, Dana explained the whole sad story.

"If Gideon hadn't ordered an autopsy, we wouldn't have known Amy had a brain tumor, which explained her irrational actions. I'm not saying your son might have had the same thing, but there may have been a physiological explanation for your son's behavior.''

''I could pray that's the reason.''

''The best parenting in the world can't fix someone's off-balance chemistry. Assure yourself that you did the best you could for both your son and Glen. Leave the rest to God.''

''Thank you for reminding me.'' He wiped his eyes with a tissue. Then he took hold of her hand. ''I guess you know I wanted you for my daughter-in-law.''

Dana fought to hold back her tears. ''I'm very honored.''

''How come no man has claimed you yet?''

''I already did,'' Jace declared in an authoritative voice as he joined her on the couch. He slid an arm around her shoulders. ''For two long weeks I've been in love with her, but couldn't do anything about it until now. We're getting married as soon as we drive to Austin so she can meet my family.''

It was a good thing Jace was holding her on the couch or she would have passed out from too much joy.

''Good for you. Does that mean you two will be living here in Cloud Rim?''

''We haven't worked out the details yet, but rest assured we'll visit you often.''

''Please do. It would make an old man happy.''

''How are you going to manage now?'' she asked.

"My nephew is arranging for someone to come and live with me."

"That's wonderful!"

"You run along now. Young people in love have plans to make."

Jace grinned and reached for Ralph's hand. "That's a fact."

No sooner had everyone said goodbye than Heidi hustled Dana out of the house ahead of the others. When they reached Jace's car, she let out a squeal of happiness and hugged Dana so hard, she couldn't breathe. Pokey kept jumping up and down on them.

"I almost died of excitement in there. You're going to get married! When did he propose? Why didn't you phone me?"

Dana shook her head. "I'd have told you, but he never asked me."

Heidi's shocked expression was priceless as she digested Dana's words. "You mean that announcement just now—"

"Yes!"

"Holy cow— Do you realize that if you two start the process right away, we could have babies at the same time?"

"Well maybe not the same day," Dana teased.

"Gideon will help. He has resources to speed up the process."

A smile broke out on Dana's face. "So does *my* husband."

"I like the sound of that." Two strong arms slid around her waist from behind. "Am I interrupting something private?'' Jace murmured against her neck.

Dana leaned against him. ''I was just reminding Heidi that she's not the only woman married to an exciting cop.''

''Except we're not married yet, my love.''

She turned in his arms. ''It feels like we are.''

''I've got news for you. There's a lot more to it than what we've been doing.''

She threw her arms around his neck. ''I hope so.''

''I love you.''

''I've been in love with *you* forever,'' she cried softly.

''Now she tells me.''

''Maybe you two should skip the trip to Austin and fly to Nevada. That's what Gideon and I did. It solved one *huge* problem,'' Heidi said before walking away.

Dana hid her red face against Jace's chest.

''You know something?'' he murmured into her hair. ''She's on to a good idea. My boss has given me three weeks off. How about we get married in Las Vegas today, then fly back for a visit with my family tomorrow. After that, we'll honeymoon in England.''

She lifted her had. ''England?''

''Yes. Prison got in the way of your getting your Ph.D. there. I thought we might look into it.''

''But, Jace, that would require a year and half at least. You're a Ranger. I wouldn't dream of taking you away from your work.''

"You're an astronomer. If I'm going to be married to one, I'd like to learn more about it."

"What?"

He nodded. "I can take a sabbatical for graduate work. I'd like to study physics—then I'd have a better understanding of what you do. I'm sure your father could recommend an honor student to operate the observatory while we're gone. Of course, if the idea doesn't appeal to you—"

"Jace, I never said that. I'm just having trouble believing this is real, that you love me."

"Let's go to breakfast and break the news to your parents. By the time we reach Nevada, you're going to know it's so real you'll be as desperate as I am to say our vows."

WHILE HER HUSBAND was in the shower, Dana lay in bed, looking around the quaint room of the little country inn in the Cotswolds where they'd known rapture.

Tomorrow morning they had to drive back to London for their flight to Austin. This was the last night of their honeymoon. These precious days and nights were a time out of time that would never come again.

When she saw his silhouette in the near darkness she trembled with desire, longing for him to join her. He dropped the towel on a chair and slid into bed, pulling her into his arms.

"You feel so good, sweetheart," he moaned the words. "You're all I think about, all I want."

He crushed her mouth beneath his.

She'd never known a man more generous. Love

seemed to pour out of him. He'd been sacrificing himself for her ever since they'd met. Now it was time to give something back.

"Jace? Can we talk for a moment?"

His body tensed. He lifted his head. "Is something wrong?"

"No. You've made everything so perfect, it's been paradise. But I've made a decision about something and want to tell you now."

She heard a change in the tenor of his breathing. "Go on."

"I found out I don't want to go to graduate school here. No one is more brilliant than my own father. Wanting to come here was the dream of a single woman still seeking adventure in far-off places. But it pales in comparison to the reality of being married to you."

"Dana—"

"Let me finish. For the rest of my life I want to be your wife as totally as I've been on this honeymoon. But you're a Ranger and you need to get back on the job, because no one does it better."

He responded by giving her a kiss to die for.

"I'll keep working on my Ph.D. through Cal-Tech. While you're at work, I'll work. When you're home, I plan to devote all my time to you. How does that sound?"

Jace answered her question so satisfactorily, it was an hour later before either of them was coherent.

"I can hear you thinking," he murmured against her neck. "What do you want to ask me?"

"Would you like to live in Austin?"

"No. I'd prefer Alpine."

"Can you do that?"

"I'll talk it over with Tom as soon as we get back."

"Oh, Jace—" She eased herself on top of him. "It's what I've wanted for a long time! I have all these things in storage. I can't wait to get them out and make a beautiful home for you."

"Do you want to start adoption proceedings right away?"

"Whenever you're ready."

"I'm ready, especially since Gideon and Heidi phoned to tell us Consuela's been set free and has taken her daughter back. We'll put in for our own little Rosita." He bit her earlobe tenderly.

"It will be so exciting to fix up a nursery."

"Everything's exciting with you. Our daughter will grow up knowing all the planets."

She smiled. "And the boys will grow up to be Rangers like their handsome father. How *did* you become a Ranger?"

"Well, for one thing, I had an ancestor who was a Ranger before the Civil War. I was named after him, and that kind of played around in my mind.

"Then when I was in fourth grade, my dog, Mutley, followed me to school as usual. But he got hit by a car out in front and died on the way to the vet. I was inconsolable until a Ranger named Gibb Barton came to the house and brought me a new puppy.

"He checked up on us every once in a while, and as I grew older I'd go visit him. My dad's an insurance agent, and both my brothers have gone into the same business. But Gibb's career sounded like the only way to go.

"In college, I majored in criminology, then went to police academy. From there I worked my way up so I could join the Rangers and be just like my old buddy Gibb."

Dana clung to him. "What a beautiful thing he did for you."

"It was." His voice had grown husky.

"No wonder you had to find the men who killed him."

His chest heaved. "Pat Hardy claimed Gibb was smiling down at us after Glen and Lewis were caught. I'm sure he was because he knew I found you in the process.

"Dana, what would I have done if you'd never come into my life?" he cried, tightening his arms around her.

"I ask that question about you constantly. Maybe it's time we stopped saying what if, and started to accept the fact that we have each other in our lives, for the rest of our lives and beyond."

He hugged her tight. "Together forever?"

"You've looked through the telescope. You've seen galaxies and universes going on to infinity. Why not us?"

"I love the way you think, Mrs. Riley."

She kissed his lips quiet. "I love you."

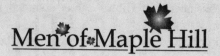

Men of Maple Hill

Muriel Jensen's new trilogy

Meet the men of the small Massachusetts town of Maple Hill—and the women in their lives:

Hank Whitcomb, who's back in Maple Hill, determined to make a new life for himself. It doesn't take long before he discovers he wants his old high school flame, Jackie Bouregois, to be a part of it—until her long-held secret concerning the two of them gets in the way!

Cameron Trent, who's despaired of ever having the family he's wanted, until he meets Mariah Shannon, and love and two lonely children turn their worlds upside down!

Evan Braga, who comes to Beazie Dedham's rescue when a former employer threatens her life. Then Beazie learns the secrets of Evan's past, and now the question is—who's saving whom?

Heartwarming stories with a sense of humor, genuine charm and emotion and lots of family!

On sale starting January 2002

Available wherever Harlequin books are sold.

HARLEQUIN®
Makes any time special ®

Bestselling Harlequin® author

JUDITH ARNOLD

brings readers a brand-new,
longer-length novel based on her
popular miniseries *The Daddy School*

Somebody's Dad

If any two people should avoid getting
romantically involved with each other, it's
bachelor—and children-phobic!—Brett Stockton
and single mother Sharon Bartell. But neither
can resist the sparks...especially once
The Daddy School is involved.

"Ms. Arnold seasons tender passion with a dusting
of humor to keep us turning those pages."
—*Romantic Times Magazine*

*Look for Somebody's Dad
in February 2002.*

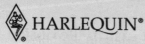

Two city gals are about to turn life upside
down for two Wyoming ranchers in

*Cowboy
Country*

Two full-length novels of true
Western lovin' from favorite authors

JUDITH BOWEN
RENEE ROSZEL

Available in January 2002 at your favorite retail outlet.

HARLEQUIN®
Makes any time special ®

Three of romance's most talented craftsmen come together in one special collection.

New York Times bestselling authors

Jayne Ann Krentz

Tess Gerritsen

National bestselling author

Stella Cameron

in

Stolen Memories

With plenty of page-turning passion and dramatic storytelling, this volume promises many memorable hours of reading enjoyment!

Coming to your favorite retail outlet in February 2002.

HARLEQUIN®

Makes any time special ®